ONE
STATION
AWAY

ALSO BY OLAF OLAFSSON

NOVELS

Absolution (1994)
The Journey Home (2000)
Walking into the Night (2003)
Restoration (2012)

SHORT STORIES

Valentines (2007)

ONE STATION AWAY

OLAF OLAFSSON

ecco

An Imprint of HarperCollins*Publishers*

Many thanks to Lorenza Garcia for her invaluable assistance when writing this book

ONE STATION AWAY. Copyright © 2017 by Double O Investment Corp. All rights reserved. Printed in the United States of America. No part of this book may be used or reproduced in any manner whatsoever without written permission except in the case of brief quotations embodied in critical articles and reviews. For information, address HarperCollins Publishers, 195 Broadway, New York, NY 10007.

HarperCollins books may be purchased for educational, business, or sales promotional use. For information, please e-mail the Special Markets Department at SPsales@harpercollins.com.

A hardcover edition of this book was published in 2017 by Ecco, an imprint of HarperCollins Publishers.

FIRST ECCO PAPERBACK EDITION PUBLISHED 2018.

Designed by Michelle Crowe

Library of Congress Cataloging-in-Publication Data has been applied for.

ISBN 978-0-06-267749-5

18 19 20 21 22   LSC   10 9 8 7 6 5 4 3 2 1

could hear the sea. That was perhaps an hour after I became paralyzed, although I couldn't be sure as I soon lost track of time. The shoreline up here is rocky and draws in the waves; it is only when you get down to the village that the beach becomes sandy. Before lying down, I had opened both windows and placed an alarm clock beside the bed so that I could see the time, but then changed my mind and put it in the drawer, removing the batteries because it has a loud tick. Of course, I needn't have put it in the drawer at all, but I didn't realize that until later.

Once I got used to the ventilator and my heartbeat slowed, I could hear the birds in the maples. Later I heard voices in the garden, clear at first but gradually becoming fainter. They were women's voices, and I pictured a pair of doctors or nurses, their shift finished, walking together to the staff parking lot, which for some reason has never been paved. Perhaps they were discussing the coming weekend, for their voices had a tone of anticipation, especially the one I imagined belonging to the younger of the two. They walked slowly, stopping twice and laughing heartily the second time. Then two cars started up, neither powerful, I imagined, and slowly began to move on the gravel in the calm sunshine. One of the women turned on the radio and rolled down the windows as she drove away.

Simone would have helped me but I couldn't ask her. First she would have tried to dissuade me, I am sure, before shrugging the way she often did, and saying that if I were bent on trying this then I should just get it over with—or words to that effect. We have been colleagues for almost eight years, and she knows that when I am set on doing something, it's not easy to get me to change my mind. Best get it over with, she would have said, insisting on administering the medication and the ventilator herself. But I couldn't ask her, not after her episode with the speech therapist. There is always the risk that something may go wrong, and Hofsinger, the department chair, isn't known for his tolerance, especially where Simone is concerned. That's why it was best she knew as little as possible.

Anthony was flattered when I asked for his help. He is young and so full of ambition that I find it sometimes painful to watch him. However, he is conscientious and hardworking and will almost certainly go far, though I doubt he will make any memorable contribution to medicine. I expect he will end up in a managerial post, like Hofsinger. The two men aren't so different, except that Anthony is a novice and has to learn to keep himself in check. I have noticed how he behaves with people he considers beneath him, and I can see which way he is heading. Simone finds him unbearable, but I can't help smiling.

Anthony didn't ask any questions; he just looked at me and then at the signed statement I handed him. He is tall and fair-haired and while he was glancing at the document it occurred to me that he could do with a visit to the barber; his hair was too long at the back. He adjusted his glasses, but I was too impatient to wait.

"I need to ask you to give me succinylcholine and keep me breathing while I lie there. This is just to confirm that I asked you to assist me and that I take full responsibility."

He wrinkled his brow as though my words puzzled him.

"In case anything goes wrong," I added.

"Nothing will go wrong," he said. "You know I worked as an anesthetist for more than a year."

"That's why I came to you," I said. "I have complete faith in you."

He straightened up.

"When? Today?"

"No, on Friday. When things are quieter."

He looked again at the statement.

"Vecuronium bromide."

"What?"

"I'll give you vecuronium bromide. Succinylcholine may cause muscle spasm, and besides, its half-life is too short. It can only be used with anesthetic."

"Let's keep this between the two of us," I said.

He nodded and said nothing more. He didn't seem curious to know what I was up to, which didn't surprise me. When she is feeling uncharitable, Simone calls him "the robot," but I simply see him as one of these scientists who primarily think about how best to do something, not why it needs doing. And that's exactly what I needed this time.

This was on a Tuesday, a week after Mrs. Bentsen, an elderly lady who had been in a coma for several months following a stroke, died. Simone had thought we should give her an MRI scan, but I agreed with Hofsinger that this was unwise. Simone took it badly, but he was right. We didn't have our own scanner at that time, and although, according to her daughter, Mrs. Bentsen was young for her age (she lived on her own and did the crossword every morning with her coffee), we couldn't ignore that she was in her eighties. I said this to Simone, as I saw no point in arguing with her over whether Mrs. Bentsen was conscious or not. I said: "She hasn't got long to live in any case." I knew it sounded harsh.

"What if she were your mother?" she asked.

"My mother's only seventy," I said, smiling.

It was then that I remembered her birthday. My father had mentioned it in a letter at Easter, but it had slipped my mind. *I should do something for her,* he had said, *give her a surprise—make her happy. She certainly deserves it. I know you're busy, but perhaps you could find the time to celebrate with us . . .*

I'd had to put the letter down and take a deep breath. At first glance, his words appeared completely innocent, and yet I felt he was accusing me of being neglectful, in his usual insidious way. Needless to say, I hadn't heard from him since, no doubt because he thought he had said enough and now it was up to me. I had put off replying, and then forgotten all about it until a month later when I was in Paris for a conference. He doesn't use e-mail, and I find speaking to him on the telephone uncomfortable, so I bought a postcard at a kiosk and sent it that afternoon.

I'm in Paris for a few days at a conference. It's cold here. I heard Chopin in a café and I thought of you both. Speak soon. Best wishes, Magnus Colin.

I remembered those lines as I stood in Mrs. Bentsen's room, watching the thin curtains stir in the breeze. Her daughter had taken her things away the day after she died, and yet I could still feel the emptiness the old lady had left behind. It usually disappears within a week or so, sooner if a new patient moves into the room. Some like to think it's the spirit or soul lingering on, but the fact is, it's only natural that those who know the patient need time to get used to the change. It isn't only believers who have trouble accepting this explanation, which is why I keep it to myself. I refrain from pointing out that anyone entering Mrs. Bentsen's room for the first time the day after she passed away would have been unaware of this emptiness. In any case, it was while I was standing in her room on that Tuesday in June, watching the curtains flutter and reflecting on Chopin, the postcard I had sent with a picture of Pont Neuf, and my mother's birthday, that I decided, more or less out of the blue, to ask Anthony to give me a dose of succinylcholine when things quieted down at the end of the week.

"I am completely in your power now," I said to him as I locked the door to Mrs. Bentsen's room, shortly after four o'clock that Friday afternoon.

His face remained impassive as he continued to set up the ventilator the two of us had just wheeled in. I dealt with the alarm clock before stretching out on the bed, and he arranged the medication on a tray, took my pulse and blood pressure, and asked me for how long I wanted him to keep me paralyzed.

"Two hours," I said. "Unless the building catches fire. Then you can give me the antidote."

He didn't reply, but put on gloves and unwrapped a slim tube which I knew he would insert into my windpipe to keep the airway open. He worked slowly, adjusted his glasses, inserted a cannula in my arm, hooked me up to the heart monitor, and asked me again how much I weighed before double-checking that he had calculated the correct dosage.

"And you want the windows left open?"

"Yes," I said. "And I'd be grateful if you could make as little noise as possible."

"In that case, you should keep your eyes closed so I won't need to moisten them."

Before inserting the tube, he numbed my throat with an anesthetic spray, which smelled like candy. He then hooked me up to the ventilator and attached the nerve stimulator to my thumb and forearm.

"Ready?"

The drug paralyzed me almost instantly. Of course I was expecting that, and yet I was terrified. My heart started hammering

uncontrollably and my clothes became drenched in sweat. I felt as if
I was hanging in midair from a rope which I couldn't grab hold of.
I had a sensation of falling and tried to kick out my legs and cry for
help, but my limbs were frozen and my voice had vanished. Only
my racing pulse revealed my anguish. Anthony checked the monitor and said something about everything being normal, and yet I
felt as if I were under an enormous weight and that Anthony was far
away, his voice almost inaudible. He dried the tears which suddenly
streamed down my cheeks and said that they were to be expected.

The only bodily function the drug affects is the power of
movement. It doesn't dull or excite the mind, or send you to sleep.
I kept reminding myself of this, trying to convince myself that I
still controlled my thoughts, that it was up to me to rally them
and slow my heartbeat. Only two hours, I told myself. Only two
hours. I thought about the white, embroidered curtains, which I
imagined fluttering every now and then in the soft breeze, the trees
outside the window, the leaves, the birds hopping from branch to
branch. Anthony walked gingerly across the floor, pulled a chair
out from under the table in the corner, and brought it over to the
bed. There he sat down and opened a book.

Gradually my heart rate slowed. The hum from the ventilator
was soothing, and blended seamlessly with the afternoon lull.
Anthony sat reading, and after a while I began to kill time by
counting how long it took him to turn each page. I hadn't noticed
the book when we entered the room, but I guessed it must be something technical or scientific, because I couldn't imagine that he was
interested in fiction or even biography. Every so often, he rose to
check the monitors before sitting down with his book again. I had
asked him not to let me know how much time had passed, and I
regretted that now. Once I heard footsteps in the corridor followed
by a knock on the door. Anthony didn't get up, but called out:
"Occupied!" in his authoritative voice. I had been right in guessing
that it was a woman; she said "sorry" before hurrying away.

Over an hour must have passed when I heard the sea. Shortly before, the windows had started rattling and the room had grown suddenly cooler. I envisioned the skies darkening, scudding clouds shadowing the lawns surrounding the hospital. I was listening for the wind when I heard the sea. At first I thought I was imagining it, but when I concentrated I heard the waves unmistakably lapping at the rocks, rather lazily, I might add.

I could not have imagined hearing the sea from the hospital, not even on winter days when it crashed against the rocks, surging onto the land, over the dirt track that takes you to the boathouses and from there into the village. Forgetting for a moment that I couldn't move, I instinctively tried to lean forward, the way people do when they are straining to hear something, but was reminded of my helplessness. This time I didn't despair, but continued to listen for sounds outside the hospital walls—for something I might not have noticed before and which I suddenly thought could mean something to me. It was odd, this strange conviction that I had missed something important, and equally bizarre the notion that now was the moment to reclaim it. I hadn't walked by the sea since that day in the fall when Malena had taken the train from Grand Central to the hospital. Of course, I should have known from her voice that something was wrong, but she couldn't have called at a worse moment. In fact, I had barely had time to pick up the phone and make a mental note of when her train was to arrive. It was another Friday, and I had the idea we might try the new restaurant in the village people were talking about, before we caught the nine o'clock train home.

The sea was breaking over the rocks, and the rays from the afternoon sun were bobbing on the waves along with a few restless gulls. I could hear our footsteps on the dirt track, the autumn breeze in the grass and the squawking gulls. And her words, which devastated me. We had reached the village by then, stopping outside the old café next to the drugstore that's still closed on Sundays. I was telling her how much I liked this little village where time seems to stand still, the main street with its corner bookstore, its barber-shop, the grocery store that sells firewood, bicycles, and toys, along with reading glasses and kitchen utensils. I was saying something about the "H" that had been missing from the blue sign above the pharmacy since I first came here almost a decade ago. And the window display that hadn't changed, either: a few perfume bottles here and there, some dried flowers, and a sun-bleached advertisement for Old Spice that could have dated from the sixties. I was about to tell her that it was the pharmacist's daughter, back from a long stay abroad, who had opened the new restaurant where I had reserved a table for us. I never got that far, because she came to a halt outside the café and tentatively took hold of my arm. And uttered those words which now echoed in my head as I lay motionless in Mrs. Bentsen's room.

I didn't stand up immediately when I started to move. First my eyelids stirred, then my fingers, and gradually, one by one, my limbs. It was strange how long it took me to get my bearings, as if I had just come back from a long voyage and had to remind myself of every detail of my surroundings because it all looked so unfamiliar, even Anthony as he switched off the equipment and adjusted his glasses.

When I finally got up off the bed, I went over to one of the windows and looked out toward the sea. You can't see it in the summer for the leaves on the trees, and yet I stood gazing out until Anthony said to me: "So, did you get what you wanted out of this?"

The next day, the first heat wave of the summer came over the city. I woke up early and jogged in Central Park, despite a little weakness, and then had brunch at the diner on the corner of Columbus and Seventy-Fourth. When I got home I tried to work, but soon gave up and, after much agonizing, finally called my parents in Allington.

never understood why we left Kingham. My father said it was because of my mother, but I didn't believe him. I suspected he had money troubles, as was so often the case, although he would have denied it.

I had just turned ten. He said she found the town depressing, and that it kept her from concentrating. She didn't want to disrupt our lives, he said, but she had put up with Kingham for too long. In addition, the climate had a bad effect on the piano, whose pitch was never as clear as it should be. Not even on a bright summer's day, because the instrument had no time to recover from those cloudy, damp periods so typical of Oxfordshire. That was why she had been unable to play for over a year, as I had doubtless noticed, and why she had to stop teaching: how could a pianist who is unable to pursue her own vocation possibly instruct others? He forbade me to discuss the matter with her, and said we mustn't let her suspect that we were anything but delighted about moving. I said good-bye to my friends Stephen, a Liverpool supporter, and Andrew, who taught me how to carve a bird out of a piece of wood, and who tolerated that I had a crush on his sister, Mary, although he had a hard time believing I could find her anything but irritating. She was a year younger than us, and had brown hair, big eyes, and a dark complexion, nothing like her two brothers and her parents who were all lily white.

Stephen and Andrew came to wave me off the day we left Kingham, and I watched through the rear window as they grew smaller in the distance. I never saw them again, but I have sometimes wondered whether they had secretly agreed not to ask me why we never played at my house. They always acted as if it were natural that we should meet at either of their houses, and treated me as an equal, sometimes even with surprising respect, possibly because I was better at school than they were, and if necessary would help them with their homework. I wrote Mary a letter before I left, which Andrew swore he would give to her, but she never wrote back and I gradually forgot about her. I sometimes wonder whether he kept his promise.

Allington in Hertfordshire is a nondescript little town with a population of around fifteen thousand. The high street has the same shops and services you find in other small English towns—hairdressers, grocers, butchers, bakers, and banks. The train from Kings Cross to Cambridge stops in Kneesworth Street; an hour from London and approximately half an hour to Cambridge. The town was almost deserted on the Sunday we moved into the house on Abbey Court, and none of our new neighbors made an appearance, except for Mrs. Tribble who lived opposite. I watched her make her way across the street to greet my parents. My mother hurried inside, while my father exchanged a few words with our neighbor, and then it started to rain. It rained all day and into the evening, and was still raining when I woke up in my new room the next morning. The house stood at the end of a cul-de-sac, and from my window I could see a large field where the local boys played football. Either my father hadn't noticed the goalposts when he bought the place, or he hadn't stopped to think about the consequences. The pitch was frequently shrouded in fog, which, like everything else in the town of Allington, held little excitement: I had difficulty imagining anything lurking in it, either superheroes or monsters. Although there were times when the sun came out, dispersing the fog, and the pitch would light up for a moment so you no longer saw the puddles and muddy patches where grass never grew.

I guessed that the old black telephone must still be in the hallway; I doubted my father would have replaced it with a new one. I could see the hallway, the table where the telephone sat, the umbrella stand, the green rug, the pictures of Chopin and Mozart above the table. The staircase to the upper floor. I hadn't been there in over a decade, but nothing had changed since I was a boy.

I counted the rings, and was about to hang up after the fifth, when he answered. We hadn't spoken in two years, and yet his voice hadn't changed. Friendly yet guarded, almost suspicious.

"It's me," I said, and then a moment later felt it necessary to add: "Magnus Colin."

"Oh, Magnus!" And then added: "Is everything all right?"

"Yes," I said. "Everything's fine."

"Are you in New York?"

"No, I'm at the hospital."

"In Connecticut? Here it's getting late, nearly dark."

I asked about the weather and their health; he saw no reason to discuss the weather, but said he had news of my mother, who for as long as I can remember has always been battling some mysterious ailment or other.

"The doctors you recommended weren't much good," he said. "But one of Margaret's German fans introduced us to a compatriot of his, whom I can only describe as a miracle worker. She hasn't felt this well in years."

My father has always referred to my mother by her first name when talking to me: he has never said "your mother," much less "your mom." It's the same with her. Vincent, never "your dad" or "your father." And I myself haven't called them Daddy or Mommy since I was a kid in Kingham. I didn't stop on purpose; I simply got used to calling them by their first names, and I had no reason to object to it. Some people find it strange—Malena certainly did—but I was perfectly at ease with it and never felt that in some way I was missing out. Our relationship had always been like that.

"Did you get my postcard?"

"From Rome?"

"No, I sent it from Paris."

"Yes, you're right. We did. Were you there for long?"

"Just a few days."

"Margaret and I spent five months in Paris once. Before you were born, of course. After that we couldn't get away. I seem to remember it was in sixty-seven rather than sixty-eight. We stayed in an apartment in a little street off Boulevard Saint-Germain. What was it called again? There was a café opposite where we would start the day with a coffee and a croissant. Margaret was playing magnificently during those months. It was as if every note had wings. The high point of course was the recital she gave at Salle Gaveau."

I walked out onto the balcony while he was talking. I live on West Seventy-Fifth Street, just off Central Park, in a two-bedroom apartment on the fourth floor of a five-story townhouse dating from the end of the nineteenth century. Most of the houses in the area were built around the same time; they are about twenty feet wide, four or five stories high, and have one or two flats to each floor. The apartment buildings on Central Park West are much taller, but they don't overshadow us too much. My balcony overlooks a back garden, and although rather small, it's spacious enough for a table and two chairs as well as a few flowerpots. Malena and I would often eat dinner out there, and sometimes when it was too hot in the bedroom, we would spread our comforter out on the floor in the living room next to the open balcony doors. It felt good making love there, with the warm breeze and the glimmer of city lights, and afterward as we held hands and listened to our heartbeats slowing, I would ask myself whether I deserved to be that happy.

When I rented the apartment, I had assumed I would be working in New York for at least a few years. I had just been hired to join a small team of neuroscientists at Mount Sinai Hospital and welcomed moving from New Haven, where I had lived while in medical school. It was therefore ironic that only six months later, we were informed that our department had been merged with a team from Yale. Since they had more money and better infrastructure, we had to pack up and join them at their new facilities outside the village of Cold Harbor, Connecticut, about an hour away from the city.

My commute isn't straightforward. It would be easier if I lived on the east side, but I've always preferred the west side. I take the subway on Central Park West and then walk to the Metro-North train at 125th Street. But it's worth the trouble. I get to enjoy the city at night and most weekends, and I use the time on the train to read or simply let my mind wander.

All this back and forth confused Vincent who had a hard time keeping my whereabouts straight.

"But who knows," I heard him say. "At this rate, Margaret may soon be well enough to travel. And then it would be perfect to take the train to Paris, although I can't say I like the idea of going in that tunnel under the Channel. How long is the train in there for, anyway?"

I have often been on the verge of moving out of my apartment, but I always change my mind at the last minute. Last March, I told the landlord I was leaving, and had started packing my stuff into boxes when I changed my mind. He had already rented it out, but fortunately for me the woman below left at the same time, so he let them have her apartment instead. Simone is right when she tells me I should move out and try to build a new life, but I have too many memories. And I fear that without the apartment to remind me, I will forget, although it stands to reason that I should start forgetting if I want to build a "new life."

"Can I count on you being here for her seventieth?"

The birthday party. I had been hoping the plan might have changed.

"When is it?"

"The weekend after her birthday. Saturday. Three o'clock."

I paused. My hesitation didn't go unnoticed. He waited. I sensed from his silence that he was expecting me to say I couldn't come. I sensed, too, that whatever excuse I gave, he wouldn't believe.

"Sure, I'll be there."

"Magnus," he said, "this isn't going to be any ordinary birthday party. It'll be an event."

"Oh?"

"God willing. But I shall say no more. Things have been happening here, Magnus. Big things."

I would normally ignore this kind of declaration, but there was something about his voice that made me stop and listen. Until he said:

"Will you come alone or with your sweetheart?"

"Alone," I managed to reply, before quickly saying good-bye.

Over the years, Simone has become convinced that Hofsinger's name shouldn't have appeared before Osborne and Moreau in the list of authors of the article in the *New England Journal of Medicine*. It's true that they were largely responsible for the implementation, and yet it can't be denied that the idea was as much Hofsinger's as theirs, and that it was due to his influence that they received the grant for such an extensive research project. Those personality traits which she most objects to in him (his overweening self-confidence bordering on arrogance, his amazing ability to wipe the floor with his opponents) are extremely useful when dealing with the politicians and bureaucrats that decide who receives grants and who doesn't. I also pointed out that his surname came before theirs in the alphabet, but I needn't have bothered as she instantly argued that none of the other authors were listed in alphabetical order, so that my name came last, hers second to last, Vanhaudenhuyse came after Murphy, and Zeiler came before McCarthy.

"In fact, you should have been one of the main authors," she said. "You certainly deserved it."

And yet she knows I don't care where my name appears on the authors list. I prefer to keep a low profile and like to be left to work in peace and quiet. It's not that I'm particularly self-effacing, but ambition and status seeking don't interest me. The shrink I saw last year tried to relate this to my upbringing, of course, but I wasn't interested in talking endlessly about those days, and so in the end I stopped going. He was in his early sixties, soft-spoken to the point where sometimes I thought I might be losing my hearing. He meant well, but didn't help me much. From his office I could see the well-lit rear windows of a music school; I would occasionally watch the supple movements of the violinists rehearsing in a bright and spacious room, and I even found myself trying to guess what they were playing.

He asked me at one point if I thought that Margaret was possibly autistic (he used the word "mildly") or suffered from some form of Asperger's. I had never considered it and told him so. "Being a neuroscientist," he said, "I think you would know." Perhaps he was trying to flatter me, but I answered that recent events would suggest that diagnosing those close to me wasn't a particular strength of mine. He smiled, but broached the subject of Asperger's again the following week, this time asking if I had ever taken a test myself. By that time I had given up on him and never filled out the quiz he e-mailed me the following day. Indeed, I don't think I ever saw him again.

The article, which marked the start of the research I have been working on continuously for the past couple of years, or since it was published in early 2006, was focused on twenty-eight patients who had suffered such extreme head injuries that their brains showed no sign of life. They were considered incapable of thought or expression and had been kept alive on ventilators, some for several years. Most were accident or stroke victims, two had contracted meningitis, and one had a rare degenerative disease. The youngest patient was about twenty and had been in a motorcycle accident, and the oldest had suffered a stroke at sixty-two. Most were men.

The aim of the research was to find out whether any of the patients might enjoy some level of consciousness despite evidence to the contrary. Osborne, Moreau, and Hofsinger came up with the idea of placing them in an MRI scanner, where it would be possible to monitor brain activity in response to questions or instructions by measuring the blood flow within the brain. The research is being carried out in three different places, with us here in Connecticut, Osborne in Cambridge, and Moreau in Liège. I remember Hofsinger saying when we slid the first patient into the narrow and, by most accounts, terrifying hole: "At least we don't have to worry that he'll feel claustrophobic."

The research consists of the following procedure: once our patients are inside the machine, we ask them to imagine playing tennis and walking through their house. When healthy people imagine playing tennis, they show activity in a region of the motor cortex called the supplementary motor area, and when they think about navigating their house, blood flows to the parahippocampal gyrus located in the medial temporal lobe, in the center of the brain. The scanner registers the activity, producing a corresponding image on the computer screen.

Hopes were high the day the ambulance brought our first patient, a carpenter who had fallen off a ladder and never regained consciousness, to the research lab. This was before the department moved from New Haven to Clear Harbor, and so the process was more cumbersome. We all waited by the window, except for Hofsinger, who behaved as if that day were no different from any other. I remember clearly that it was raining yet warm. Malena called to wish me good luck just before the ambulance drove up to the building. Her voice cheered me as always.

For weeks we had tested the equipment which we developed

in conjunction with our colleagues in Cambridge and Liège. The software had been a bit unstable to begin with, but the programmers had made improvements and now it was behaving perfectly. Simone and I had taken turns lying inside the scanner and imagining we were playing tennis or walking around our respective homes, and the appropriate areas of our brains had lit up on the screen as anticipated.

And so it was all the more disappointing when the equipment failed at the first attempt. We had finally installed the patient inside the scanner, after some difficulty with the ventilator cables and tubes, and Hofsinger had taken up his position in front of the microphone connected to the scanner, ready to address the patient. He was, of course, aware that this was a potentially historic moment, and although his speech was formal as always, his manner was almost jaunty.

He was taken aback when I told him that we had a problem. He stood still for a moment, glaring at me, demanding an explanation. Given that he had scarcely taken any part in the preparations, I saw no reason to go into a long story about what might have gone wrong.

"I'll let you know the moment it's fixed," I said.

He glanced at his watch before walking out. I suspected the software was to blame, and after a brief inspection it turned out there had been a glitch introduced the evening before when the programmers decided on their own to try to shorten the response times even more. With software, it isn't uncommon for one thing to go wrong when another is fixed, and they were quick to discover the fault and correct it. I found Hofsinger in his office and he took up his position at the microphone as before, while I sat in front of the screens next to the programmers and some other technicians, and gave him the signal when we were ready.

"Good morning, my name is Dr. Hofsinger. You are in an MRI scanner . . ."

He explained the procedure and asked the p[...] low his instructions. He tried to sound at once aut[...] reassuring, which he is good at. But it didn't work. No ma[...] how many times he told the man to imagine that he was playing tennis or walking from room to room, the screen showed no response, either in the motor cortex or in the parahippocampal gyrus. Even so, we didn't give up, and continued the next day—with the same result.

Our colleagues in Cambridge and Liège fared no better with their patients, and there is no denying that some members of the team were a little dejected when we compared notes during a conference call at the end of the week. They had no reason to be, of course; it was only to be expected that most, if not all, of our patients were irrevocably lost, their brains so damaged that they contained no conscious thought.

During the weeks that followed, expectation gave way to despair when none of our patients, or those in Cambridge and Liège, showed any response. It was as if we had invented a sophisticated way of trawling for fish only to discover there were none left in the sea. Hofsinger made an occasional appearance, leaving me in charge of dealing with the patients. It can't be said he missed anything, because patient number twenty-two, as he was referred to in the article, wasn't one of ours but our colleagues' in Liège.

He was twenty-four years old and had been in a car accident five years before. There was nothing to suggest that he had any more life in him than the other patients; sometimes the corners of his mouth would twitch, and every now and then he would grind his teeth, but so did the others, and such gestures are merely unconscious nerve impulses. Yet he thought about tennis when Moreau told him to, and at Moreau's behest conjured up in his mind the image of a house through which he pretended to be walking. Not just once or twice, but over and over again, ree days in a row, until it became clear that he had been locked inside his paralyzed body all these years.

Hofsinger and I flew over from New York and Osborne traveled from Cambridge, and after resting for an hour, we met at the lab and watched Moreau talk to his patient, as the different areas of his brain lit up on the screen. Hofsinger doesn't understand French and asked me what Moreau was saying, as though wanting to make sure the questions were the same ones he himself had asked our patient.

We had a celebratory dinner at a small bistro near Rue Fond Saint-Servais. It had rained during the day, but by evening the sky had cleared and there was a splendid sunset as we sat outside on the terrace. There were ten of us around the table, and Hofsinger made an overly long speech, comparing the human brain to a labyrinth, no less mysterious than outer space. He had drunk a few glasses of red wine, and his words, pompous yet eloquent, were undoubtedly lost on most of the Belgians, who spoke little English. In the middle of his speech I received a text from Malena, and I couldn't resist picking up my phone. It said: *If you examine my brain, you'll see I'm thinking of you,* and then she added a smiley face.

I called her later that night from my hotel room. She was on her way to a dance performance and was heading toward the subway on Central Park West. I could hear the murmur of traffic and had the impression she was late, so I quickly said I hoped she had fun, when all I really wanted was to listen to her voice. She sensed it, and I heard her slowing down as she told me what wonderful weather they were having, how Central Park was in bloom, and how much she loved me. Then she blew me a kiss down the phone and I thought I heard her say once more that she loved me, but by then she was on her way down into the subway and the call broke up. I could see her threading her way deftly through people on the stairs, and I knew she hadn't held back when she blew me that kiss, that she was unembarrassed amid all those strangers. I thought about how different we were. I would never be able to do that, and still I loved her more than I ever thought I'd be capable of.

I felt empty after I hung up. I had been like that at the restaurant earlier that evening, only now it was worse. I told myself I was probably tired after the journey; jet lag always affects me. And yet I couldn't help thinking there might be a deeper problem. Earlier, while Hofsinger was talking, I had started to reflect on patient number twenty-two. We were acting as if we had performed some miracle, and yet there he lay in the hospital ward, where he had lain for the past five years, trapped inside his body, with no hope of change. I tried to tell myself that at least he could listen to music or the radio or news from his friends and family when they visited him, but I wasn't convinced.

It came as a shock. I had taken part in one experiment after another, and although some of our patients had pointed us in the right direction, until now there had been no real results. I should have felt proud, optimistic, like my colleagues, in particular Osborne who was over the moon and kept repeating that we had saved patient number twenty-two, who had "practically been buried alive," as he put it. But instead I was discouraged.

The hotel wasn't far from the center of Liège, but when I returned from the restaurant and went back to my room all I saw through the window were deserted streets and, beyond the low-roofed houses, the river. It had started drizzling again, and the streets were slick and the lights in the neighborhood hazy. I knew it was hopeless to try to sleep and I was too agitated to read or watch television, so I grabbed a light jacket and went out.

Before I knew it, I found myself heading toward the hospital. It was only a short walk, and I had no problem remembering the way from my previous visits.

The patient was alone in the room, the hum of the ventilator scarcely breaking the silence. A soft lamp glowed in the corner, but around his bed lights from the medical equipment dotted the shadows. I paused in the middle of the room, before walking toward him. There were no personal effects around, nothing that offered any idea of what his life might have been like. Someone had left a newspaper on the chair by the window, one of the nurses, I imagined. On the front page was a picture of a train crash.

I had been overcome by a sudden urge to see him, and yet I realized now that I had nothing to say to him, nothing that could interest him or make his life easier in any way. He appeared to be sleeping, and I took care not to wake him. I felt drowsy myself and sat down. It was still raining, the drizzle was now a downpour and rain was streaming down the windows. Before I knew it, I was asleep.

It was past four in the morning when I woke up. The newspaper had vanished and someone had placed a pillow under my head. It took me a moment to realize where I was, but as I stood up and looked at the patient, it suddenly occurred to me how we might try to communicate with him. It was as though I had always known, as though the idea had come to me long ago and was waiting for this moment to reveal itself. My response seemed to confirm this: I didn't get excited the way I often do when a new idea pops into my head. I simply opened the door quietly and walked into the night.

As I might have expected, Simone heard about my "antics," as she called them. She didn't tell me how ("It doesn't matter," she replied when I asked), but clearly Anthony had been unable to stop himself from telling her that I had asked for his assistance, not hers. He wouldn't have used those words, of course, but said enough for her to take offense. She looked at me in silence, with that schoolmarmish expression that shows she is at once disappointed and concerned, then asked me, as she had done more than once during the past few months, whether everything was all right. I said yes, even though "everything" is a big word, hoping she wouldn't ask further, demand to know what I had been thinking, because my explanation would make no sense to her. And so, I replied:

"I could hear the sea."

I was sitting at my desk; she was standing by the door. It had been open but now she closed it.

"Magnus," she said, "what on earth are you talking about?"

I could barely look her in the eye, but didn't want to seem evasive.

"While I lay there paralyzed, I discovered that I could hear the sea. You should try it sometime."

"You mean being injected with succs and placed on a ventilator?"

"Vecuronium bromide," I corrected, and tried to smile.

"It doesn't help them, Magnus. Nor you. You must try to . . ."

She fell silent. I saw her eye alight on the photograph of me and Malena which I had pinned to the bookshelf above my desk. It had been taken in Florence, on Ponte Vecchio, six months before she died. We were on our way to the Uffizi and had stopped to look down at the river. She had asked a passerby if he would take a photo of us. She has her arms around me and a playful expression on her face.

I glanced at the photograph, then at Simone. I was keen to end the conversation.

"You should go out and find a man so you can stop worrying about me," I said.

She smiled weakly, and, of course, I regretted what I had said, especially after everything that's happened between us. But I had the feeling she was going to put her arms around me the way she sometimes had after Malena's death. I wanted to avoid that.

The telephone rang. I hurriedly picked it up, but Simone stood still, listening to me go over the results of the latest research with Osborne. Out of the corner of my eye, I saw her thrust her hand into the pocket of her white gown while she continued to stare at me, as if she were trying to see into my mind. She must have had a chewing gum wrapper in her pocket; I could hear it rustle. I took notes while Osborne was talking, although I knew he would e-mail me a detailed report.

The idea I had had that night in Liège proved more complicated to put into practice than I had thought. And yet it couldn't be simpler. With patients able to imagine playing tennis or walking around their house, we would try to communicate by asking them yes or no questions. For yes, they would be instructed to imagine playing tennis. For no, they would be told to think about walking through their house. I had explained it to the three wise men, as Simone calls them, over breakfast the day after my visit to patient number twenty-two, and they quickly embraced the idea, especially Osborne. Moreau and Hofsinger gave the impression of regretting they hadn't thought of it themselves, and Hofsinger said in a detached voice: "That seems like a logical next step."

Patient number twenty-two was occasionally able to respond to those questions, but the same can't be said of those who came to us subsequently—one here in Connecticut and two in Cambridge. They had more severe brain damage, and in addition the software proved less reliable than we had anticipated. Still, we carried on undaunted, and recently Osborne had told us he had high hopes for a female patient from Dover, who promised to be even more lucid than patient number twenty-two. Or so he thought, until suddenly she stopped responding to the simplest questions.

I gave Simone an account of the call, going into far more detail than was necessary to try to prevent her from picking up the thread of our own conversation. While she didn't seem to be paying full attention, I assumed I had succeeded.

When I thought she was leaving, she paused in the doorway.

"How could you hear the sea?"

I looked at her, maybe a little puzzled, and she repeated the question.

"An hour had gone by," I replied, "when suddenly I heard the waves."

She frowned.

"I wasn't imagining it," I added.

"Let me know if you get any other weird ideas," she said as she walked out, "preferably before you act on them."

Later that day, when I needed to speak to her about something, I couldn't find her anywhere. I called her cell phone, but it was switched off. Finally, one of the nurses told me she had seen her go into Mrs. Bentsen's room a while ago.

When I opened the door, she was lying on the bed with the windows open. She gave a start when she saw me, but said nothing and decided to lie still. I didn't leave, and before I knew it I was listening for the waves as well.

On our last evening in Florence, Malena and I went to a concert in the gardens of a small castle, just outside the city. We were running late, and she asked me to hurry her as she got into the shower. She would often do that. She said she had no sense of time—like all Argentinians. When I alerted her, she would always reply in a playful voice, devoid of anxiety or panic: "Already? Oh my God!" Sometimes, for fun, I would lie and say it was later than it really was, but it always turned out that she knew better. "Really?" she would begin, before adding: "No, that can't be . . . You're teasing me."

The hotel overlooked the Arno; the building dated back to the Renaissance. The windows were tall, running from floor to ceiling. I opened one and looked down at the men on the river-bank with their fishing rods as I dressed. I could hear her turn off the shower. The sun was setting behind the hills, which turned from red to blue as dusk settled over the city. I walked over to the bathroom to move her along, but paused the instant I saw her. She was standing naked over the washbasin, putting on some facial cream. She was on tiptoe to get closer to the mirror, and I gazed at her pale brown back and hips, her calves, her dark hair, still wet, which fell over her shoulders and always gave off a whiff of spring.

When we had returned to the hotel that afternoon, I had dozed off for a while in the warm breeze from the river and dreamt that I was walking in a forest. I thought about that forest as I watched her, and couldn't bring myself to say that it was eight o'clock. I didn't want the moment to end, but she had sensed my presence, and smiled when she turned around and saw me. She said nothing, simply opened her arms as I went over and embraced her, kneeling to kiss her belly, then moving my head down and kissing her there, too, clasping her to me. She ran her fingers through my hair, and I told myself that as long as I had her I could endure any ordeal or disappointment, any adversity. Before we met, I had been prone to take failure badly, especially in the lab, and was quick to blame myself when things went wrong. I would panic unnecessarily, and occasionally, when I was very low, I imagined that I might have inherited from my mother the traits I feared most.

I awoke before dawn alone in bed. The concert had finished at about eleven, and we decided to ask the cabdriver who brought us back to drop us off halfway to the hotel so we could walk the rest of the way. It was a starlit night, and the full moon shone on the red rooftops of the city and the squares, where people at outside cafés spoke to each other in half whispers. We were crossing Piazza della Signoria when she came to an abrupt halt. I felt her hand pull on mine and instinctively tugged to prevent her from falling. She clutched her right ankle, then stood up straight and smiled.

"How clumsy I am."

She insisted she had tripped, and I didn't give it another thought, although the ground looked smooth to me. She was wearing low-heeled shoes and a skirt she had bought earlier that day, and I looked down at her feet, so perfectly formed. We carried on across the square, threading our way through the streets down to the river and back to the hotel.

When I awoke that night she was standing in the moonlight before the open windows. I watched her raise one leg, stretching out her arm, then lower it again and step to the side, before raising the other, her movements fluid, as if she were standing in water. The moonlight enveloped her, but stopped short of the bed where I lay motionless in the dark watching her.

In the end I walked over to her. We stood in silence gazing down at the river and the moon reflected in it, seemingly floating idly downstream.

On the phone, Vincent told me my old room was being used for something else now—he didn't explain
what, although I could tell he was hoping I would try
to wheedle it out of him—but that if I wanted I could sleep on
a mattress on the floor. In fact, I was relieved. I didn't want to
stay with my parents and had already been thinking of excuses. I
had reserved a room at a bed-and-breakfast on Tenison Road in
Cambridge, halfway between the station and the tennis courts,
and rented a small car. I had told my father my flight arrived
in the morning, and that I would drive straight from London
to the party, which was to start at three thirty. He had urged
me not to be late, for I might miss "the big surprise," which was
carefully timed. He paused for a moment, hoping I would ask
him to elaborate, but I didn't. I had discovered long ago that it
was better to ignore my father's antics.

I hadn't lived long at Abbey Court in Allington. The year
after we moved there, I went to St. Joseph's, a boarding school in
South Cambridgeshire. I liked it there, made good friends, and
went home only at half-term and during the summer holidays. I
did well academically and was good at football and swimming.

I acted in a few school plays and took part in the science club activities. I think I more or less faked an interest in plants because Murray, the school gardener, used to hire five boys to help him over the summer. I suspect he knew, and guessed my reasons, but I worked hard and grew fond of him and his wife, Beatrice. They lived a stone's throw from the school, in a small brick house with a fountain in the garden, and when in late July the school closed for the holidays and my coworkers went home, I was allowed to stay with them for two weeks before going back to Allington. I had to get written permission from my parents, but that was never a problem.

I didn't sleep much on the plane and had difficulty staying awake at the wheel of the rental car. I pulled over after half an hour to buy coffee and drank it in the parking lot before setting off again. The weather was cloudy but dry, and quite warm. I glimpsed patches of blue sky to the east, but the west was overcast, and here and there veils of rain hung from the clouds, brushing the green hills. I was remembering Murray and Beatrice, both long dead, and their house, and the fountain, when suddenly it occurred to me that I might have time to go there on my way to Cambridge, where I had planned to stop off at the bed-and-breakfast, take a shower, and change before leaving for Allington. It was eleven o'clock, and this detour would take only forty-five minutes, an hour at the most.

I drove off the motorway at the first opportunity, heading north, first through the suburbs, then through villages and country roads. The drive is prettiest between Stanstead Abbotts and Standon, where the road narrows and disappears for a stretch into a forest. I slowed down when I came to the River Rib, pulled over at the side of the road, and threaded my way along the path until I reached the riverbank. There I sat down, leaning against the trunk of a big tree. The weather had cleared, and every so often the sun would shine through the clouds onto the river and the surrounding fields.

It wasn't strange that I ended up dozing off in the calm by the river, but of course it spoiled my plans, including my intended detour to Murray and Beatrice's house. By the time I woke up, it was almost two o'clock, and huge raindrops were breaking the smooth surface of the river. I couldn't feel them beneath the thick canopy of the tree overhanging the water, but now I leapt to my feet and sprinted back to the car. It bucketed during the remainder of the journey, and as I drove into Cambridge, the windshield wipers were scarcely able to keep pace.

At the bed-and-breakfast, I took a quick shower before hurriedly putting on a suit I hadn't had any reason to wear for months, a blue shirt we had bought in Florence, and a tie. I can't stand such outfits and loosened my tie with the intention of straightening it again once I arrived at Allington. I still had to buy flowers; I didn't want to show up empty-handed at the party, but had been unable to think of a gift Margaret might like. I stopped off at a florist's shop on the way out of town and grabbed a preselected bouquet, as I didn't have time to wait for the shop assistant to put together anything fancier.

It was half past three when I drove into Allington. There were few people in the center of town, and most of the shops were shut. I had no feelings about the place, good or bad. All I could think about was the time.

For some reason, I had been expecting a bigger gathering, and was surprised to see plenty of parking spaces on the street. I pulled up outside Mrs. Tribble's old house and turned off the engine. She had moved many years ago and there were children's toys in her garden now, and a bicycle propped against the fence. I was barely ten minutes late; even so, I felt as if somehow I had let my parents down. I paused for a moment, retrieved the flowers from the passenger seat, and hurried across the street.

I had to ring twice before Vincent came to the door. He had on a brown suit that looked too big, and a yellow shirt with a brown tie. His gray hair didn't seem to have thinned much, but the lenses in his square, steel-rimmed spectacles looked thicker than before.

"I was starting to think you weren't coming," he said as he opened the door. "Was your flight late?"

I was about to say yes, as I would doubtless have done when I was younger, but announced instead, in a louder voice than I had intended:

"No, I fell asleep."

He looked at me, almost startled, and then I saw the corners of his mouth twitch as if he were about to smile.

"Come in," he said. "It's a small gathering. Let me introduce you to our guests."

I looked around as I followed him to the living room. Apart from a few wet umbrellas in the stand beside the front door, nothing had changed since I was a boy. The telephone was still on the table in the hallway, Mozart and Chopin on the wall above, the green rug on the floor.

The living room is double, but not particularly spacious. In the bigger room facing the street there is a three-piece suite, a coffee table, a small fireplace, and against the wall a sideboard with a collection of family photos on it, including some of me as a child. In the smaller room overlooking the back garden, there is the grand piano, and the walls are covered with photographs of Margaret at different times in her life, of Rachmaninoff, Liszt, and Vladimir Horowitz, who according to Vincent was the only twentieth-century pianist, besides Margaret, capable of playing Liszt, especially the sonata in B minor.

My mother was nowhere to be seen and there were four guests in the lounge, three men and a woman. I had already met Christopher Llewellyn Hunt, director of the Cambridge School of Music, where Margaret had once taught, and his wife, Hilary. I had never met the other two, a tall man my age and an older man with a beard and thick, well-groomed hair. I knew my parents had always considered Hunt one of their staunchest supporters, and I remembered that Vincent used to call him when things weren't going so well for Margaret. Which was often. Hunt always appeared sympathetic and told Vincent what he wanted to hear—that Margaret was a genius and would one day receive due recognition. She had held several recitals at the school concert hall, and Hunt would write flattering things about her in the program. I remember attending one of them between Christmas and New Year's Day when I was a teenager. The hall had been almost deserted. Rain had turned to snow.

I realized I was still holding the flowers when I went to shake the couple's hands, so I asked my father to take them. He did so, setting them aside without a glance, and it was then that I noticed in my hurry I had forgotten to write on the card. It was too late now, and pointless for me to feel remorse.

I knew Vincent would introduce me to his guests in the most grandiose terms, but still he made me squirm. He referred to me as a "famous neurologist" working at "the leading neurological research institute in the States," and told them he had lost count of all the plaudits I had earned and papers I had published, despite my young age.

"We hardly ever clap eyes on him, he's so busy," he added. "But science must come first, isn't that right?"

The older man introduced himself as Philip Ellis, and said he and my father were in business together, though he didn't say what business. Vincent offered no explanations, either, but I assumed my father had founded yet another record label specializing in classical music. Ellis wore a large red stone on the ring finger of his right hand. He smelled of tobacco, and at the corners of his mouth his gray beard was stained yellow.

The other man was a German, Hans Kleuber. He spoke with a heavy accent and had a slight stoop, and when he bowed to shake my hand, I thought he was never going to straighten up again. Vincent told me and the Hunts about him. Ellis seemed to know him already. Kleuber owned one of the largest collections of records in the world, Vincent said, having set out to acquire all the piano music that mattered. They had met roughly a year ago, when Kleuber wrote to him inquiring about "a few" recordings from the sixties and seventies.

"Three hundred," said Kleuber, grinning. "And Vincent was able to throw light on all but ten or twenty. Incredible, but true."

There was no hint of sarcasm in his words, and I wondered how much Kleuber knew about my father's past. I got my answer a moment later when he added:

"Of those three hundred records, only about fourteen were released by Mecca."

Mecca was the record label my father owned in the late seventies, the type that rereleased recordings by well-known artists under made-up names and sold them cheaply. Thus, for example, Beethoven's Fifth Symphony with Herbert von Karajan conducting the Berlin Philharmonic was reattributed to the Vienna State Orchestra conducted by Wilhelms von Eggertz, repackaged, and sold at less than half the original price. The Vienna State Orchestra and Wilhelms von Eggertz were both my father's inventions, as were the conductors Romano Ferrere and Claudio Mascarpone, the Helsinki District Symphony Orchestra, the violinist Marta von Klapper, and the vocalist Benjamin Gross. Earlier on in his career, Vincent had failed with two similar enterprises, but with Mecca he had found modest success. He took out a loan, mortgaged the house he had recently inherited from his parents, and decided to move up the food chain, signing deals with four well-known artists, including Heinrich von der Heydt and Camilla Launer, whose career was only beginning. But the musician he seemingly paid the most attention to was Margaret. The two of them had just met.

Vincent fetched a bottle of Champagne and made a great show of popping the cork before he filled the glasses waiting on a tray next to the fireplace. Everyone could see that it was a bottle of Dom Pérignon, and Hilary indulged him by mentioning the fact.

"Only the best," he said. "Only the very best . . ."

There was still no sign of Margaret, and I assumed he had explained her absence before I arrived, so I asked no questions. We raised our glasses, "To Margaret," and then Vincent asked me to follow him into the kitchen. He took the empty Champagne bottle with him, and I carried the flowers.

On the kitchen table, under plastic wrap, were some sandwiches and finger food from the delicatessen in town, and next to them two silver trays, both from Vincent's parents' estate. He picked up a tumbler full of colored cocktail sticks and asked me to arrange the finger food and sandwiches on the trays, with the sticks in them. In the meantime, he went to the fridge, took out a bottle of sparkling wine, and opened it over the sink. Then he fetched a funnel and decanted it into the empty Dom Pérignon bottle standing on the dish rack. I pretended not to notice, but instead of the usual contempt, this act aroused feelings of pity, and regret at being there.

"Where's Margaret?" I asked.

He disposed of the empty bottle of sparkling wine under the sink.

"Upstairs. She's getting ready."

With this he glanced at his watch and gave a start.

"We must sit down," he said when we were back in the living room. "I hadn't realized the time."

He indicated the sofa and chairs, then rushed upstairs. I could hear the familiar old creak of the staircase and had a sudden fear that he might slip. Hilary and Christopher Llewellyn

Hunt sat together on the sofa, Ellis in one of the armchairs next to them, while Kleuber and I perched on two chairs from the dining room. No one said a word until Kleuber leaned over to me and whispered: "Terribly exciting, isn't it?" I nodded, although I was starting to feel uneasy and wished I could disappear.

It was at least ten minutes before Margaret came down. In order to avoid having to walk past us, she entered via the kitchen, through the connecting doors behind the piano. Kleuber came to life and started clapping, and we all joined in. Vincent followed behind, taking his usual seat in a corner by the piano.

She sat down without looking at us. I thought I saw her bob her head, but I may have been imagining it. I was only too familiar with the tension in her face and the tremor in her hands before she clasped them in her lap. For a moment I thought she was about to push the stool away from the piano and flee, but then her shoulders slowly lowered, her face relaxed, and her eyes fixed on the keyboard. We watched her with bated breath, Kleuber craning his long neck, captivated before she had even struck the first note.

Rachmaninoff's Sonata No. 2. "Monstrous" is the word I heard her use to describe it once when I was a boy. I remember that day well. It was summer, and I had been playing football in the field by our house with some of my friends. She was going through a bad patch at the time, and I was doing my best to stay out of her way, make myself scarce. I arrived home and heard a torrent of words coming from the living room, frantic wails of despair, stifled exclamations, choking sobs. "I can't, I just can't . . . It's monstrous, he's monstrous, and anyone who can play it is monstrous . . ." My father was trying to calm her down, in a gentle voice that only made things worse. "Stop! Stop! You don't understand . . ." As often, I had entered from the garden, but instead of hurrying upstairs to my room, I walked over to the connecting doors and peered into the piano room. I don't know why: I was used to such scenes, and thought they no longer affected me. She must have heard me, because suddenly she swung around and looked at me over her shoulder. I have never forgotten her expression, although I may have misinterpreted it at the time, for I felt as if she had spotted the reason for everything in her life that had gone wrong. She gave a loud cry and fled through the living room and up the stairs.

Vincent stooped to pick up the sheet music she had flung on the floor, then looked at me. For a moment he seemed unsure whether to stay and comfort me or follow her upstairs. Then he put the music aside, turned away, and walked out after her, head bowed.

At last Margaret looked up from the keyboard and raised her hands, with a movement so slow as to be almost imperceptible. She held them suspended midair, fingers drooping as if all her muscles had gone limp, eyes closed. She remained like that for a few seconds, in absolute silence, and then, as if a tide had washed over her, she slammed her fingers onto the keys with perfect assurance, and the room was filled with the opening bars of the sonata, which in my memory evoked only anguish. I hadn't heard the piece since that summer long ago, and yet I knew every single note the instant she played it, and I remembered the parts where she slipped up, as I sat in my bedroom reading the books I had borrowed from the library, and the football magazines I had bought at the newsstand next to the butcher, waiting for the summer holidays in Allington to end so I could go back to St. Joseph's.

I was on tenterhooks throughout her performance, half expecting her fingers to seize up, for her to fall apart. But it didn't happen, not during the fast, strenuous first movement, nor the slow, lyrical second. I had heard her sail through them, but never the last movement, *allegro molto,* dramatic, almost frenzied where it reaches the high notes. More than once I had heard Vincent and Margaret talking about it after she fled to the bedroom in despair, with Vincent close behind, consoling her. That always took forever, but afterward they would discuss the piece and what had gone wrong, and he would offer words of encouragement. If I was around, she acted as though nothing had happened.

She had aged, and yet her slender frame remained youthful, her back straight as an arrow. She moved constantly, even during the slow passages when her fingers scarcely brushed the keys, her arms, elbows out to the sides, rising and falling like giant spider legs. My father had always said she was like a sculptor, not a painter. That the notes were like clay in her hands, from which she could fashion whatever she wished: people, cities, hills and valleys, fleeting thoughts. At the time, I had taken no more notice of this remark than of his many other utterances, but as I sat there in the living room next to the transfixed Hans Kleuber, I finally understood what he had meant. Only it wasn't cities or people or hills or valleys I saw, but rather a wall rising slowly between us. And as it grew higher, so my anxiety increased, for I was convinced that at any moment she would strike that wrong note which would cause havoc: her thoughts would collide with her fingers, the wall would collapse on top of her, and she would run screaming from the wreckage.

She performed the shorter version of the sonata, which is about twenty minutes. The *allegro molto* is just over seven minutes, but seemed to take forever. I was exhausted by the time she played the final notes, bathed in sweat, my hands clasped so tight my fingers hurt. Kleuber leapt to his feet—"Bravo, bravo!"— and the others followed; everyone but me. She rose to her feet, smiling, as if there had been nothing to it and she had simply been playing a popular tune, beaming as she came toward us.

I took hold of myself and stood up, but Kleuber was already beside her, showering her with praise. Hilary and Christopher Llewellyn Hunt were close behind, then Ellis, a man with a knowing look who seemed to keep his thoughts to himself. I stood motionless, and rather than wait for me to approach, my mother flung out her arms.

"Colin, darling"—she rarely called me by my Icelandic first name—"how wonderful to see you! How long has it been since your last visit?"

We embraced fleetingly, and before I could reply, she thrust me from her, as if she had suddenly noticed something important, and said:

"Your tie needs straightening, my dear boy."

I had resolved to do it before getting out of the car, but in my haste I had forgotten. Usually, I wouldn't have let it get to me, but now I felt as if I had done something wrong. I clutched at my neck, fumbled for my tie and attempted to straighten it in the middle of the room.

"There's a mirror out in the hallway," she said as if I had never been to the house before.

The hum from the living room reached me as I stood before the mirror adjusting my tie and attempting to collect myself. I noticed how pale and tired I looked, but focused my gaze on my collar and tie. I had made a mess of it and had to take the tie off and start over. I heard Margaret raise her voice as though about to deliver the punch line, and Kleuber burst out laughing, but I couldn't make out the words.

I remained rooted to the spot after I had finished fixing my tie, unable to make myself go back into the living room. The window beside the front door caught my eye and I glimpsed the rental car parked across the street outside Mrs. Tribble's house. I fumbled in my jacket pocket for the keys. My feet turned toward the door, and before I knew it I had my hand on the latch. I glanced over my shoulder, turned the handle, and walked into the pouring rain.

As I got into the car outside Mrs. Tribble's house with the intention of starting the engine, I was suddenly over-whelmed by the same feeling of powerlessness as when I had lain hooked up to the ventilator, listening to the sea and Malena's voice in my head. I looked at the rain on the wind-shield and the keys in my hand, but was incapable of moving. It was as if I didn't know where I was heading and so couldn't set off. During the past few months, I thought I had made some progress: I no longer felt indifferent about everything, and was able to lose myself in my work, enjoy my first coffee of the day in the quiet kitchen or out on the balcony, find bright moments even though the darkness was never far away. But now I was en-veloped by a gloom that penetrated my brain, and for a moment I felt one with it. I didn't try to move, but instead closed my eyes and started listening for the sea and Malena's voice down in the village, as though casting around for a light amid the shadows.

For weeks I had forced myself to stop thinking about that day, but now I couldn't stop myself. The rain beat down on the car, calm and steady, but apart from that all was quiet. Perhaps I was too impatient or my thoughts too restless, because however hard I tried, I couldn't conjure up her face or hear her voice. I was seized by a sudden fear and dropped my keys noisily on the floor. I slowly picked them up and started the engine, turned on the windshield wipers, and gazed out into the grayness, at the empty field where we played football when I was a boy, the now dilapidated goalposts and the crows flapping overhead in the mist.

When I was about to drive off, my parents' door opened and my father looked out. He saw me immediately and our eyes met for a moment before I turned off the engine and took my cell phone discreetly out of the glove compartment. He waited for me while I crossed the street, but I beat him to it, showing him the phone in my hand and explaining that I had to take a call from the States and didn't want to bother everybody. He looked at the phone and then at me as if he couldn't figure me out. He didn't like it and, as we returned to the house, tried to regain the upper hand by grabbing the Champagne bottle as we walked into the sitting room and handing it to me. It was empty.

"Do me a favor," he said loud enough for everyone to hear. "Fetch another bottle of Dom Pérignon from the fridge. And toss this one while you're at it."

I looked around. Margaret was standing next to the fireplace talking to Hilary and Kleuber. She was excited and spoke in a loud voice, explaining something to them as she showed them first the backs, then the palms of her hands.

I went into the kitchen, opened the fridge, and took out a bottle of Codorniu Vintage Brut Cava, the same sparkling wine my father had poured into the Dom Pérignon bottle earlier on. There were three more on the bottom shelf next to the butter and eggs. I uncorked it over the sink and stood still for a long time, the Cava in my right hand and the empty Dom Pérignon bottle in my left, before finally grabbing a funnel and forcing myself to follow my father's example.

No sooner had I entered the sitting room than Vincent tapped his glass and cleared his throat. An unnecessary gesture in such a small gathering, but doubtless that was how he had envisioned the moment.

"Dear friends. When Margaret agreed to celebrate this turning point, it was on the condition that we would invite only our closest friends. Naturally, I had prepared a lengthy guest list, but as you know, Margaret doesn't like to be in the limelight . . ."

I was standing behind the others, and couldn't help lowering my eyes as he spoke. My tie was too tight and I winced with each word. Were the others unaware of what was going on? I wondered. I looked up, contemplating them one by one. Christopher and Hilary Llewellyn Hunt had always shown my parents unswerving loyalty, although I couldn't recall there being much contact between our two families. If they had any doubts, they certainly gave no sign of it as they stood side by side next to the fireplace. Kleuber hadn't known Vincent and Margaret long, and besides was so thrilled to have the honor of being among the chosen few, so childishly eager in his appreciation of Margaret, that there was no room for suspicion. Ellis wore his usual expression, as if he were constantly trying to stop himself from smirking.

Vincent went on talking. When at last I was able to look at him and at Margaret standing beside him, a dreamy smile on her face, I tried to imagine how they might appear to me if I were seeing them for the first time. He was in full swing, discussing the merits of one pianist after another: "Rubenstein was born with perfect piano hands: broad palms and fleshy fingertips, his little finger almost the same length as his middle finger . . . He played the romantics with a rare artistry, but was never much good at Bach and Mozart . . . Schnabel and Backhaus were serious, sturdy pianists like others of the German school, but they lacked imagination and inspiration . . . Horowitz came closest to Rachmaninoff himself, that pure tone came solely from his fingers, for he scarcely touched the pedals . . ." He emphasized each word as if he were explaining a hitherto unknown truth and barely drew breath between sentences.

I lost the thread of what he was saying more than once, and it was only toward the end that I realized his speech had been carefully crafted. It was the women's turn now, Annette Essipoff and Teresa Carreño: "Essipoff moved her fingers and wrists so beautifully, she was marvelous to watch . . . Carreño hammered the keys like a Valkyrie, masculine and forceful . . ." He spoke in a hushed, deep voice, the way he always did when he had something important to say. Then he fell silent, looked at Margaret, who bowed her head, then at us, pausing for a few seconds before raising his voice once more.

"We are gathered here today not merely to celebrate Margaret's birthday, although that is reason enough, but because in this modest dwelling something extraordinary has taken place. Something momentous, if I may say so, although, naturally, you must judge for yourselves."

That summer had started promisingly. April rains had given way to a sun-soaked May, and I had kept to my plan of going to more live events than the year before, especially those that took place in the open air. The first week of June the Lee Konitz Quartet played in Tompkins Square Park, and the weekend after I saw an old Hitchcock movie on the big screen in Bryant Park. I went by myself both times and enjoyed being alone in the crowd, but Simone invited me to *The Tempest* in the Delacorte Theater in Central Park in the middle of the month. She had bought two tickets at a charity event and wanted to show her gratitude for my support over the previous weeks. The worst was over, and yet understandably the accusations had taken their toll. When I glanced at her in profile as we stood in line, I noticed she had lost weight.

We didn't speak about her problems that evening, and I did my best to lighten the tone of our conversation. In May, following a two-month inquiry, the medical council had cleared her, and although this was reason to celebrate, we were both aware that she was guilty of making a serious error. The council had said as much but concluded that it was wishful thinking rather than any intentional deceit on her part that had gotten her into hot water. As her superior, Hofsinger hadn't taken part in the inquiry, but he made it clear that he thought Simone had gotten off lightly. She knew from the start that he was prepared to fire her if there was the slightest possibility that her actions reflected badly on him, and she had the impression that he had been secretly hoping the medical council would give him reason to do so. I think she was exaggerating, but he certainly wouldn't have hesitated to give her the sack if he thought it necessary.

Simone had been in charge of the patient, a man in his mid-thirties who had been in a coma for many years, and had deduced from the images that he might be less brain-damaged than previously assumed. Before taking things any further, she showed the images to Hofsinger and me, and we both thought she had a point. Simone is cautious by nature, a level-headed scientist, and she made it clear that she saw no reason to be overly optimistic, although, naturally, she thought it correct to run more tests on the patient.

Two weeks later the speech therapist Simone had hired to assist her handed in his first report. Although it wasn't nearly as categorical as his later comments about the patient, the report was still big news, for in it the speech therapist claimed that the patient had twice shown signs of attempting to say something.

With hindsight, Simone should have stopped there, instead of taking the man at his word, although in her defense, they had previously worked together and she trusted him. I hardly knew him, but he certainly didn't come across as a flake. He was short, sprightly, and immaculately dressed. He wore glasses, his graying hair neatly combed to the side, and he spoke slowly, even under pressure. People with a grudge against Simone would later maintain that the prospect of finally getting attention had clouded her judgment. However, those accusations were unfair: Simone had been successful in her work, coauthoring several articles and assisting with others, although admittedly she hadn't gained much recognition yet. But it was only those who disliked her who said such things, and indeed her mistake only emboldened them.

The speech therapist would sit with Simone's patient in front of a computer screen and help him place his fingers on the keyboard. At first, the messages were short and simple (*hi, thanks, my name is Stephan*), but then he began to describe his feelings in detail. His descriptions were of course harrowing, and moved everyone in the lab. TV and newspaper interviews followed—with Simone, the speech therapist, and the patient's family, who believed he had been rescued from hell. His wife explained how her life had fallen apart after she lost her husband, and his daughters wept openly in front of the cameras as he wrote on the computer screen how much he loved them, and how hard it had been for him not to be able to tell them that for so many years. Simone did her best to shield the family from the media, but everyone was so thrilled that it proved almost impossible to remain silent.

The shock came when it was discovered that the speech therapist, not the patient, had manipulated the keyboard. One could debate endlessly whether the therapist had acted deliberately, but the conclusion reached by the medical council based on psychologists' reports was that this wasn't the case: somehow the man had convinced himself he was doing the patient's bidding. Of course, Simone was devastated, and the resulting media coverage was unforgiving. The scorn of some of our colleagues was even worse. I did my best to limit the damage, and stood up for her within the department. I also managed to persuade the editor of a well-known science journal to refrain from publishing a malicious article about the mishap, written by a respected colleague, just before the issue went to print.

The media frenzy soon died down, but the appearance of the

article would have had lasting consequences for her career. She was therefore extremely grateful for my support, although too distraught to tell me so at the time. She was given three weeks' leave, and traveled over to France, where she spent a few days in Paris before visiting her parents in Cassis. We exchanged e-mails daily while she was away.

I now ask myself if this was a warning sign. She has always been a strong advocate for her patients—Anthony sarcastically calls her Mother Teresa when he's annoyed with her—but I never thought her advocacy would cloud her judgment. Instead, I blamed the therapist, who had most likely fooled not only Simone but himself as well. I left it at that.

I told her she owed me nothing when she invited me to see *The Tempest,* although I was grateful to her, of course. She had bought good seats, in the middle of the upper circle. We arrived early, and gazed at the empty stage and the trees circling the open-air theater, reaching to a sky tinged with red. It was warm, but Simone had come prepared with a scarf in her bag. Before we left the lab, she had suggested I wear a light sweater, or at least take one with me. Some people considered her bossy, but I appreciated her concern, because I tend to be absent-minded and doubtless wouldn't have considered the evening chill.

I noticed the woman with the white shawl the moment she appeared in the circle. She paused for a moment, looking around, then nudged her male companion, saying something to him. I assumed from looking at her that this was her first time there. She had her back to me and I could barely make out her profile, and yet strangely my heart missed a beat. I waited for her to turn around, edging forward in my seat, but then the boy in front of me stood up, and by the time he sat down again, she was already descending the steps in search of her seat. When she sat down, her companion leaned toward her, pointing at the stage. She nodded, and they chatted in a relaxed manner which suggested they were good friends. I tried in vain to make out from their gestures how close they might be.

I didn't realize Simone had been saying something until she prodded me.

"A penny for your thoughts."

The Tempest has been a favorite of mine since we performed it at St. Joseph's. I was fourteen at the time, and played Ariel, the spirit who assists Prospero by means of magic and trickery. I was surprised how much of the text I remembered. The production at the Delacorte had received rave reviews and those who didn't have time to stand in line for tickets all day were fighting over them online, paying hefty prices. Simone was clearly pleased to be able to invite me to such an event, and I was ashamed that I barely managed to concentrate on the play. I tried, from the beginning, but my eyes kept wandering down the circle, lingering on the cheek, which I could see if I tilted forward slightly.

For the first hour we enjoyed daylight as the sun slowly disappeared, a blue shadow spreading over us. I kept glancing down the circle but could no longer see her, and I found myself eagerly awaiting intermission.

I didn't usually behave like this. I had lived with a woman once, many years before, but only for a short time. She was a doctor as well, a hematologist, both beautiful and talented. We got along well, but she said she felt I didn't love her. It was a damning judgment and yet I couldn't really argue, as I hardly felt anything when she announced that she was leaving me. I imagined I might miss her at first, but instantly saw the advantages of living alone. She was hurt, and I didn't begrudge her parting words the day I helped her move out. She said she thought I was incapable of love, that I needed help, that it was about time I took a good look at myself. It was unlike her to talk that way—she was usually restrained and understanding, and I felt guilty that she had lost her composure. She regretted that

I didn't attempt to defend myself, and said that if anything it confirmed her fears.

Since then I had been guarded in my dealings with women, and didn't rush into things. My relationships didn't last long, seldom more than a few weeks, and even when they appeared to be going smoothly, at the slightest mention of future plans I would withdraw. The women could read the signs, and I regretted when these affairs ended. I was fully aware of my limitations.

And so I was completely unprepared for the feelings roused in me that evening during *The Tempest*. They terrified me, and I tried to ignore them, without success. When Ariel appeared onstage in the guise of a harpy, I knew it was nearly time for intermission. I started to shift in my seat and rose to my feet the instant the applause died down.

It had turned cold, as Simone had predicted, and we decided to warm ourselves with a cup of hot cocoa. We edged our way through the crowd toward the exit, and from there down to the concession stands selling refreshments on the platform behind the seats. I glanced about as we descended the circle steps, and again as we reached ground level, but saw no sign of her. Simone would sometimes tease me about how distracted I could be, and I tried not to let it show while we waited in line.

We finished our hot chocolate and Simone went to the restroom. We were being called to our seats, so I eased my way through the crowd to the entrance.

I saw her when I was still at the bottom of the steps. She was a little ahead of me and had wound the white scarf about her neck against the evening chill. Her dark hair was caught beneath the scarf, and I watched as she eased it loose, tucking it behind her ears with slender fingers and light, nimble movements. A gap appeared between the people in front of me, and before I knew it I had slipped through and was standing beside her as we reached the seating area. Then, strange as it might seem, I became calm; my heart stopped pounding and the chattering voices around me died down, until it seemed that the two of us were standing there alone.

I have often wondered whether I would have dared to approach her had the man behind me not pushed me, causing me in turn to bump into her. I like to think I would have followed my urge (I was going to say "desire," but that's not the right word), although it is against my nature. I dislike pushiness and find men who chase after women they don't know tasteless. My friends in Cambridge used to make fun of me sometimes for being a prude, but that had no effect on me.

She had been holding an envelope, which she dropped on the floor. I noticed the words *The Juilliard School* printed in one corner. We stooped at the same time to pick it up.

"I apologize."

We both seized the envelope and she smiled as we straightened up.

"Thank you," she said.

Her voice was bright, her dark eyes warm and kind, her smile so friendly I couldn't help but feel profoundly at ease. We had reached the level where our ways parted and yet I instinctively followed her down the steps.

"Let's hope it has a happy ending," I said.

"I beg your pardon?"

"For Prospero and his family," I said.

"Are you concerned for them?"

"Is it possible not to be?"

She laughed.

"I haven't seen the play for so long, I don't remember the ending," she said.

She sat down. Her companion was waiting for her. I gave him a sidelong glance. He was wearing bright green trousers. I sensed from their behavior that they weren't lovers. It was probably wishful thinking, and yet I felt relieved.

I scarcely took in the second half of the play. I was reflecting on how easy it had been to talk to her, the woman whose name I didn't know, whom I had never seen before, and how good it felt to know she was near me. I thought about her eyes, her dark hair which she brushed behind her ears, her effortless gestures. She expressed such an open cheeriness that I was almost taken aback. It was as if nothing bad could happen if she was around.

I made sure we approached the exit at the same time.

"A happy ending," I said.

She nodded with a smile, and her companion and Simone looked at me as one.

"We literally bumped into each other during intermission," she explained to the man.

"My name's Magnus," I said.

"I'm Malena," she said.

They walked ahead of us down the stairs. On the bottom step I noticed that she paused for a moment, then she turned around. We looked at each other for a split second; that was all.

When Vincent finally broke the news, there was a look of concern on Llewellyn Hunt's face. I saw his wife glance at him as though unsure how to respond, but then she smiled and joined in with Kleuber's applause. Ellis's expression remained inscrutable; he was clapping as well, and I noticed the ring on his thick finger as his fleshy palms came together. For my part, I was confused, as if I were still sitting outside in the car watching the crows above the misty football field, straining to hear Malena's voice the day she came to see me.

Vincent announced that over the past four years, Margaret had been secretly recording some of history's greatest piano work, enough material for twenty-four CDs, which he proposed to bring out one after the other. The recordings had been made under his direction there at the house, in my old room, which was currently filled to the rafters with all sorts of equipment. Margaret's range was astonishing, he said, for she had recorded both lyrical and melancholy works, epic and grandiose pieces, works that required speed and strength, others where each note must be given the freedom to come alive by itself before the next note is played.

"During the past four years," he explained, "when most people assumed Margaret had retired for good and expected never to hear of her again, we have recorded all the Goldberg variations, all Beethoven's and Schubert's piano sonatas, all Chopin's and Liszt's works for solo piano, and many more by Schumann, Scarlatti, Tchaikovsky, Mozart, Mussorgsky, Mendelssohn, Saint-Saëns, and, of course, Rachmaninoff."

He might have been referring to a world-famous pianist who had suddenly vanished from sight but was now ready to make a triumphant comeback, much to the joy of her admirers who had lamented her absence all these years. But the fact was, my mother had never fulfilled her potential, or rather, she had never received the recognition which she and Vincent felt she deserved. Many things, and people, were to blame, most notably the cliques controlling the world of classical music behind the scenes, who had systematically prevented her from enjoying the acclaim she was due. It was they who kept her from giving recitals in the most prestigious concert halls, they who wrote disparaging reviews about her in newspapers and magazines, although without being too harsh, for that might arouse suspicion, they who awarded grants to other pianists, not half as good as she, they who took every opportunity to push her aside, knowing that she was indomitable and served no one but art, no matter who they were, what position they held, or what the consequences might be.

This is what I heard most days at the house in Allington, in that room where Vincent was now so eagerly talking about Margaret's return, in the kitchen, or coming from their bedroom when they thought I was asleep. They would try to contain themselves when I was around, but the house isn't big and their conversations would frequently end with Margaret bursting into tears, screaming, and howling.

"It's so unfair, so horribly unfair!"

She would vent her anger on Vincent, whom she accused of being too soft, incapable of putting up a fight. I remember a conversation they had one evening upon their return from London, where Margaret had given a couple of recitals at a tiny concert hall in Chelsea. The first had been attended by a music critic from *The Guardian*, a man who had reviewed Margaret five years before and whom she considered stupid and spiteful. Vincent, however, insisted that although much of what he had written might be considered misguided, on the whole his review had been positive.

"Positive!" Margaret cried when they arrived back from London. "Positive!"

Vincent kept every review, every article, and knew all the important ones by heart.

"He said your playing was inspired," he insisted.

"In parts," she protested. "Inspired in parts."

Silence.

"And you suck up to that little fool, thinking it will do some good!"

It seemed my father had met the critic during intermission and taken the opportunity to praise one of his recent reviews of Arnold Bax, an obscure British composer of modern music who Vincent believed deserved more recognition. He probably thought he could kill two birds with one stone, as he attempted during their pleasant conversation to suggest that the critic might repeat the same exercise with Margaret, who, like Bax, hadn't been given the respect she deserved.

Although Vincent thought he had succeeded, the results spoke for themselves. The critic did review the concert, but his remarks were bland and unlikely to change the world's opinion of Margaret's talent. And besides, although he found no fault with her playing, and even said a few polite words about her interpretation of Mendelssohn's "Nocturne" from *A Midsummer*

Night's Dream, the review was uninspiring, brief, and appeared in the pages "where they place items of no consequence," as Margaret put it.

Vincent knew it would only make matters worse if he tried to protest, so he changed the subject and started telling her about a man he had met at her second recital, an admirer who had also been to the first recital and was scarcely able to contain his enthusiasm. They were in the bedroom by then, and the woman who had looked after me while they were out had gone home. The door was closed, but I swear I heard every word they said. And yet I have to confess that I sometimes wonder whether I didn't let my imagination run away with me, or whether I misheard bits of their conversation, because at that point she had lowered her voice, as though making it clear she had reached the heart of the matter.

"Things might have been different if I hadn't met you. I might have been . . ."

My father was rarely lost for words, and I waited for him to say something, but he didn't. It was she who went on speaking after a silence.

"You were in such a hurry to have a child. Couldn't it have waited?"

In general, I have always wished my father would have left unsaid most of what came into his head, but this time I waited breathlessly for him to reply. I don't know whether Margaret's words came as a shock to me, but somehow I doubt it. Looking back once more to that evening, it seems more likely that they confirmed what I had long suspected but refused to recognize. That is why I desperately needed him to say something that would make her take them back: "How can you say such a thing, Margaret?" or "We both know you don't mean that." But he kept quiet, possibly because he was also weary, possibly because he feared she would repeat her words, perhaps even more vehemently, rather than back down. I have often played their conversation out in my head, with a variety of different endings. But that is mere conjecture; everything that needed to be said had been said, and neither had anything to add.

When I came downstairs the next morning, they were both sitting at the kitchen table reading the newspaper as though nothing had happened. Meaningless as it sounds, I have a clear memory of Vincent chomping on his toast the moment I entered. He was usually the first to say good morning, as she always sat with her back to the door, but this time she seemed to sense my presence, because she turned and smiled.

"Are you up already?"

Of course I had been awake for hours, having barely slept a wink, but had avoided coming downstairs.

"Sit down with us and have some breakfast."

It was completely out of character; she never spoke to me like that, and I couldn't help thinking that this charade was a continuation of their discussion of the night before, as if she were saying to Vincent: "See, even though you ruined my career, I've never taken it out on the boy."

Vincent droned on while I dredged up those scenes from the past. He lavished Margaret with praise, gave detailed descriptions of her interpretation of each work. Finally, he took us upstairs to show us the recording studio in my bedroom, and gave us each a copy of the first CD, which he said they would soon be distributing: Liszt's Mephisto Waltzes.

Kleuber couldn't contain himself, and asked Vincent whether he wouldn't play the CD for us, the beginning at least. Vincent needed no prompting, and we installed ourselves once more in the sitting room. I had the feeling the Llewellyn Hunts weren't too happy about Kleuber's proposal; Christopher in particular seemed suddenly uneasy. For my part, all I wanted was to flee, but I consoled myself with the thought that at least I would be spared any memories connected to the music, because I couldn't recall ever having heard Margaret play the waltzes.

It was still raining outside. I sat in the chair by the fireplace and listened as the soft drizzle merged with the music. Perhaps it was the story of Faust at the wedding feast that made me suddenly think about Florence, about Malena standing in the moonlight that seeped in through the window, her reaction when I put my arms around her and we gazed at the moon in the river and I asked her to marry me. I remember thinking how long it took before she replied.

Christopher Llewellyn Hunt seized the opportunity after the first waltz to rise to his feet.

"Wonderful news," he said. "My heartfelt congratulations. Alas, we must be leaving. A reception at the college. Duty calls."

He spoke hurriedly yet courteously, and I followed them to the door, as discreetly as possible. When I fumbled in my pocket for the car keys, I noticed Margaret looking at me. She said nothing, but I could tell from the way she smiled that she knew what the score was.

I duly took my leave, congratulating my parents, assuring them I would listen to the new CD at the first opportunity, and promising I would be back soon. I told them I was flying early the next morning, and on my way to Cambridge I called the airline to change my flight.

I lay down as soon as I arrived at the guesthouse in Cambridge but couldn't fall asleep. At three in the morning I got dressed, took my things out to the car, and set off for Heathrow. On the way I swore I would never come back to Allington.

I came across the invoice for the rental car yesterday morning while tidying my desk. It was underneath a mound of papers along with the plane ticket and the Mephisto Waltzes, which Vincent made sure I took with me before I left. Simone says she can't understand how I can work in this mess, but that's nothing new. Although in most other ways I'm considered meticulous and well organized, I have always found it difficult to keep my desk clear.

I was wondering whether I would ever actually play the CD when Anthony came in with some papers for me to sign. A great music enthusiast, he instantly noticed the Waltzes and asked me what it was. I was at a loss as to what to say, for I had never had any reason to discuss my parents with him. It occurred to me to change the subject, to simply say it was a gift before putting it in a drawer, but I found I couldn't.

"Your mother?" he said.

I nodded.

He seemed excited.

"I wasn't aware you came from a musical family. We've never spoken about music."

"I inherited neither the talent nor the interest," I said.

He appeared to take my comment at face value, but continued to look at the CD on my desk.

"I'd love to listen to it sometime."

I handed him the CD.

"Here. You can have it."

"Are you sure?"

"I have another copy," I lied.

He was extremely grateful, almost reverential, as he took the CD from me and started to read the cover. Anthony's manner has never given me cause to complain, and yet somehow at that moment I sensed a change in his attitude toward me. I can't explain it exactly, but I perceived certain deference, a trace of obsequiousness, which took me by surprise.

After he left, I wondered whether his opinion would change after listening to the Waltzes. Simone had told me that he is an active participant in online music forums, mostly classical but some jazz as well, and has strong views, which he airs freely, especially when he thinks his favorites, in particular Mahler, are being unduly criticized. Otherwise what he writes is knowledge-able and impartial, she says, although he occasionally comes across as pedantic and arrogant. I suspect she is being a little unfair, and yet I can't deny I rather regretted having spoken to him about Margaret and given him the CD of the Waltzes. On the other hand, I hadn't had much of a choice.

When Malena awoke after our first night together at my place, she came across an old LP in my bookshelves that I had forgotten about. It was the only recording of Margaret I pos-sessed, Mendelssohn's *Songs Without Words,* from 1972. This was on a Saturday in early August, about a month after *The Tempest.* I had opened the balcony doors and was making coffee in my galley kitchen. At nine in the morning it was already hot, and Malena had slipped on a checked shirt of mine that reached down to her thighs. She had casually gathered her hair in a bun, and I was gazing at that, and at her slender neck, fully exposed, the baggy shirt draped over her slim shoulders, and her cheek, turned toward me as she read the cover. And then suddenly she looked at me and said:

"Is this lady a relative of yours?"

I gave a start. She turned the cover toward me so I could see it better, but there was no need.

"Yes," I said. "She's my mother."

Margaret's surname was Bergs, and she never spelled her first name the Icelandic way, Margrét, so there was no reason why Malena should connect her with me. Margaret C. Bergs—the *C* stood for Conyngham, of course, which is my surname, but Malena had no way of knowing that. And there was no mention on the cover of Margaret being from Iceland; she had never considered that worth flaunting.

"What made you ask?" I said.

She looked straight at me. I did my best to appear unfazed, but later she confessed I had failed.

"I told you I'm a witch."

I mustered a smile. The day after *The Tempest* when I had called her to invite her out to dinner, she had suggested we first go to a performance at Juilliard where she said she taught modern dance. I was still reeling from my audacity of the night before, when, to my astonishment and that of Simone, I had asked Malena for her telephone number. I had quickened my pace when we came out of the theater, catching up with her just as she was about to disappear amid the crowd into the darkness of Central Park. I was so astonished at my own behavior that I felt as if I were standing outside myself as I walked up to her and made my request. And yet she made it easy for me, reaching into her bag for a pen and paper and noting down the number, while Simone and the man in the green trousers stared at us.

"There you are," she said simply, handing me the piece of paper.

We arranged to meet outside the hall. I arrived early and waited on the sidewalk in the warm, humid evening. I had found it hard to concentrate on my work that day, and had taken an early train because I didn't want to risk being late. On the way, I thought about what I should say to her. Our telephone conversation had been brief; I had had enough difficulty plucking up the courage to call, and she was in a hurry. I felt I needed to begin by explaining that I wasn't in the habit of accosting women I didn't know, and that my conduct at *The Tempest* was incomprehensible even to me. I didn't want it to come out wrong, so I wrote down on a piece of paper what I wanted to say, read it over and over, changed it until I was satisfied with the result. I told myself it was important from the outset to clear up any possible misunderstandings.

I hadn't been waiting long on the sidewalk when I started to have second thoughts. The words which an hour before had seemed so meaningful on paper, sounded different in my head. How could I tell her my behavior had been silly? By doing so wouldn't I imply that I was fickle, unable to stick to anything? Wouldn't she conclude that the feelings that had made me approach her at *The Tempest* were insubstantial and might simply have disappeared, like dust in the wind?

Those were my thoughts as she walked up the street. If she could read them on my face she didn't let it show. She waved, smiling when she saw me, and my worries instantly disappeared. I no longer felt any need to explain and could see the words I had written on the piece of paper for what they were. And yet she hadn't even spoken, and almost half a block still separated us.

She seemed to know everyone and was clearly popular. She introduced me simply as "my friend Magnus," as if there were no need for any further explanation. It occurred to me that she didn't know my surname, but she didn't seem to care. I didn't know hers, either.

At the beginning of the dance performance, she leaned over and told me she was worried about one of the dancers, a fair-haired young girl who I guessed was about twenty. That was all she said, and I thought it only natural that a responsible teacher should be concerned for her student's welfare and imagine all kinds of possible mishaps. But when the girl limped off the stage a little later, I couldn't help asking Malena how she had known.

"I'm a witch," she replied, and carried on watching the performance.

She put the Mendelssohn on the record player and listened to the first few bars.

"There's a family likeness," she said.

"What?" I said.

"Between you and your mother. A strong family resemblance."

I didn't respond, but poured two cups of coffee and asked her if we shouldn't sit outside on the balcony. I felt uneasy, and sensing this she put down the record cover. She changed the subject the moment we stepped outside, but I was still pensive.

"My parents," I said. "One day I'll tell you about them."

"There's no need."

"I'm just not ready."

I feared she might interpret my words to mean that I didn't think we were close enough for me to open myself to her, and I was about to say something to contradict that, but she spoke first:

"I don't need you to tell me more, Magnus."

She sat on my lap, placed one forefinger at each corner of my mouth, and gently pushed them upward.

We both smiled.

"Because you're a witch," I said.

"Exactly, because I'm a witch."

We went into the bedroom and made love while Margaret carried on playing Mendelssohn in the living room.

My work has suffered over the past few months. Of course I've been aware that progress has been slow, and yet only now as I start writing my yearly report to Hofsinger and the medical council do I realize how disappointing my performance has been. Simone's and Anthony's conscientiousness reflects well on me because I oversee their work, and I emphasize all they have done in my report. But it is hardly enough.

Hofsinger turned a blind eye during the first month or so, but he has begun to insinuate that he thinks my grieving process, as it's apparently called, has gone on long enough. Of course, he doesn't put it like that, but I can read between the lines. He is right.

I had the impression when I woke up this morning that Malena was lying next to me. It is like that sometimes for the first few seconds after I emerge from sleep, less now than before. I usually come to my senses before too long, but occasionally I find myself stretching my arm toward her, grasping at thin air. I am amazed it should still be happening. Her face never appears more clearly to me than in those fleeting moments.

My poor performance means that our colleagues in Cambridge and Liège have taken the lead. We all benefit from one another's work, but of course there is some rivalry between us. Hofsinger wasn't very happy when Osborne told us during last week's telephone conference about a patient they had received from Birmingham Hospital, a veteran of the Iraq War who was considered incapable of thinking or speaking, but had been able to reply to Osborne's questions rather quickly and without major contradictions.

Hofsinger looked at me while Osborne talked about the soldier, stating that he was in better shape than patient number twenty-two. I wrote down anything I thought significant and avoided his gaze. The greater Osborne's enthusiasm, the bigger the frown on Hofsinger's face. Osborne hadn't mentioned this patient during a telephone conference we had had a fortnight earlier. And yet to judge from his account, their research on him must have started before that.

Hofsinger inquired about the soldier's history. Osborne gave him the details and described his condition when he returned from Iraq and was taken to Birmingham Hospital.

"And when did you say he came to you?"

"About a month ago," Osborne said, leafing through some papers to make sure. "Yes, that's right, the seventeenth."

Hofsinger raised his eyebrows, looked at Simone, then at me, to make sure we realized what we were contending with. But Osborne is an honorable man, and has never gone behind our backs; indeed, I could hear from his voice that he had no idea what lay behind Hofsinger's questions.

As I had expected, Simone followed me to my office after the telephone conference to complain about Hofsinger.

"He's not happy," I said.

"You can say that again. What has Osborne done wrong?"

"He's disappointed with our performance," I said.

Silence.

"My performance. My work has suffered since . . ."

Simone tried to protest, mentioning the projects she and Anthony had been working on for the past few months.

"We both know I've scarcely had a hand in them," I said.

"You two were so close," she said then.

I gave a start and turned away from her, pretending to look for a book in the cabinet by the window so she couldn't see my face. Her words startled us both, and she clearly regretted them, but she couldn't take them back. She had always been careful talking about Malena, and almost never mentioned her of her own accord.

"Forgive me," she said as I took a random book from the shelf and walked back to my desk. "It just came out."

It wasn't long before our names became as one. Malena and Magnus, our friends would say, Magnus and Malena, as if we were no longer two separate beings. Her colleagues, mostly connected to the dance or ballet world, used to call us M&M. They found it funny, and we didn't mind, as the nickname sort of confirmed how we felt.

We were never apart after that evening at Juilliard. When we left the auditorium and decided to get something to eat at a restaurant on a side street close by, it felt as if we had been in the same situation and made the same decision countless times before. I felt as if I were opening a book in the middle and picking up the thread from there, without any need to flick back through the pages in order to remember the characters or the plot, because everything was clear as day.

I was surprised by how spontaneous she was in conversation, how she seemingly had no need to ask me anything or to explain anything about herself to me. She was frank, without being blunt, and her bright laughter rang in my ears. Even so, I found out that she was from Buenos Aires and had come to

New York to study dance before she started teaching herself. She made fun of her own accent, insisting it must be the reason why the waiter brought her chicken when she had ordered fish. When I was going to wave him over and point out his mistake she told me not to bother.

"I'm sure the chicken will be fine, too," she said.

She tucked into her meal, and I couldn't help remembering an incident I thought I had long forgotten. I hated the fact that this memory should come back to haunt me at that precise moment, and yet I couldn't get it out of my mind.

I was twelve or thirteen at the time and the occasion was my mother's birthday. Vincent had reserved a table at a restaurant in Cambridge and we drove there through the misty darkness. I remember Vincent taking off his glasses and trying to polish them with his tie. He isn't a good driver and I had a bad feeling about this, but kept quiet. Margaret had been silent the whole way, and saw no reason why she should help him with his spectacles.

The restaurant was half empty and we were shown to a table by the window. Outside, a streetlamp glinted in the mist, but apart from that everything was dark. The place reeked of damp and had seen better days, the carpet was threadbare, and the blue wallpaper had been patched. The waiters wore black suits with white shirts and black ties, but their clothes were old and baggy.

"Well," said Vincent, once they had brought the menus, "let's see. You can order anything you like from the left-hand side of the menu, Magnus, anything at all."

On the left were the house specials, a choice of three first courses, three main courses, and ice cream for dessert. I forget what I ate, but my mother ordered the salmon. Or so she maintained, after the waiter brought her lamb chops.

"Well," said Vincent, leaning over his plate to smell the food, "this looks delicious."

I started eating, but Margaret sat still, without moving a finger. Vincent didn't notice at first. When he finally caught on, he asked whether everything was all right, as he raised his fork to his mouth and began to chew.

"I ordered the salmon."

"Are you sure?"

He ought to have known better than to question her. Which he wasn't doing, since his tone was innocent, as one might say, "Really?" or "Is that so?" when something unexpected happens.

She didn't answer, but stopped him when he was about to call the waiter over.

"No," she said.

"What?" he replied.

"You don't believe me."

"Margaret."

"You're probably right. I just imagined that I ordered salmon."

"I didn't say that. Of course I believe you. I was deciding what I wanted when you ordered and I didn't hear you, that's all."

Silence.

"I'll ask the waiter to bring you salmon."

"No!"

Vincent gave a start. As for me, I had stopped eating and was staring into my lap. I could see out of the corner of my eye that the people at the next table were looking at us.

We left before the dessert. Margaret didn't touch her lamb chops, and when the waiter came to take the plates away he asked whether the food hadn't been to her liking.

"Oh, yes," she replied. "It was delicious."

Why did these memories assail me at that precise moment when I had never felt happier? Why did I think about the lamb chops on my mother's plate when Malena picked up her knife and fork and laughed about the time when she found herself in a cab bound for Brooklyn before she realized the driver had misunderstood her directions?

"I was going home," she said. "It must have been my accent."

"Spain?" I asked.

"Argentina. England?"

"Yes. But half Icelandic."

She smiled.

"What is it?" I asked.

"You believe in elves, don't you?"

"I wasn't brought up there," I replied, not seeing a reason to mention the time we'd spent in Reykjavík. I hadn't thought about those days for a long time, and had no desire to dredge them up.

"Of course elves exist," she said. "They have to."

"Forgive me," Simone repeated after a lengthy silence.

"Do you remember when Malena and I went to Iceland?" I asked. "She was always on the lookout for elves. She assumed that being Icelandic I would be able to see them. Can you picture her?"

I must have smiled because Simone's face relaxed and all at once she looked relieved.

"Yes," she replied. "I can picture her."

"How could I not have realized she was dying?"

We are expecting a new patient. I told Hofsinger this morning and didn't hesitate to say yes when he asked me whether I saw a reason to be optimistic. I probably should have been more circumspect, but in the light of recent events, I felt I had no choice. I don't blame him for losing faith in me. And yet I am genuinely more optimistic than I have been for a long time, because what I have read about the patient bodes well. Admittedly, the report isn't all that detailed. The woman is coming to us from a local hospital in New Mexico, where the facilities are quite basic: for example, she hasn't yet been given a CT or an MRI scan and is unlikely to receive one until she gets here. All things considered, the information looks promising, although she has yet to be examined by a neurologist.

Our last two patients were a disappointment. Although initial examinations suggested otherwise, neither ended up showing signs of consciousness. They came to us from a hospital in Boston, with whom we enjoyed good relations, but since then Hofsinger has decided to break those off. He doesn't know that on both occasions I was to blame.

As a rule, we visit and examine the patients before taking them on, so we can judge their condition for ourselves. Of course the process isn't infallible, but since the research we do is both costly and involved, it has been deemed necessary. I have been the one to carry it out from the beginning, and I can't deny it has often proven useful.

I never visited the two patients in Boston. I tried, but couldn't. The first time, I managed to leave my apartment, descend the stairs, and open the door to the street, determined not to give in. It was raining, a light but continuous drizzle, and I paused on the stoop, staring out into the grayness. It seemed to have swallowed everything up, leaving no sign of life, and the silence which rarely makes its presence felt here in the city was oddly profound. I thought about the train ride ahead, the thoughts I would carry with me, the grayness that would envelop me during the journey, and I felt utterly deflated. I turned around and walked slowly back up the stairs.

The second time I didn't even make it out of bed. Outside the sun was shining.

As I was responsible for all communications with the hospital and the head doctor, who has always been gracious toward me, my colleagues never discovered my failure. I managed to avoid having to lie about my movements, because no one would ever have thought to question my honesty. But of course, I was deceiving them by omission; of course, I was not only betraying them but myself as well. I never imagined myself capable of that.

But that's in the past. I look ahead to the future now, and all of a sudden I feel in control of myself. Without exaggerating the progress I have made, there has been a definite change. I notice it, for example, in my attitude toward my job. Not long ago, I would simply have shrugged if Hofsinger had told me my services at the hospital were no longer needed. I might even have felt relieved, said good-bye the same day, scarcely bothering to remove my belongings from my office. But things are different now. I feel as if my job is all I have, and I'm almost certain we can help this patient who is on her way to us.

It was Anthony who went to examine her. I suggested he do this, and he was delighted. I am sure Simone was a little offended, but she soon got over it, and besides, she isn't fond of flying. I reminded her of that, implying that I had taken it into account. Hofsinger asked whether I trusted Anthony with the task, and I told him it was time we put him to the test. Naturally I felt like a fraud as I listened to myself speak, but I brushed those thoughts aside.

The woman is about thirty years old, five foot seven, currently weighs ninety-two pounds, though she was probably twenty or thirty pounds heavier prior to the accident. She was found at the side of the road close to Las Cruces, the southernmost part of the state, twenty yards from a ruined motorcycle. She wasn't carrying any identification. There were skid marks on the road, and wreckage from the motorcycle and another vehicle, an automobile, suggested a collision. The police are no closer to discovering what happened, although they assume the woman was a passenger. She wasn't wearing a helmet.

The accident happened two months ago, and the police still don't know the woman's identity. Anthony says the nursing staff at the hospital assume she is Mexican, here illegally. In any case, despite announcements in the media, no one has inquired about her, and the police have given up or perhaps lost interest in trying to find the driver of the motorcycle or the automobile which left the scene of the accident. The motorcycle had been stolen.

"What surprises me most is that they didn't pull the plug on her," Anthony said, handing me his report after he returned from his trip. "I expect the doctor who looked after her prevented it. He is still young and idealistic."

The young doctor's remarks were a testament to his keen sense of observation and conscientiousness. He noticed that the patient started blinking five weeks after the accident and concluded she was emerging from her coma. He also noticed that she had moved her eyes up and down, and knew enough to assume this meant she was conscious. He must have researched the subject, for he writes as if he is explaining it to himself: "I imagine she awoke from a deep sleep yesterday. The first time I saw her blink was when I looked in on her late in the afternoon. It was fleeting, and she soon fell asleep again. Yesterday evening, one of the nurses saw her not only blink but also move her eyes. I witnessed this myself this morning. She moved her right eye, I couldn't see her left . . . It's possible she is fully conscious, able to hear us, to smell, to feel the sheet brushing against her skin as we spread it over her . . .

"This morning I stroked her brow and then her cheek, and asked her to blink if she could feel it. At first I saw no change, but then the right eye opened—slowly and with difficulty—before closing again. I called the nurse and repeated the procedure but this time she didn't respond. I assumed that sleep had claimed her once more . . ."

I asked Anthony if the doctor had added anything when they met.

"He wasn't there," he said. "A well-deserved break, I was told. Works hard, takes good care of his patients."

I wondered whether the young doctor's reflections had found their way into the report by accident; they are handwritten on a folded sheet of lined, yellow paper in the middle of the file, unrelated to the rest of the report. I have the feeling he slipped them in deliberately.

Just as I was about to walk out of his office with the sheaf of papers under my arm, Anthony cleared his throat.

"I listened to that CD you gave me," he said. "Three times. Congratulations."

Although I had been living on West Seventy-Fifth Street for about four years when Malena and I met, I can't say I knew my neighbors. On the floor below me lived an elderly lady in a rent-controlled apartment, and above me was a French couple, Monsieur Chaumont and his wife, who corrected me the first time I said good morning to her:

"Not Chaumont," she said. "*Roullard*. Estelle *Roullard*."

She gave me an offended look, and from then on I was careful to have as little to do with her as possible, at most nodding if we met on the stairs. Monsieur Chaumont taught French at a nearby high school; he was small and dapper, always wore a pocket handkerchief and elegant brown shoes with his gray slacks or blue suit. They had a lapdog which they walked daily around the neighborhood, dressing it in a woolen sweater in winter.

Monsieur Chaumont had once knocked on my door to ask whether I, too, was without hot water, but that was the extent of our relationship. They moved about quietly and never disturbed me, and the dog mostly refrained from barking, or couldn't be bothered to.

I was therefore taken aback when one evening I came across

Malena merrily chatting to my French neighbors out on the sidewalk. I was coming from work and looking forward to seeing her;
she had moved in with me that week, having brought over some
of her clothes the weekend before. I had plenty of space in my
wardrobes, but used the opportunity anyway to donate some of
my old clothes to the Salvation Army, as I wanted her to bring as
much as she could, everything if possible. They were speaking in
French, and they all said, *"Bonsoir!"* when they saw me, Malena,
too. I don't speak any French and felt unable to respond in kind,
so I simply nodded. I stood next to them in silence until the
conversation ended, and the couple walked off down the street,
the dog on a leash between them, and Malena and I went inside.

"What a nice couple," she said.

"Glad to hear it," I said.

She laughed.

"They said they don't know you."

"They're quite right."

"What a curmudgeon you are."

"Me?"

I told her about my exchange with Madame Roullard.

"She's a poet," she replied, as if that explained everything.

First she brought her clothes, then a few books, her kettle (she
found mine hopeless), her family photographs, a painting of dancers by an Argentine artist, a friend. Then more clothes. Her father
had passed away, but she spoke regularly with her mother and
sister, sometimes on the telephone but more often on Skype. They
both lived in Buenos Aires. She had so many friends I couldn't keep
track of them all, and I would occasionally forget who was who.

"You remember Edelmira, we met her at that Turkish restaurant in Brooklyn with Gustavo and Mia."

Sometimes I remembered, sometimes I didn't.

"Short?"

"No, tall."

"Dark-haired?"

"No, blond."

She rolled her eyes, laughing, and said she had never met anyone who had such a bad memory for people.

There was never a harsh word between us and we never had to refrain from speaking our minds to avoid having a quarrel. Not once. We engaged in frequent, affectionate banter, and knew how to appreciate each other's idiosyncrasies.

"How could I be so dumb?" she would say to herself at the slightest provocation, for example when she forgot her keys or her MetroCard, which happened often. She would invariably respond by resolving to take herself in hand—"This can't go on!"—and asking me if I could help her. "No," I would say, "it amuses me too much, seeing your expression when you're angry with yourself."

She was in the habit of talking to herself, always in Spanish. I enjoyed listening to her, although I could understand only the occasional word. I felt I was seeing her in another light, as if a side of her was being revealed that would otherwise have remained hidden. I saw it, too, when she spoke with her mother or her sister and, of course, even more so when we made love/had sex. I don't know whether she realized, but at those moments she always spoke in Spanish, sometimes with her eyes closed, though more often gazing into mine. I won't deny that I was curious to know what she was saying, although, to begin with at least, I found it more arousing trying to imagine.

In the end, I felt I had no choice but to learn Spanish. We had known each other for almost six months, and I was bothered by not knowing her language, especially when we were with her Spanish-speaking friends. They often made an effort to speak English for my sake, but that made me uncomfortable. I would encourage them to carry on talking in their language, saying that I liked listening to them and I could understand enough. I was exaggerating, of course, but they, and above all Malena, were grateful.

I am almost embarrassed to admit that something Simone said probably spurred me on. I tried to make light of it at the time, but the memory of it haunted me longer than I would have wished.

It was a Monday morning. I was telling her about my weekend, an afternoon with Malena in Williamsburg and the purchase of a new sofa for the living room and an oriental rug to go with it.

"Has she moved in with you completely?" asked Simone.

"No, she's keeping her apartment, although she is hardly ever there."

"Why?"

"Her rent is low."

Simone said nothing, but I could tell she didn't find the explanation convincing.

"She says people should move house in spring. Not in fall or winter. She's superstitious."

"Pardon?"

I smiled.

"Superstition is part of her culture. I find it rather amusing."

That was when Simone looked at me and said in her solemn way:

"How much do you know about her?"

She quickly added that she didn't mean to imply anything, only that I should be careful. I thought I knew what was behind this: she had once lived with a doctor who had a drug problem, which he managed to hide from her for several months. This experience had obviously had a profound effect on her, made her overly skeptical, and yet her words preyed on my mind. I reproached myself for entertaining suspicious thoughts—and Simone for putting them in my head. I don't intend to make too much of them, but I suspect they partly explained why soon afterward I resolved to try to learn Spanish.

Malena's response was measured. She appreciated me taking the trouble, but said she felt almost guilty, that it would be far easier for her to improve her English and to encourage her friends to do the same. I hadn't said anything to her about it before I bought the books and CDs, because I was of two minds and only decided on the purchase when I found myself in our bookshop late one Saturday afternoon. I told her that, and she kissed me on the cheek and whispered something in Spanish, which, of course, I didn't understand.

I dutifully sat at my desk every evening before going to bed, and followed the instructions in the book for exactly fifty minutes. This method had received good reviews online, and people claimed they had learned the language in two months. If Malena went out to dinner or to a performance with her friends, I would use the opportunity to study before she came home, but mostly she was there in the apartment with me while I did the work. She would occasionally offer to help, but otherwise left me to my own devices. I had expected her to show more interest in my endeavor, but I didn't say so. I supposed the situation made her uncomfortable; she was an unassuming person and didn't like me to go out of my way because of her.

That was what I supposed, and yet secretly I was beginning to suspect that she felt I was getting too close to her, in some way invading her privacy. The more I progressed, and started showing off, just for fun, by using a few simple words and expressions, and later more complex sentences and comments, the more I noticed that she increasingly responded in English. She behaved differently, too, when we met her friends; they were delighted that I was struggling to learn their language, and encouraged me, taught me new words and useful expressions, and corrected me when necessary. She seldom took part in those exchanges, and either remained silent or turned away and spoke, in English, with others in the group.

I tried to make light of her behavior and didn't find fault with it for fear she might pull away from me. I studied less and less when she was at home, and finally stopped altogether. Instead I would read on the train on my way to the hospital and listen to the CDs on my way home. I took advantage of the fact that one of the nurses is Mexican and practiced talking to her whenever I could. She corrected me pitilessly, and I memorized her comments or wrote them down.

"*El gorila es feliz,*" I repeated after her, stressing the *r* in *gorila* and the second syllable in *feliz. Estoy feliz.*

There were many bizarre sentences in that textbook.

I was making steady progress, but was careful not to let it show when Malena and I were together. We never spoke about my Spanish studies, and I kept the books and CDs in my backpack rather than leave them lying around. Nor did I publicize it among her friends, although I had started being able to figure out what they were saying, and I always pretended to be absorbed in something else whenever she spoke to her mother or sister. That was less than before, and I suspected she called them more often now from the school, where she shared a small office with her companion from that night at the Delacorte, Alexander Kosloff, the ballet teacher in the green trousers.

This may sound strange, but in other respects our relationship was perfect, with no shadows lurking. We enjoyed every moment we spent together, and when I was alone I only had to imagine her and my mood would lighten. We were so close that our friends would make fun of us for being like an old couple. I eventually became more outgoing, and she, who was the life and soul of any party, became more content to spend a quiet evening at home.

We made love with the same passion as when we first met but were now also able to navigate each other's thoughts. It never occurred to me that this might be a bad thing, until I started trying to memorize her words during these moments so that I could look them up later. Of course this was a silly idea, but curiosity got the better of me.

She clearly read my mind, and in bed that night didn't say a word. I had feared my memory might let me down, her words might become muddled in my head, so I listened and watched intensely, waiting for her lips to part. They did, and I glimpsed the tip of her tongue as usual, but when no words followed I became flustered.

She must have noticed, but she didn't let it show. Afterward, we lay next to each other, staring up at the ceiling, and I reached for her hand, fearing I might be losing her. But she responded, passing warmth and affection from her palm to mine, so I calmed down, promising myself I would set my Spanish studies aside.

Maria, the Mexican nurse who had been helping me, shook her head when I told her I was taking a break from my studies, and said it was a mistake, just when I was hitting my stride. Malena's friends noticed my waning interest and stopped teaching me slang words and other useful expressions, while Malena went on as before, avoiding speaking Spanish in front of me.

She maintained her silence, too, when we were in bed, and I accepted that that wouldn't change.

She found her voice again on a Friday evening. I remember it had begun to rain on my way home, and when I got off the train the sky looked as gray as the streets. She was trying on a new dress in front of the mirror in the bedroom when I arrived and called out to me the moment she heard the door.

"Does it suit me?" she asked.

We made love with the rain falling on the windows, and before I knew it, the words came. The same ones as before, I assumed, and yet they seemed to have an added urgency, as if she had something important to say. Afterward, I noticed tears in her eyes for the first time. I was startled, but she smiled and said:

"I just feel so good."

We ordered takeout from the Italian place on Columbus, and I went to fetch it while she set the table and lit some candles. I didn't take long, but when I returned I could hear she wasn't alone.

Madame Roullard was standing by the kitchen table.

"They've been invited to Iceland," Malena said as I walked in. "To a literary festival."

Madame Roullard said something in French.

"To a poetry festival," Malena corrected herself. "She wants your advice."

"I haven't been to Iceland since I was a child," I said.

Malena handed me a typewritten sheet of paper. In French.

"She brought us a poem as a present," she said, as if that might somehow revive my knowledge of Iceland.

I thanked Madame Roullard, went into the living room, and fetched two illustrated volumes about Iceland which someone had given me.

"Merci," she said as I handed her the books, but I could tell from her expression that she considered them rather a meager offering.

She left and we sat down to eat. Malena read the poem aloud, translating it for me, and then stuck it on the fridge where it remains to this day.

"It's very beautiful," she said.

> *Où même mes pensées ont peur*
> *De l'errance*
> *Sans un compagnon?*

"I'm afraid I can't be of much use to them," I said.

"I'd love to go to Iceland."

"Really?"

"With you."

"Someday," I said, dissembling. "Maybe someday."

Anthony was waiting for me yesterday when I got to the hospital. My Metro-North train had been delayed, traveling at half speed and, on top of that, coming to a halt twice on the way. In addition, I had managed to leave home later than intended—on purpose, I might add. He had clearly been asking after me, because the moment I entered my office and took off my backpack, I heard a nurse call out to him: "He's here."

The new patient was due to arrive that afternoon, a couple of days later than expected due to problems with paperwork. Simone complained that after Anthony's trip to New Mexico, he was behaving as if the woman were his sole responsibility and was jealously guarding all information about her.

"I decided to give him this opportunity," I said, "so I can hardly start interfering now."

She raised her eyebrows and shook her head, but said nothing.

"Things will change once she gets here," I added. "Until then, we have to let him run the show."

I had started the day brimming with optimism. I had slept well, and when I opened my eyes to the light, I felt no pang in my stomach, no wave of dread welling up in my breast. I had lain still, half expecting that strange feeling of contentment to disappear and for the numbness to take over. But it didn't, and I felt in control of my thoughts, able to steer them away from memories that saddened me.

The coffee tasted unusually good. I browsed the newspaper and opened the balcony doors, despite the cold weather. Before shaving, I turned on the radio and listened to some jazz and a soft-spoken woman reading a summary of the news. Perhaps I was afraid my peace of mind would disappear the moment I left the apartment, so I delayed getting going, even though I was eagerly awaiting the new patient's arrival.

I had barely had a chance to take off my jacket and scarf when Anthony entered my office. He was clearly excited.

"I need to show you something," he said.

I assumed it would be about the new patient, and I hoped everything was all right, although I couldn't tell from his expression.

"On the computer," he added.

I typed in my password, and he shifted restlessly as the screen lit up. Then he leaned over, seized the mouse, and in no time had opened a webpage I had never seen before. He typed a few words, paused, then pointed at the screen and told me to read.

It was a forum on Yahoo! for classical music enthusiasts. I immediately noticed my mother's name and a picture of the CD I had given Anthony. I could see from the first few comments that everyone who had listened to it had loved it. Many boasted of having "discovered" her, and two of the forum members squabbled over who had first drawn attention to her. Others wanted information about her background and how to buy her CD. The one with the most posts declared he had been in touch with the record company, run by her husband, only to discover more CDs were about to be released.

Anthony stood next to me while I read.

"You haven't seen this?" he said as I straightened up.

"No," I said.

"I didn't think so."

I made a mental note of the name of the forum.

"This doesn't happen very often," he said.

I had stopped reading but was still gazing at the screen. He brought up another website.

"Look, same here."

I only had to glance at the screen to see he was right.

"Do you know which other CDs are about to be released?"

I shook my head. He hesitated, then cleared his throat.

"Do you think it's possible to get ahold of them in advance? I'd pay, of course."

His request didn't surprise me, and I didn't resent his audacity; he meant well enough, although it was obvious he wanted to be able to boast in front of the others about having beat them to it.

"If it's not too much trouble," he added.

I told him I would look into it.

Before leaving, he told me that everything was ready for the patient's arrival; he was expecting her in the early afternoon.

"I'll let you know when she's here."

I shut the door behind him, sat down at my desk, and continued to read about Margaret on the forum. I can't say I found anything new: people didn't seem to have a problem with repeating themselves over and over, siding with those who agreed with them, finding fault with those who didn't, and generally trying to impress. Even so, many of them were knowledgeable and articulate, and I imagined you could get hooked on this if you had the requisite interest.

My eye alighted on a brief comment posted by Anthony. His analysis of Vladimir Horowitz's and Margaret's interpretations of the Mephisto Waltzes had caught the attention of many on the forum. He spoke about the differences in accentuation before declaring that to his mind they were the two best interpretations of the work he had ever heard.

I stopped reading and leaned back in my chair. I was surprised at how relaxed I felt; as a rule, the slightest mention of my parents was enough to make me uneasy. I had been expecting the usual despair to overwhelm me as Anthony stood beside me, and more so when he left me sitting alone in front of the computer. Yet it was like when I woke up that morning and lay in bed convinced my contentment couldn't last: this serenity persisted.

This state of mind inspired feelings of tolerance and even sympathy. I started to reflect on my mother's life, all the disappointments I had witnessed as a boy, and I told myself that although her words and deeds had often hurt and I knew I could never forgive her, I could imagine how she herself felt. Especially in light of what was emerging: that she had indeed been unfairly judged. She had been trapped inside her own body, I told myself, like my patients: she wanted to make contact with the world; she felt she had something to say, something to contribute, and yet no one listened. She was ignored, sometimes even belittled, while others less deserving were idolized. And meanwhile, time went by. Perhaps people like her shouldn't have children, perhaps she had only done it to please Vincent or to be like other women, perhaps she had always known she couldn't serve both art and me.

She had attempted to lure me into her world, the world of music. I couldn't have been older than four, yet I remember clearly the two of us sitting side by side at the piano, she trying to teach me. I remember how gentle and positive she was at first, how attentive and encouraging. I made every effort, because I could feel that if I did there would be many moments like that, she and I alone at the piano on those peaceful afternoons, with nothing to disturb us.

She tried to control herself, to hide her disappointment when she realized I had no talent, but she couldn't. The smile vanished first from her eyes, then from her lips. Her words of encouragement became orders, her praise cries of despair. "No, no, no, not like that! For heaven's sake!" Sometimes she would get up and disappear into the kitchen to simmer down, and when she came back she would say in a gentler tone: "Shall we try again?"

In the end she gave up. I remember that one day when I sat down at the piano at the usual time, three o'clock, she walked straight past me without saying a word and went upstairs. She had just been practicing herself; I had heard her from my bedroom, where the babysitter was playing with me. When I called after her, Vincent appeared and sat down next to me. There would be no more piano, he said; Margaret had to rest. "What about tomorrow?" I asked. "No," he said, "Margaret has to rest then, too."

I don't think it had ever occurred to her that a child of theirs might not be musically gifted. I can just imagine Vincent trying to persuade her to have a child, conjuring up images of a close-knit family whose world revolved around music, above all her music. Perhaps she reckoned that two devotees were better than one, because people grow old and there is no knowing what can happen in a lifetime.

I am not justifying her behavior; my sympathy doesn't stretch that far, though I welcome this feeling of serenity. But I am trying to understand her, especially now that it has dawned on me, possibly for the first time, how underrated her talent has been. I even feel ashamed for having doubted her, for having so often found her pathetic.

I saw before me the old black telephone in the hallway, the

umbrella stand, the green rug, the pictures of Chopin and Mozart above the table. I could almost sense my parents' presence
and imagined hearing an occasional note emanating from the
piano. I still felt calm, but even so I hesitated before picking up
the phone and dialing the number that hadn't changed since I
was a boy.

While I was a medical student at Yale, I was invited to take part in a study of how the brain perceives music. It was the subject of much conjecture at the time, and still is, although some progress has been made, and the work looked promising. The professor leading the research, Thomas Stainier, was barely forty but had already made a name for himself. He had been awarded a grant from the MacArthur Foundation when he was quite young, and was expected by some to go far, possibly all the way to a Nobel. We students respected him, not least because he rode a motorcycle and played in a rock band. We would occasionally see him on his bike, more often than not with a woman riding pillion, arms clasped around his waist, wearing only a tiny black helmet for protection.

Many students were eager to work in his lab, so I can't deny I was proud when he approached me unexpectedly and offered me a place. We had met at a departmental meeting the weekend before, and had gone with a few other people to a bar in New Haven, where I had drunk more than normal. Not too much, but enough to loosen my tongue. Most of the people working with him had some knowledge of music; they had taken it as a subject together with biology as undergraduates, which is probably why I felt I had to say yes when he asked me whether I knew anything about music. I quickly added that I had never studied music myself, and was in fact talentless, but had been brought up in a musical family, and I told him my mother was a pianist.

"So it's in your blood," he said, and sounded so emphatic that for a few days I believed him.

When, a week later, I turned down his offer, he simply stared at me for a moment without saying anything. I expect he wasn't used to people refusing him anything, either in his professional life or his personal life. He was above attempting to persuade me, but felt it was worth trying to probe a little—or perhaps to bring me down a peg or two.

"Are you rebelling against your mother?"

"No," I said.

"Do you feel you would somehow be following in her footsteps by undertaking this research?"

"No," I said.

"If as you say you have no talent for music, aren't you curious to find out what part of your brain determines that?"

I didn't like his questions, but I tried not to let it show.

"Dr. Kirschner has offered me a placement," I said. "I'm more interested in what he's doing."

Stainier's research lab was in a different wing from Kirschner's, but even so I frequently bumped into him during my years at Yale. He would always grin and call out when he saw me: *Conyngham,* he would say, addressing me by my surname, and occasionally he would whistle a little tune for his own amusement.

The truth is that for years I read every article he published, and followed his research with interest. Not only did he endeavor to explain which part of the brain perceived the various characteristics of sound, but also how music stimulates emotion and memory, and why some people like rock while others prefer jazz. He was very productive, and those working in his department complained of long hours and sleepless nights. He, on the other hand, showed no signs of fatigue.

I had long since graduated and started working with Hofsinger when I heard that Stainier had given up medical research and opened a bicycle repair shop in a small town on the Hudson River. No one could explain the reasons for his disappearance, but I was told it was sudden. He was at the height of his career.

I started thinking about Stainier after I called my parents this morning. Vincent didn't take long to pick up, and far from detecting any hesitation or suspicion in his voice, I found him brimming with self-confidence.

"Hello, Vincent."

"Magnus! I'm expecting a call from a journalist."

"Shall I ring back later?"

"No, no. Are you in New York?"

"No, I'm at the hospital."

"In Connecticut?"

"Yes."

"By the sea?"

"Yes. I just saw some of the online comments about the CD."

"Not only online. It's everywhere."

"A colleague of mine showed me some forum," I said, but Vincent's attention seemed to be on my mother, whose voice I could hear in the background.

"I'm sorry," he said to me, then called out to Margaret, probably louder than necessary: "It's Magnus Colin! He's calling from the hospital!"

He resumed talking to me.

"Do you remember my speech at the birthday party?"

I said I did.

"Momentous. Isn't that the word I used?"

"Yes, I seem to remember you did."

"At last," he said, "at last she is getting the recognition she deserves."

"Yes."

"We knew. But they've been working against us for years. For decades. You might learn something from scanning the brains of all those who ignored her."

I don't know whether this was meant as a barbed comment, but the fact is, I felt ashamed. I had long since concluded that Margaret was essentially mediocre.

"We're waiting for a journalist from the *Guardian* to call. He wants to come to the house. Don't you think we should say yes?"

My mind was beginning to wander, but I managed to murmur that I saw no reason why not.

"You caught your plane all right?"

"Sorry?"

"We haven't heard from you since."

"Yes," I said. "I did."

"Good, good. Right. Well, we mustn't talk for too long— this fellow might be trying to call."

"Of course," I said. "I only wanted to . . ."

"This is just the beginning, Magnus. Just the beginning. We're releasing two more CDs at the end of the month."

"Can you send them to me?" I blurted out.

He called out to Margaret: "Magnus wants Schubert and Liszt!"

"If it's not too much trouble," I added.

"Perhaps this will enable you finally to start listening. We did our best at the time."

There was no trace of accusation in his voice; he spoke as if he were simply reiterating an established fact which we had often discussed. Even so, I was taken aback, lost for words until he brought up the journalist from the *Guardian* again. Then we said good-bye and I managed to tell him to send my regards to Margaret.

"Yes, and send mine to your sweetheart. What's her name again?"

"Malena," I said, in a voice so low as to be almost inaudible.

"Give her my fond regards. And those of Margaret."

I had pushed my office door shut, and when I hung up I could feel the silence. I sat motionless at my desk, picked up a pencil and twirled it between my fingers. I felt uneasy, yet maintained my calm. Ought I perhaps to reconsider my attitude toward Vincent and Margaret? Was I the one who had been difficult, judged them too harshly all these years? I had certainly never believed that Margaret possessed the sort of talent which suddenly seemed so self-evident. Was it true that I had always dug my heels in, refused to take part in their lives, sulked whenever they tried to give me advice, and declared a silent war on them? I had never thought of it this way, but all at once I was beginning to question myself. Why hadn't I the courage to tell them Malena was dead? Why hide it from them? Out of disrespect, or was I just no more capable of facing up to reality than before?

So I sat for a while, dredging up events from the past, trying to see them differently. I was dazed, and, of course, failed to get to the bottom of anything, and yet the seeds of doubt were sown, and my pity—or was it contempt?—gave way to remorse.

I should never have called them. For whatever reason, my conversations with Vincent invariably end in some kind of unpleasantness or upset. Perhaps I'm to blame, not he. Or maybe we both are. In any event, I always torment myself afterward, raking over what we said and interpreting his every word, possibly in the worst way.

Was he belittling my work when he said I might learn something from scanning the brains of all those who mistreated

Margaret? Was he implying that I was among them? That is what I was thinking when the image of Thomas Stainier and his motorcycle flashed into my mind. Why would he disappear like that when every door was open to him? What truth had he discovered that had prompted him to give up everything?

I was about to google him when Anthony opened the door.

"She's here," he said.

She was lying where I had lain, in Mrs. Bentsen's room. Two nurses were attending to her when Anthony and I entered, plumping up her pillows, tucking in her sheets, making sure the machines were functioning correctly. They looked up when they saw us but said nothing, and the silence was profound. The windows were open and the room felt cold, so I closed them before walking over to the bed.

I sensed it the moment I saw her face. This wasn't a suspicion or a hunch—it was an absolute certainty. The woman was conscious: she could hear me walking toward the bed, she could feel my presence. I was expecting her to open her eyes at any moment and speak to me. I imagined her voice echoing in my head, her accent when she asked where she was. I even saw her raise her hand and brush away the lock of hair that had fallen across her brow, before turning to me and smiling.

Who knows how long I might have stood there, motionless, had Anthony not cleared his throat and handed me the patient's notes.

I looked at the most recent entry. No surprises: the journey from New Mexico had been without incident.

As a rule, we speak to our patients as if they are fully conscious, and we keep doing so until we discover otherwise. And, of course, we are careful not to talk about them in their presence as if they can't hear us. Before coming to fetch me, Anthony had explained to the woman where she was and what tests she would be undergoing. So far he hadn't detected any sign of a response.

Written in the margin of the lined yellow paper was the name Adela. Anthony had discovered that the young doctor had called her that when it became clear her identity remained unknown. When I asked him whether he knew why the doctor had chosen that name, he simply shrugged.

"Possibly he just started with the letter *A*."

I didn't think the name suited her, but I felt I had no choice but to carry on with it. Even so, I avoided using it when addressing her.

"My name is Magnus Conyngham," I said. "I'm one of the doctors who will be taking care of you here, and I'd like to welcome you."

I repeated some of what Anthony had already told her, then asked if she could open her eyes; I said we had seen in the report we had received from New Mexico that she was capable of that.

"Only if you feel up to it," I said. "There's no pressure."

We drew closer to the bed, stood motionless, and scrutinized her eyelids. For a moment, I thought I saw a slight tremor in the upper part of her right eyelid, but I was probably imagining it, because neither the nurses nor Anthony noticed anything.

After a while, we looked at one another and decided to call it a day.

"Don't worry," I said. "We know you can hear us."

We always talk that way to our patients, yet perhaps there was something in my tone that made both Anthony and the two nurses pause. I only realized it myself when I saw their response, and even then it took me a moment to catch hold of myself. I thought I ought to say something, but waited until we were out in the corridor.

"She's conscious," I said.

I am cautious by nature and so they were all the more surprised at my announcement.

"At least everything would seem to point in that direction," I said, backpedaling a little. "She was able to blink relatively recently. And we know what that means."

"You don't think that might just have been a nerve spasm?" asked Anthony.

"No, not from the way it was described. I think the muscle in her upper eyelid is simply tired. The journey must have taken its toll on her."

After they left, I sat down at the computer. The page was still open to the forum Anthony had shown me, and I closed it and searched on Google for news about a car accident in New Mexico. I found two articles from *Las Cruces Sun News,* both brief. The first was purely factual, while the second speculated that the driver of the motorcycle had gotten in the car he had collided with and left his passenger behind, perhaps believing she was dead. Witnesses were asked to come forward, as well as anyone who might be able to identify the woman who was said to be in a coma. There was a photograph of her, taken at the hospital. It was grainy.

I found a story in the *Las Cruces Bulletin* and on some websites, all short and showing certain apathy. The same photograph followed all the articles, and the more I saw it, the less I thought it resembled our patient.

I kept thinking about her during the departmental meeting later that day, discreetly looking at her photograph on my phone. When I tried comparing it to the image in my memory, my mind played tricks on me, recalling Malena's face instead. I felt uneasy, but I didn't put the phone away.

It was dark when the meeting ended. Most people had finished work for the day, and there was a line of cars from the hospital down to the main road. I dropped some papers off at my office before heading down the corridor to the west wing, toward Mrs. Bentsen's room.

There were three nurses on night duty, the others had gone home. I greeted them as they sat over their coffee cups at the nurses' station in the center of the corridor. It was quiet on the ward at that time, only five patients, four of them in comas.

"I looked in on her," one of the female nurses said. "Nothing to report."

It was gloomy in the room; the overhead light was switched off, the only illumination coming from the equipment beside the bed. I stood still for a moment by the door before walking over to the bed and turning on the small table lamp. It cast a soft light on her face and neck, the cables attached to her, her dark hair.

"It's Dr. Conyngham," I said at last. "It's evening now, and dark outside. You are alone in the room, the windows face east, out to sea . . ."

I described the room, spoke about the accident, told her that no one had been able to identify her. Whenever I paused I had the impression that she was waiting anxiously for me to carry on. And so I did: I told her what we had in mind with our research and warned her it would take time and that we all needed to be patient.

I spoke to her no differently than I would to any other person in her situation, not on that first evening. Obviously, I spoke simply and honestly.

When I was about to switch off the light on the bedside table and say good night, I thought I saw something move out of the corner of my eye. I quickly turned around and asked her whether she had blinked. I tried to sound calm but my voice quavered.

"Can you do that again?"

That's when I saw it. A slight movement in her upper right eyelid, a mere tremor that attested to an enormous effort.

"I see it," I said. "I see it. I know you are trying. I know you understand everything I say. We will make contact with you. We won't give up until we have made contact with you."

I was too overcome to go on. I said good night a second time, fetched my jacket from my office, and hurried to the train station.

I slept little that night and was up before dawn. I ground some coffee beans in the kitchen and tried to clear my mind. On the way up to Connecticut, I gazed out the train windows as the houses emerged one by one out of the early morning gloom.

I dreamt about Malena last night. I dream about her often. Only this time it was different. Instead of seeing her from a distance as I usually do, we were together in Iceland. We were in a car, like the one we had rented when we went there, but bigger and a different color. I think this one was green. The one we had rented was red. I remember laughing at her when the man at the Hertz counter showed us what was available.

"You decide," she said. "I'd just like it to be red."

The car in my dream was green and we were driving in places I didn't recognize. I have forgotten them now, apart from the fishing village where we had stopped when I woke up. There were boats moored in the harbor, an island out in the fjord, shaped like a snail or a cat curled up, and the sea was a mirror. We were standing beside a small house down by the harbor, and she said: "I want to live here." She said words to that effect quite a few times when we were in Iceland, so it wasn't strange that they should be repeated in my dream, and yet there was a gravity about them that surprised me.

Malena's interest in Iceland didn't dwindle after Madame Roullard and Monsieur Chaumont returned from the poetry festival in Reykjavík. According to her husband, Madame had been appreciated and admired by the audience; the festival had been well attended and organized; the hotel room, clean if rather rudimentary. They spoke about the landscape, the immensity, and Madame said she had been so moved by it that while she was there she had composed three poems. Two short and one long. Malena told me this, because as before I had little to do with the couple myself. Their conversations took place mainly in the stairway or when Malena bumped into them in the neighborhood, and always in French.

The trip came sooner than expected. After Florence we had intended to keep going south, perhaps to the Greek islands. Even so, we hadn't booked a flight or a hotel, preferring to leave it to chance. I mentioned Crete or Corfu, and Malena said something about Icaria, which I had never heard of. It was only later that I understood what she was thinking.

And so I was astonished when all of a sudden she changed her mind and proposed we go to Iceland. That was the morning after I woke up and saw her standing in the moonlight by the window overlooking the river. I was thinking about her movements, those slow, gentle dance steps during the night, her face when I walked over to her and put my arms around her. She had started weeping and I didn't understand why. When she told me they were tears of joy, I wanted to believe her.

Her suggestion came out of the blue. We had been discussing our plans for the day, a trip to Lucca or Pisa, dinner on the way home. I was still in bed and she had just climbed out of the shower.

"Let's go to Iceland," she said, all of a sudden.

I tried to talk her out of it. We can go next summer, I said, organize the trip in advance, we don't even have the right clothes with us now.

"And what about the itinerary, the flights, and the hotel?" I said.

She shrugged and twisted her hair up in a towel—we could buy the clothes we needed in Iceland, and book everything online.

Our round-trip tickets to Rome had been cheap, but we couldn't change them. It had taken me some time to find them and I was about to calculate how much we stood to lose, when I saw the expression on her face and paused. When we first met, I had described her to Simone as someone with a thirst for adventure, adding that this was just as well because I was probably too set in my ways. I don't remember the context, nor does it matter. But as Malena and I stood there by the hotel room window, in almost exactly the same place as the night before when I had taken her in my arms in the moonlight, I glimpsed in her face not a thirst for adventure but rather a look of despair. It was there just for an instant before she caught hold of herself.

"Forgive me," she said. "I know I should have mentioned it before."

She said she wanted to see the soil I had grown from. She had said this before, and I had pointed out that my Icelandic roots didn't go very deep, apart from those preserved in our genes, invisible to all, including me. But this time I didn't speak along these lines, didn't say a word about my roots or my genes. Instead, I got dressed and went down with her to the dining room. We sat at the computer by the window overlooking a tiny square where farmers were selling their produce, and the morning sun shone onto the table between us.

She wasn't herself for the first few minutes, silent and distant. I told her I had nothing against going to Iceland if she was so set on it, and tried to lighten up the conversation. But it was as if she knew she had let her mask slip and realized I had glimpsed the anguish on her face.

She slowly collected herself, and the smile returned to her face. We switched on the computer, bought plane tickets to Iceland from Milan, rented a car at Keflavík Airport, and booked our first night at Hotel Borg. We had five days at our disposal. She said she wanted to see the countryside and already seemed to know exactly where we were going. I was amazed by how well-informed she was, and said so.

"Estelle told me where they went, and I looked a few things up online," she said, trying to play down how prepared she was.

Soon after we moved to Allington, I developed an obsession with learning about Iceland. I wasn't very happy at the time; I missed Kingham, and I found Margaret more incomprehensible than ever. She seldom mentioned her mother country of her own accord, and usually changed the subject when I asked her about it. Only when she was at a particularly low ebb would she sometimes say that perhaps she would be better off in a backwater like Iceland, since nobody in England wanted her.

Vincent had never shown the slightest interest in Iceland, and so it was hopeless asking him anything. He said there were few reasons to go there, although the mountains were beautiful. He mentioned Hekla in particular. I suspected it was the only one he knew.

I went to Allington Library, which was on top of the hill on the other side of the football field. The only book I found on Iceland was Auden and MacNeice's travelogue, *Letters from Iceland,* published in 1937. I hadn't heard of it before, of course, and I sat down with it by the window, filled with anticipation. But my heart sank when I opened the book and found that the first chapter was written in verse, "Letters to Lord Byron," part one of five. However, as I leafed through the book, things began to look up, because I found some photographs and discovered that the book wasn't made up entirely of obscure poetry.

On my first visit to the library, I mostly looked at the photographs. Although in my opinion there were too many of horses, some were instantly memorable: for example, a photograph of two boys watching a man cross a river on a ropeway, a farm on a windswept hill, and a man playing the accordion. I also came across a line from a poem that stayed in my mind as I headed home: *This is an island and therefore unreal.*

In the weeks and months that followed, I went to the library every Tuesday and Thursday after school and sat by the window reading Auden and MacNeice's book. The poems which at first had seemed so dense became clearer to me, and in the end I could recite many of them by heart. I never took the volume home with me, because I didn't want to give Vincent or Margaret the chance to know I was reading it, and besides, it felt good sitting by the window in the peace and quiet of the library, watching the activity outside the garage across the street and the train as it came sweeping around the tracks into the town.

After reading *Letters from Iceland,* I considered myself knowledgeable about the country, undaunted by the fact that the book had been written nearly half a century before. I wasn't surprised that Margaret had abandoned such a tough, unforgiving place, for I couldn't possibly imagine her in any of the landscapes evoked by those two poets, whether urban or rural. And what about Vincent? He would never survive there, of that I was certain.

That is what I told myself, relishing the fact that I alone possessed this information without their knowing it. I was convinced I was an Icelander by nature, taking after my late grandfather, a sailor about whom my mother spoke little.

When a year later Vincent told me one spring day that Margaret had been invited to give a recital in Iceland and to stay on and teach a class to a few chosen students, I was amazed that she accepted. And yet considering the difficult winter she had

had—few triumphs and many more disappointments—perhaps
it wasn't so surprising.

An Icelandic Ph.D. student at Cambridge, Ísleifur Kristófers-
son, helped organize the trip, working with his friends at the
Reykjavík Music Society to arrange the recital and the class.
Vincent helped with publicity materials, and Margaret even
gave a short interview over the phone to the public radio.

I thought about those days when Malena and I landed in Keflavík. I remembered the old terminal, long vanished, low shacks
that could have been from the time of Auden and MacNeice,
and Ísleifur and his friends who came to meet us dressed in their
short overcoats. They drove us into town and I watched the lava
fields out the window and Keilir, the mountain which I instantly
recognized from *Letters from Iceland*. My heart leapt when it
suddenly appeared through the mist, which was nowhere else to
be seen on that clear day.

When Malena and I had checked into our hotel we took a
walk through the center of town, before heading up Bankastræti
to buy some warmer clothes. I had already told her about Margaret's recital at the old cinema, Gamla bíó. She had asked about
my trip with my parents, gently of course, and I couldn't avoid
telling her more than I wanted. I seized the opportunity and
walked with her to Ingólfsstræti, where I thought the cinema
had been, and was relieved to discover I was right. She contemplated the building, even stepping into the middle of the road
and gazing up at it. It was less imposing than I remembered,
though I didn't say so. She tried the door but it was locked.

Standing there on the sidewalk, I was struck by the thought
that I had never been there before. At first I made little of it,
tried to brush it aside, but when that failed I became anxious.
I glanced down the street, as though in search of some land-
mark that might put me back on the right track, and yet neither
Arnarhóll looming close by or even Mount Esja on the far side of

the bay looked familiar to me. And yet there the mountain was beneath the blue skies, just as it had been the evening Margaret held her recital in the cinema, regal and suitably distant.

Malena was looking at the poster on the door, the image of a man in a green suit standing in what looked like an orange field, arms outstretched, either singing or calling to someone not in the picture.

"Is he an elf?" she asked, turning toward me.

"We should have gone to Greece," I said, turning on my heel and walking away without looking back.

begged her forgiveness. We were back in the hotel room. I was sitting on the edge of the bed, she was standing by the window. I had walked until I reached the hotel, then at last I looked behind me. She wasn't far away but had stopped calling out when she realized I wasn't going to slow down.

She had her back to me, her arms folded as she looked out over Austurvöllur square, or pretended to. The afternoon sun was shining on her, and I thought I saw a tinge of red in her dark hair.

"I don't know what came over me," I said.

She had never seen me lose my temper before; I very rarely do. I expected her to be hurt and angry, unsure for the first time what to make of me, possibly blaming herself for having forced me to come to Iceland; I envisioned a difficult trip ahead and felt sick when I thought about how I had behaved.

And so I was taken aback when she turned around and smiled.

"I knew we were meant to come here," she said. "I knew we needed to."

I should have felt relieved, of course, and yet there was

something in her manner that prevented me. I had always been able to smile when she talked about being a witch and things like that, and besides, her tone was then conscientiously mischievous, so I never took her seriously. But now I couldn't help remembering the expression of despair clouding her face in Florence, and it struck me that she might think my behavior had somehow evened the score. Surely I was imagining things, and I reproached myself as I sat on the edge of the bed looking at her, and yet a seed had been planted which I didn't like.

That evening, in a little restaurant down by the harbor, I saw that she had prepared this trip very carefully. She didn't admit it, of course, but made it look as if we were planning our itinerary together as we tucked into mussels and cod. Naturally, still ashamed for what had happened earlier, I did my best not to show that I knew. Our first stop would be Snæfellsnes, where she wanted to walk up the glacier, and from there to Stykkishólmur, where we would take the ferry to the island of Flatey. There was a small hotel on the island, she told me, perfect for an overnight stay. She wanted to visit the highlands, too, and thought it best to take the ferry from Flatey to Brjánslækur, and then to drive from there to Skagafjörður and on up to Sprengisandur. She had somehow managed to find out as well where we could rest on the way, and when we got back to the hotel, she showed me a photograph of a tiny hut beneath a rocky hill.

I did my best to respond with enthusiasm to her ideas, although I couldn't understand why she had kept her travel plans secret from me. She must have spent weeks elaborating them, down to the very last detail, it seemed. It reminded me of the days when I used to sit in the library in Allington reading Auden and MacNeice, unbeknownst to my parents. Why had she played the same game with me?

I tried to hide my misgivings and was as cheerful as I could allow myself to be, asking questions that affirmed my interest and eagerness. She replied informatively and showed me photographs on websites with cars crossing powerful rivers on Sprengisandur, of Snæfellsjökull under a bright blue sky, people climbing Drangey in Skagafjörður.

"I've seen so many pictures now, there's no need for us to go there," I said, jokingly, then instantly regretted it.

She shot a glance at me. I smiled and then she tried to smile back. We were on our feet, and I put my arm around her, but no matter how tight I held her, a breach of some kind seemed suddenly to have separated us. I was about to ask what was the matter, but she broke the silence first.

"Look how beautiful the evening light is," she said.

Did I sense that we would never see Drangey or Sprengisandur except in the pictures on the website? Sometimes I think so, but that may just be my imagination.

We set off early in the morning in good weather. I slept little in the light nights, and yet I wasn't tired. We chatted all the way to Snæfellsnes (she especially), and after a while I felt everything was as it should be. Yet it was almost as if we didn't trust the silence. Malena marveled at everything she saw, every rock, every river cascading down the mountains to the sea, old bridges by the sides of the road, having no purpose anymore, sheep grazing on the verges, and horses in the farmers' fields. I told myself that I had won her back, her natural joyfulness and childlike excitement, her laughter as she clasped my arm, crying out: "Oh look, Magnus, just look at the waterfall, up there on the mountainside!"

The flash of despair I had seen on her face in Florence belonged to the past; it no longer had any place in my memories, no more than my anger of the day before, which I had persuaded myself was nothing more than travel fatigue. We stopped beside a brook outside Borgarnes, had sandwiches, and drank water from the stream as the breeze caressed the yellow grass and our cheeks.

She fell silent as we drove along the Snæfellsnes peninsula on our way to the glacier. I remembered a few things about it from when I was a boy, and I told her of Jules Verne and his book *Journey to the Center of the Earth,* and mentioned people's long-held belief that the glacier possessed magical powers. I don't recall whether I actually joked about these superstitions, but if I did it would have been good-natured anyway. She nodded a few times, but I sensed I wasn't telling her anything she didn't know. She was busy looking out for the glacier, despite my assurances that you couldn't really see it from the south of the peninsula until you were almost upon it; she seemed restless, anxious that we might somehow miss it. I said as much.

"I doubt the glacier has moved," I told her, patting her thigh. She smiled absent-mindedly, almost mechanically, and kept staring out the window.

She said nothing when the glacier finally appeared, but I could hear her breathing becoming slower and deeper. I stopped for a moment so she could take in the scenery, before continuing up the hill to where we parked the car by the side of the road and got out.

It was as if she had a plan, but wasn't quite sure where to start. Finally, she rummaged in her bag and took out a bundle of papers I hadn't seen before. She sifted through them for a while, and I decided not to ask any questions, zipping up the jacket I had bought the day before. There was a cold breeze, and we gazed at the sea far below. At last she looked up and said, as if it were the logical continuation of a discussion we had been having: "The energy from the glacier is strongest here on the eastern side, but we need to climb higher up."

I followed her up the foothills, toward the snow that glittered in the sunshine, but she seemed to find the going hard, and our ascent was slow. At last she stopped and sat down on a rock. I asked her whether her foot was still hurting.

"Still?"

"Since Florence," I said. "Since you twisted your ankle."

"A little," she replied. "I'll be fine."

After a short rest, we turned around and started to climb down. I walked ahead. There were more people on the glacier than we had expected, most of them tourists, but soon she stopped again and asked me not to wait for her. I assumed she was trying to feel the power of the glacier, and I didn't want to put her off by looking over my shoulder.

We drove over the moor and caught the ferry from Stykkishólmur to Flatey. It was clouding over by then, but still dry. We stayed on deck during the crossing. It was cold out in the fjord and she wound her scarf more snugly about herself. Seabirds wheeled above the boat, and a man on the bench next to us claimed he had seen an eagle through his binoculars.

By the time the ferry docked at Flatey, the wind had died, and a few drops of rain fell from the sky. We placed our luggage in a small car sent from the hotel, and were told that otherwise no one drove on the island. Malena still seemed to be limping, so I asked the driver whether she could get a lift with him to the hotel. She interrupted before the man had a chance to reply, insisting there was no need. I could see she was annoyed, but she forced a smile and said: "How beautiful it is here."

From the harbor to the hotel was a short distance, down a gravel road, past some low dwellings, farmhouses, and fish flakes. On the side of the road not far from the hotel was a chicken coop, and a tiny church on a knoll where sheep were grazing. Malena walked slowly at first, and I was careful not to go too fast myself, pausing every now and then to look around, the rain still only a light drizzle. Halfway down the road, I noticed her pace suddenly quicken. She seemed almost surprised at first, pausing as though unsure of her footing, then she brightened up, gliding ahead, light on her feet, as if she had sprouted wings. I said

nothing, but remembered how good I felt when she looked over
her shoulder, grinning from ear to ear, and said:

"I'd love to live here."

I smiled back at her.

"Let's move here . . . Seriously."

"Seriously?"

"Yes, why not?"

"If that's what you want."

"Do you mean that?"

"You know I'd follow you anywhere."

We rested a little in the attic room which awaited us in the
tiny hotel. White curtains fluttered before the window, through
which the sounds of the sea seeped in. The boats idled in the
harbor and children were playing by the shore. I fell asleep.

It had stopped raining by the time we finished our dinner,
so we decided to go for a stroll around the island. We threaded
our way along the road next to the shore, on the north side
where the hotel was, then turned east, leaving the houses behind as the hayfields took over. Malena marveled at the light
summer evening, the stillness and the scenery, and said again
that we should settle on the island.

"I can teach dance," she said, "and you can set up a doctor's
office where we live."

"Where will that be?"

She looked around and pointed to a black timber house
down by the shore.

"There."

I told her that few, if any, people lived on the island in winter.

"Then I'll dance for you," she said, and I waited for her to
say that I would tend to her when she had a cold, or fell ill, but
instead she said: "And you can fish."

I smiled, and we threaded our way along a narrow sheep's
trail, she in front. The sun came out over the fjord, lighting up

the sea and the clouds that were slowly breaking apart. When we reached the nesting fields, we turned south, crossing the island diagonally, the arctic terns following us, screeching relentlessly and swooping above our heads. I handed Malena a stick with which to protect herself from the diving birds. She found it amusing, and I said something about terns being good at protecting their young.

All was well until we reached the southern shore and were about to head back to the hotel. When she tripped, we had just glimpsed the remains of a wrecked ship on the beach ahead of us, and she was running toward it. I was watching her and saw the way her feet gave way beneath her (one or both, I am not sure) as she pitched forward onto a boulder by the path. She cried out in pain, and I rushed over to her. I could see immediately that she had broken her left arm in the fall.

I grappled with her for a long time where she lay on the ground, finally helping her to her feet and holding her up as we made our way back to the hotel. It seemed to take forever; the terrain was uneven so she paused with almost every step.

There was no hospital or even a doctor on the island, but the staff at the hotel rallied and found a fisherman to take us on his boat back to the mainland. Malena waited in the lobby while I packed our things. Before closing the door behind me, I glanced out the little window. The sun was sinking toward the horizon, the rippling waves washing the last rays up onto the land, leaving them behind on the pebble beach.

While I sat in the waiting room at Stykkishólmur staring out into the night at the veils of mist above the harbor, I remembered all the injuries Malena had struggled with that year. I hadn't given them much thought and she had dismissed them as unimportant, although they had clearly prevented her from dancing most of January. For three weeks in a row she had stayed mostly in her apartment, insisting it was easier as there is no elevator in my building. When I offered to move in with her while she was convalescing, she thanked me but said she didn't want to upset my routine. She claimed she was getting better and would return to my place in a few days. Of course we saw each other during that time, but not as often as I would have liked. She talked about being busy at school, and besides she was constantly going to physical therapy and yoga. I told her I was glad she wasn't limping but she pulled a strange face and told me that the pain was intermittent. Of course I took her words at face value.

I found out later that she had been undergoing tests during that three-week period, at the end of which she was given a diagnosis. On the twenty-ninth of January, to be exact. That evening we went to the opera, and although she was more fidgety than usual, I remember thinking she was enjoying life again. We spent the night together, lying awake for a long time in each other's arms, as after a long separation, and when I awoke the next day to go to work, she didn't want to let go of my hand. I remember how happy that made me, and I reproach myself now for having been so blind.

It was about two in the morning when we left the hospital in Stykkishólmur. I had been intending to find us a room for the night, but Malena wanted to drive back to Reykjavík immediately. I called Hotel Borg and booked a room and we set off in the red rental car that was waiting for us by the harbor where I had parked it the previous day.

She tried to rest, drowsy from the painkillers. I don't think she fell asleep, but she kept her eyes closed, perhaps so she wouldn't have to talk. In fact, I was relieved at first, because that enabled me to enjoy the still night. Horses slept in the fields, and I saw sheep scattered about like white specks in the semi-twilight, the blurred contours of the distant mountains, a pale moon above the ocean. Peace and quiet with no one around but us, her breath measured, and I was strangely relieved that our Icelandic trip would soon be coming to an end.

I don't know why I was then seized by this sudden uneasiness. Nothing had changed as we approached Borgarnes, nothing I could put my finger on—the night was as calm as before, the moon was still shining on the sea. It was as though I was incapable of allowing myself to feel good and was searching for a way to shatter the calm, to call darkness down upon me. Why?

As it was, I began to think about the time when I was in Iceland with Vincent and Margaret. Until then, I had been fairly successful in keeping those memories at bay, yet now they assailed me, relentlessly, no matter how hard I tried to ignore them.

The trip had started well. Ísleifur and his colleagues had arranged for us to stay in a small apartment on Sjafnargata, where we settled in before going to dinner at the home of Ísleifur's parents. We received a warm welcome, Margaret played the piano, much to the delight of the company, and Vincent gave a short speech in which he announced that Margaret's recital was a token of her gratitude to her land and people. Her success should encourage other Icelandic musicians, for it showed that with talent and determination they, too, could as well as anybody else have the world at their feet. He gave a toast, and when Ísleifur let slip that it was his mother's birthday, Margaret sat down at the piano and played "Happy Birthday," improvising a few amusing variations to the hilarity of everyone present.

The next day Margaret was interviewed by a few journalists. Vincent was never far away, interposing comments here and there, to put things in context, he said, because Margaret was too self-effacing. The interviews appeared the day of the recital, and Margaret translated them for Vincent over their morning tea; I was standing within earshot. It amazes me sometimes that they let me listen to those fictitious accounts of Margaret's life, those tales about her career, instead of telling me to go outside and play. And yet it was as if they were listening to the gospel truth, and simply wanted to make sure no one was straying from the script, casting aspersions, or splitting hairs.

"Excellent," Vincent remarked every now and then as Margaret read aloud, "brilliant, well written, elegant, hits the nail right on the head."

The recital was well attended and Margaret got a standing ovation. The reviews were complimentary, although Margaret felt that one of them—written by a young composer—could have been more positive.

"A novice," she explained. "Studied in Germany, apparently. Just got back."

I remember it was the sentence "Strange we haven't heard more about her" that she took exception to, because in all other respects, according to what I heard, the review was fine.

"Not bad at all," said Vincent, picking up the other newspapers to try to distract her.

"But that's the biggest broadsheet," said Margaret.

"Read the sentence again," said Vincent.

"'Strange we haven't heard more about her.'"

"Might he not be saying that it's a shame your countrymen haven't been following your career more closely?"

"Is that what it sounds like to you?"

"There's nothing else in the article that suggests any animosity."

"But no enthusiasm, either. No generosity. Only a tedious account of my repertoire and a dispassionate description of my performance.

"No, that's not true," said Vincent, who had been taking notes while Margaret read aloud. "A professional performance . . . Well received by the audience . . . Hoping this marks the beginning of further concerts in Gamla bíó . . . Not bad at all, Margaret."

She was persuaded for the time being, and we went for a walk around Tjörnin, the pond in the city center, and later that day visited my aunt Berglind, whom I had met for the first time at the recital. She was older than Margaret and didn't look like her at all; she was short, rather stout, with a kindly face, and seemed almost shy of my parents. She spoke no English, Margaret explained, and hadn't finished high school. Her husband was tall and skinny, and rather reserved. His name was Friðrik and Margaret told us he was a cabinetmaker. They had three children: two had left home, which left Jóhann, who was a year older than I.

The same thing happened with us cousins as it does with

most children; although we spoke different languages we instantly seemed to understand each other. While the grown-ups drank coffee and tried to make conversation, we went first into his bedroom, the walls of which were lined with pictures of Manchester United football players, and then into the yard, taking with us the ball Jóhann kept under his bed. The two of us kicked it around until a third boy joined us and then others later until we had enough players for two teams.

I wouldn't be exaggerating if I said that Jóhann and I became fast friends, and before we left, I persuaded Margaret to ask her sister whether he and I could meet up regularly during the rest of our stay. They lived on Ásvallagata, so it wasn't far to go, and I wouldn't need any help getting there. Of course, Berglind said, and I could see my parents were delighted about this new relationship, as it meant they no longer had to worry about keeping me busy.

Margaret's class started the following day and should have lasted two weeks. For the first few days, I had breakfast at Sjafnargata before leaving for my cousin Jóhann's house, where I would stay until bedtime. But this involved a lot of useless to-ing and fro-ing and we cousins, naturally, concluded that it would be better if I moved in temporarily. Our parents raised no objections and I stuffed my clothes in a bag and moved to Ásvallagata, where I slept on the floor in Jóhann's room.

I still look back on those days with a smile on my face and a happy heart. Simple family life was something new to me; it reminded me of a smooth river running gently into the sea, washing the grassy banks, reflecting the bright sky and the birds flying overhead. At least, that is how it seemed to me many years later when I was at Cambridge and would rest my biking legs on the banks of the River Rib and reflect on my life. I also realized that it was my experience there that helped encourage my exile from my parent's house—for what else could

I call my escape to the attic room in Murray and Beatrice's house?

I can still smell the pancakes Aunt Berglind used to make to accompany the afternoon coffee, and the odor of wood in Friðrik's workshop in the cellar; I can hear Friðrik's quiet voice and Berglind's humming along to the radio, which she always had on in the kitchen. They were relaxed and cheerful, completely different from how they had seemed in my parents' company. Friðrik let us build a boat in a corner of his workshop and Berglind showed me photographs of my grandparents and of her and my mother as children.

Everything went like clockwork until exactly one week into our stay in Iceland, when disaster struck without warning. Vincent knocked on the door when we were in the middle of lunch: boiled fish and potatoes, prepared by Friðrik, because Berglind worked in the mornings. And freshly baked lava bread, which was delicious with butter. Friðrik and Berglind were listening to the news on the radio while slowly eating their food, but Jóhann and I were in a hurry because our friends were waiting for us to resume playing football on the field up at Landakotstún.

"You have to pack your things," he said when Berglind opened the door. "We're leaving."

"Leaving? Where to?"

"Home."

"Home?"

"You must pack your things."

He turned to Friðrik and Berglind and tried to explain that we had to go back to England earlier than planned.

"Due to unforeseen circumstances, shall we say, nothing that can be done about it, I'm afraid."

He spoke fast and didn't think of simplifying his language so they had a hard time understanding a word of what he was saying. Finally, he managed, through gestures, to make it clear to them why he was there, at which the couple exchanged glances and then looked at me, doing their best to put on a brave face.

"I'm not going," I said to Vincent.

"Magnus . . ."

"I'm not leaving here. You two can go."

"Magnus Colin. This is beyond my control . . ."

"I'm going to stay. I'm going to live here."

I don't remember ever having rebelled against my parents or truly spoken my mind to them, however much I longed to do so. Consequently, Vincent didn't know what had hit him. He had never lost his temper with me and didn't then. He seemed bewildered.

"Magnus Colin. Not you as well . . ."

"Take her home and leave me here. I never want to see either of you again."

I didn't shout, but my voice was trembling with rage and I remember fighting back the tears. I think I would have won that contest had Vincent not broken down, right in front of the four of us there in the hallway.

First he closed his eyes and lowered his head; his body began to shake, but when his crying became audible I felt every ounce of strength drain from my body. These were quiet, breathless sobs, signifying utter defeat. It was as if myriad failures had all of a sudden converged, forcing my father to appear more sincere than I had ever seen him.

I collected my things, shook Friðrik's hand, and allowed Berglind to take me in her arms. Jóhann and I looked at each other for a moment, but when I felt the tears begin to trickle down my cheeks I opened the door and walked out of the house without looking back.

I didn't say a word in the taxi up to Sjafnargata where

Margaret and the suitcases were waiting for us, nor on the way to the airport. They were silent, too, and it was only later when I put together snatches of their conversation that I found out what had happened. Then Margaret's words as we boarded the plane echoed in my head:

"I shall never come here again."

Vladimir Ashkenazy set the cat among the pigeons.

He was married to an Icelandic woman and had become an Icelandic citizen in the early eighties, but was living in Switzerland when this happened. He was still considered one of the world's leading pianists, although by then he was mostly conducting. Icelanders respected and admired him; he was even dearer than a son of their own, because he had chosen to become one of them, preferring them over the superpower with which he had cut all ties. He was a citizen of the world, and he brought that world with him to this small island in the north, with his playing and his appearance—his tousled hair and exotic features, his name. Local musicians vied for his attention, and even those who never listened to classical music were in awe of him.

Until then, the course had progressed without incident. There were eight students in total, and although Margaret later insisted they were all talentless, I could tell from my father's timid rebuttal that she had liked them well enough. Ísleifur and his colleagues, the perfect hosts, made sure Vincent and Margaret were entertained every evening, and my father even made a deal with a record shop owner to import everything on the Mecca label. Things couldn't have been better; even the weather was in a good mood and the sun made an appearance nearly every day.

Ashkenazy arrived unannounced. No one knew he was in the country, Ísleifur later explained to my father. My mother was in the middle of teaching when one of the students looked out the window and saw his idol enter the building. He gasped, unable to stop himself from announcing the news to the whole class. There was a small commotion among the students and someone opened the door and looked down the corridor. Soon afterward Ashkenazy appeared with the director of the school, who had been waiting for him by the entrance.

Margaret was upset by this disorder among her students, although I suspect she would have gotten over it had the director not insisted on pausing in the open doorway.

"I expect you two have met before," he said. "Vladimir Ashkenazy, Margaret Bergs."

Margaret hesitated, but Ashkenazy shook his head, smiling.

"No, I don't believe we have."

"But surely you must know of each other."

Silence. The students looked first at him then at her, while the director appeared bewildered, as if he realized that he had made a blunder.

"Bergs?" Ashkenazy said.

"The pianist, Margaret C. Bergs," insisted the director.

As Vincent later pointed out, a civilized human being would have put an end to the embarrassing situation simply by replying: "Yes, of course, how silly of me. Pleased to meet you. I've always been a great admirer of yours." Nothing more. A few words, a handshake, and a friendly smile. After which he would have continued on his way with the director, while Margaret resumed her class, and no harm would have come of that meeting.

"I'm so out of touch," he said instead. "It's shameful, really. Forgive the interruption."

The students knew exactly what had happened. The silence was excruciating and in the end Margaret marched out and went straight to Sjafnargata, leaving her coat behind in the classroom.

That was at ten o'clock. At twelve, Vincent picked up her coat, then came in the taxi to fetch me.

We have never spoken about what happened between us in Ásvallagata. Not a single word. And yet our relationship changed because of it, and was never the same again. He became cautious, not discussing anything with me but the most ordinary matters. He also spoke differently to Margaret when I was around, was wary, and took care not to say anything that was blatantly untrue, not even when he was trying to placate her. I had never been an insolent child, but every now and then I would make it clear that they no longer had the upper hand. I confess I enjoyed this; perhaps it was a sign that I had reached adolescence.

Vincent's response was to pack me off to St. Joseph's that fall. It was late, but fortunately Christopher Llewellyn Hunt knew the headmaster. And so I stayed in my parents' house only a few weeks after our return from Iceland, although the time went by very slowly. Margaret was either bad-tempered or silent. She didn't touch the piano, and once she stayed in bed for three whole days. She didn't speak to me much. I contrived to spend most of my time with my friends, playing football from morning until night, or else I stayed in my room. That spring, Vincent had given me an old record player with a built-in speaker, along with a few records from his Mecca label. He was hoping I might be tempted to learn to enjoy proper music, as he called it, but until then I had left it to gather dust. It wasn't the records he had given me that changed my mind, but rather a Led Zeppelin album lent to me by a friend's older brother.

I remember clearly the day I first ventured to put *Physical Graffiti* on the turntable. It was just before supper; the album had been in my room for a few days, but I hadn't dared take it out of the sleeve before then.

The response was almost immediate. I hadn't turned the volume up, but the sound carried easily in that house. They were downstairs, in the living room, where they had been sitting since I came home. I stood by the door, listening as much for any noise that might come from downstairs as to the music itself, watching out of the corner of my eye as the black disc went around and around, and automatically tapping my feet to the rhythm.

At first there was dead silence, but then I heard my mother say: "Where's that noise coming from?"

"From outside, wouldn't you say?" my father replied, and I heard him open the front door.

Then they understood, and lowered their voices, although Margaret had always found it difficult to speak in a whisper.

"Do something!" I heard her command Vincent. "Do something!"

I sat on the bed when I heard him climbing the stairs. He came up slowly, pausing twice on the way. He tapped gently on the door, paused, then entered before I had time to decide whether to reply or not.

He looked drained.

"Magnus Colin . . ."

I waited.

"This won't do."

I didn't answer.

"You'll have to turn it off."

"Why?"

"You know why. This noise . . ."

"It isn't noise to me. And I don't care what you think."

He stood in the doorway looking lost, glancing once over his shoulder down the stairs to where I guessed my mother was watching him. He then turned his attention to me and the record player, before finally trudging over to it, lifting the needle slowly, and replacing the album in its cover. I sat still, gazing at him in silence. I was expecting him to take the record with him, but after holding the sleeve in his hand for a moment, he put it down and walked back to the door.

"I'm sorry," he said, and before he closed the door, he added: "I've applied for a place for you at St. Joseph's. I know you'd like to go there. Perhaps it's for the best."

I played the record again only when they were out. That didn't happen often, and I made sure I took it off before they came home. It was like in a cold war: they knew about my weapon, and that was good enough for me.

That chapter would doubtless have been closed had my friends and I not walked down to the center of Allington at the beginning of August to buy some refreshments after football. The shop was in a square that had a jumble sale on Saturdays where you could pick up all sorts of things, including cheap, secondhand editions of the football magazine *Shoot*. We lingered there before going back to the pitch, drinking our Cokes and browsing through the magazines. As we were about to leave, I spotted some records next to fountain pens and picture frames. One of them caught my eye. It was Beethoven's piano concertos played by Vladimir Ashkenazy with the Chicago Symphony Orchestra.

Before I knew it, I had parted with a pound and the record was in a plastic bag. I put it under my jumper while we were playing, and sneaked it up to my room when I got home. After dinner, I put it on the turntable, and played it all evening without interruption.

Margaret wasn't there the next morning at breakfast and

Vincent was silent. I wolfed down my egg on toast and went out to play with my friends until the afternoon. When I got home the record had vanished and I never saw it again. Margaret was nowhere to be seen, and it was only when my father and I sat down to dinner that he told me she had gone away for a while. He waited for me to ask where, but I didn't. I found out later that she had moved into a guesthouse in Cambridge, not far from the park. She stayed there until I left for St. Joseph's two weeks later.

Although I never discussed it with her, I kept thinking about those days when Malena and I got back from Iceland and she announced she was going to Buenos Aires to recuperate. She told me about a physical rehabilitation center for dancers and athletes where she had been twice before, once when as a child she suffered a torn ligament, and later when she sprained her ankle. "They work miracles there," she told me, and her choice of words didn't strike me as odd; people say these kinds of things. I asked if I should go with her, but she simply caressed my cheek, giving me a kiss as she thanked me and reminded me that I needed to attend to my own career. She didn't want to be a burden to me, she said. That stayed with me, too.

I took her to the airport, carried her bags from the taxi, and helped her check in. After saying good-bye, I watched her pass through the security gate, and waited for her to turn around, but she didn't.

A tiny tremor in the upper right eyelid, a slight but definite quiver.

"Definite?"

I was sitting at my desk, while Simone stood leaning against the book cabinet.

"Yes, definite," I replied. "I saw it with my own eyes. Not once but twice."

"When?"

"Last night."

"Just you, not Anthony?"

"Yes, just me."

We had started running tests on our patient that morning, first the CAT scan, then the MRI down in the basement. We needed the most precise information about the nature of the brain damage she had suffered, and Anthony was concerned there might be an occlusion or a potential rupture, but I was convinced the woman's injuries were restricted to the brain stem, and that she was otherwise fully conscious and able to think clearly.

"Convinced?" Simone demurred.

"I see no reason not to be," I said.

"So you mean she doesn't even have a bruise or any other short-term problems."

She resented the fact that I hadn't told Anthony to consult with her, and I sensed she was dying to remind me that my judgment hadn't been exactly reliable recently. Simone can be merciless when she feels affronted, and I was fully expecting her to bring up the two patients from Boston at any moment. I thought I could read it on her face as she stood leaning against the cabinet, arms folded, staring at me.

"I never went," I blurted out.

"What?"

"To Boston. I never went."

She raised her eyebrows, but then she gradually understood.

"I didn't examine either patient, and the second time I didn't even make it out of bed."

I neither lowered my gaze nor bowed my head as I made my confession, but rather looked her straight in the eye and spoke as clearly as I could.

"Why . . . ?"

"I couldn't handle it," I said before she finished her sentence. "I couldn't handle anything."

She looked down.

"Why didn't you ask me to go?"

I couldn't answer that question, not properly, not in a way that would make her feel better. So I said nothing, and silence descended between us until she quietly walked out.

Among other things, the tests revealed that the new patient was severely concussed. The cortex showed signs of bruising, but there were no occlusions or ruptures in the middle artery. However, there was clear tissue damage in the brain stem, although we couldn't tell how serious from our initial examination.

Anthony went over the results with Simone, the nursing staff,

and me. I affirmed how pleased I was that everything seemed to
support the theory that the young woman was locked in her
own body, fully conscious, although unable to move or speak.
I praised Anthony for a job well done, and said this boded well
for our research, adding that we could soon start trying to make
contact with her. Anthony lapped up the praise and agreed with
my conclusions, and the two of us rose to our feet as if there were
nothing more to say.

Simone had listened in silence while we were talking, an
impassive expression on her face, but now she cleared her throat.
We were almost at the door.

"I'd like to look at the images," she said.

She offered no explanation, but it was clear that she had
some reservations. Anthony and I stopped in our tracks, and I
could see him bridle at her overbearing tone. She was trying my
patience, too, and I was tempted to tell her that, but thought
better of it. Instead, I was about to say something about two
pairs of eyes being better than one, but she spoke first.

"Has the patient shown any response?"

Anthony looked at me and then shook his head.

"But she opened her eyes before she came to us," he said, "and
Magnus saw a tremor in her eyelid, which you already know."

"But you didn't."

Silence. Anthony thought she was criticizing him and
frowned but said nothing. He didn't realize her anger was di-
rected at me, not him.

I decided to put an end to the conversation, and said with as
much calm as I could muster:

"Have a look at the images, then we'll compare notes."

When I stepped into my office, a small package was waiting for me. It was wrapped in brown paper and I recognized
Vincent's ornate, flamboyant handwriting. It had been more
legible when he was younger, but it was shaky now and not easy

to decipher. He had asked for my business card at my mother's birthday party and had copied what was on it, making sure he underlined my title, *Assistant Professor, Cognitive Neuroscience and Imaging,* with a different color pen. To anyone else he would undoubtedly have seemed like a proud father, and yet I remembered only too well all the business cards he had made when I was a boy. They had bristled with titles, too.

I was taking the packaging off when Anthony walked in.

"What on earth is the matter with her?" he said, closing the door behind him.

"She's annoyed with me," I said. "Don't worry about it."

I didn't want to talk to him about Simone, who, in spite of everything, is extremely dear to me, and so I quickly changed the subject. The contents of the package provided me with the perfect excuse: two CDs, one of them double. Liszt and Schubert, just as my father had promised. Both had my mother's photograph on the front, hand cupping her cheek.

"This is for you," I said, passing him one of the CDs.

He gave a start.

"Liszt," he said, and started to read aloud from the back. "'*Gnomenreigen, Liebstraum, Funerailles . . .*'"

I was about to hand him the Schubert as well, but I pulled back. Perhaps he noticed the gesture, because he stopped reading and looked up.

"Schubert," I said. "You can have him, too. After the weekend."

He thanked me, and yet I could sense he was going to find waiting for the Schubert difficult. He glanced at the CD in my hand, then caught hold of himself, slipped the Liszt into his pocket, and told me he would listen to it as soon as he got home. Right now the tests were waiting; he would tell me how things were going at the end of the day.

"And don't forget to make sure Simone has access to the images," I said.

At midday, I interviewed some medical students applying for an internship, and afterward Hofsinger and I met with the other heads of department to discuss budgets and related matters. The meeting was long and I found it hard to concentrate, although I think I succeeded in not letting that show.

At five o'clock, when I finally had a free moment, I hung my lab coat over the back of the chair and walked down to the village. There were people sitting at tables outside the café, warmly dressed to be sure, and the doors to the restaurant were open while inside waiters were setting the tables for dinner. In the window of the drugstore a revolution had taken place: instead of the faded Old Spice poster, there was now sunscreen lotion and a picture of children flying a kite. The old perfume bottles remained along with the dried flowers, and yet to me it felt as if everything had been turned upside down.

I walked quickly to the appliance store next to the supermarket. Of the two stereo systems the sales assistant showed me, he recommended the one that was more compact, weighed less, and had a radio as well as a CD player.

I walked back along the shore, and although I couldn't help thinking about the day Malena took the train up and we walked down to the beach and then into the village where we stopped outside the café, I felt fine.

I had been gone longer than I intended. It was after six when I returned to my office and the corridors were quiet, most of the staff having gone home. Anthony had been looking for me, and when he couldn't find me had sent an e-mail instead. He said that the tests hadn't revealed anything new, but would resume tomorrow. He was on his way home to listen to my mother.

It was still bright outside and the lights hadn't yet been switched on. The room was silent apart from the hum of the ventilator. Although the patient lay like an effigy on the bed, I felt that she was aware when I opened the door and walked in. I coughed gently.

"You've had a busy day," I said.

I walked over to the bed and studied her face in the twilight. Her features seemed sharper, but I told myself I must be imagining it. I spoke to her about the tests and told her to be patient, this was a lengthy process, but she could be sure that we were on the right track. I was about to ask her to try to move her eyelid, but changed my mind. It wasn't fair to burden her with that after all the tests she had undergone that day.

I took her hand and stroked it without saying anything before plugging in the stereo system and opening my mother's CD.

"I hope you like this music," I said to her as I pressed the play button.

I listened for a while. The music floated around the room, enveloping us, merging with the darkness, transmitting beauty and calm. I walked back over to the bed and looked at her. All of a sudden, it was as though her expression had changed, as though some inner light had surfaced.

"I know you can hear," I said, clasping her hand. "I can see it in your face."

I would probably have stood beside her bed until the last strains had died down had one of the night nurses not entered the room.

We exchanged a few words, then he turned his attentions to the patient, checked the monitors, adjusted the pillows under her head. I asked him not to switch the music off, said good night to them both, and closed the door quietly behind me.

Before leaving home, I grabbed the rental agreement I had received over a month ago. The old lease had expired and the owner was planning to raise the rent to market prices. I thought this was perfectly fair and intended to sign the document and send it back to him, but hadn't gotten around to it. I had been wondering whether it might not be healthier for me to move, to break away from all the memories that lived with me in that apartment. I had pretty much decided to make the leap, but that was before I started feeling better. Now I was of two minds, and as the train wove its way through the Bronx, I began to read through the contract. It was a boilerplate agreement, but I couldn't really concentrate. I was thinking about the tremor in her eyelid.

Monsieur Chaumont brought up the subject of the new contract when I met him on the stairs over the weekend. I didn't tell them about Malena's death until a month after it happened, purposely avoiding them. Madame Roullard had left four or five messages on my answering machine (in French, naturally), but I was in no state to return her calls. She had knocked on my door twice as well, but I didn't trust myself to let her in, and was content to look through the peephole instead. It was only when I ran into them outside the house that I told them the news. I was on my way out and they were arriving home. I was brief and then hurried away.

Monsieur Chaumont was outraged by the new contract. He was very excitable, and spoke about injustice and robbery, told me also how thieves had broken into the apartment of a fellow countryman and stolen two hundred euros which he kept in an envelope in the fridge. I couldn't see how that was relevant, and not wishing to draw out the conversation, I didn't ask.

"Aren't you going to contest it?" he asked. "Shouldn't we join forces?"

"I'm afraid I've already signed it," I lied.

He was disappointed, but before we parted he said to me:

"Madame Roullard has just written a poem about Malena. She misses her. It's very moving."

The contract didn't take long to read when I finally put my mind to it, and after reflecting for a moment when I reached my office I signed it, stuck a stamp on the envelope, and put it in the mail. At ten o'clock I met Hofsinger and gave him the gist of the tests Anthony had done on Adela, made sure I sounded moderately optimistic but didn't promise too much. He posed all the predictable questions, and was pleased when I replied that so far we hadn't discovered any cause for concern.

Then he asked: "Why do you call the patient Adela?"

I explained that she had acquired the name at the hospital in New Mexico.

"I don't approve of allotting arbitrary names like that," he replied.

I said I knew what he meant, and that I didn't think the name suited her, either.

He appeared baffled by my choice of words, but said nothing and instead looked at the report.

"I shall refer to her as patient number two hundred and twelve."

I nodded. Before taking my leave I mentioned Osborne and Moreau. We hadn't told them about her and perhaps it was time we did, I said.

"No, let's wait," he said. "As we should have done on the last two occasions."

Patient number two hundred and twelve had been taken for tests when I looked in on her. However, the stereo was in its place, though switched off. I opened it to make sure the CD was still in there before closing it again and pressing play.

I was surprised that the music should touch me as deeply as it did. I had arranged to meet Simone at eleven o'clock but realized the time only when I was already a quarter of an hour late. Then I hurried out, but the music stayed with me, as did the memories and doubts it had awakened. Why had I never allowed myself to feel the mournful tenderness of my mother's playing, the boldness with which she tackled fear and despair? I was more familiar with the music than I had realized, for she had often practiced Schubert's piano concertos, but perhaps I hadn't listened to them properly before now. Or been too young. Could that be the explanation?

Simone wasn't in her office but had left a note on my desk asking me to e-mail her when I was free. I sat at the computer and was about to tell her to come by when it occurred to me to open the website Anthony had introduced me to. I wanted to see whether there were any new posts about Margaret, assuming it wouldn't take me long to read them.

It wouldn't be an exaggeration to say that over the past few days the posts about the Mephisto Waltzes had increased tenfold, and in addition a passionate debate about my mother's interpretation of Liszt was taking place. I could see that Anthony's name figured prominently as he led the discussion for the most part. In his first post, from ten o'clock the previous evening, he said he had listened to the CD three times and was still euphoric. He spoke of Margaret's intuition, clarity, and perfect balance, her search for beauty and transcendence, the profound stillness concealed between the notes, imbuing them with meaning and intensity. He started his review with the words: "I am honored to be among the first to write about Margaret C. Bergs's interpretation of Liszt . . ." and though I couldn't help smiling at his need to draw attention to himself, my amusement was soon replaced by an odd mixture of gratitude and remorse, which had been eating away at me lately.

When one forum member ventured to suggest that Jorge Bolet had at least done an equally good job of interpreting Liszt's work, especially in his 1972 recording, which had just been rediscovered in the RCA archives, Anthony was quick to respond. His comment was posted at two in the morning, and this time he declared that he had just listened to the CD five times in a row and was convinced it was a masterpiece. "I feel I could be hearing Liszt himself play, so lucid is the interpretation, so pure and unpretentious, free of the need some musicians have to impose themselves to the detriment of the composer."

On the next page were some reviews of the Mephisto Waltzes from respected magazines and websites such as *Gramophone, International Piano,* MusicWeb, and Classics Today, along with articles from several newspapers. The reviews were all positive but only a taste of what was to come. I read them from beginning to end—they were all to the point—then clicked on the link to my father and his partner's company and bought five copies of each CD.

I felt strange afterward. I am not naturally impulsive and yet I had instantly typed in my credit card number and my address, and opted for express delivery despite the extra cost. But now, as

I leaned back in my chair and looked at the confirmation of sale on the screen, I started to question myself.

Had I needed the comments on the forum and the magazine reviews to be convinced of my mother's genius? Was I just any other member of the herd, incapable of making up my own mind, so immature that I had been allowing distant events to cloud my judgment? Or did I simply have no ear for music? Had I only been entranced by her interpretation of Schubert because I had been told to? And did I believe that in buying these CDs I was somehow atoning for my dismal behavior?

I shook my head to rid myself of these thoughts, stood up, and tried to reassure myself. Hadn't the *Gramophone* reviewer proclaimed that my mother had undergone a transformation, and that her Mephisto Waltzes bore no comparison to her interpretation of Chopin's piano sonata no. 3, the last work she recorded before disappearing from view? Did he not say that she had matured as an artist, her sensitivity deepened, her approach to pitch, rhythm, and sorority reached a level not previously heard in her performance? Was it any surprise then, that I, a mere layman, hadn't glimpsed her talent before now?

I carried on in this way for a while, blaming and justifying myself by turns, never getting to the bottom of things needless to say, leaving myself hanging in the air. And that's where I was when Simone cleared her throat in the doorway. I gave a start, and must have had a bewildered expression when I looked up because she said:

"Is something wrong?"

I could see on the computer that it was almost twelve, and I felt guilty for neglecting her. But instead of making up an excuse, I decide to tell her the truth (or part of it at any rate) in the hope of disarming her.

"My mother," I said, handing her the Schubert. "She's become an overnight success."

She looked at the front and back of the CD then at me.

"I wasn't expecting this," I said. "It feels like everything has been turned upside down."

Some weeks after Malena died, I confided in Simone that I hadn't told my parents about her death, and I wasn't sure whether I would or not. It was a mistake, of course, because remarks like that demand further explanation. I had immediately tried to change the subject and answered her questions evasively, but I couldn't help telling her more about my parents and my upbringing than I would have liked. More than I had ever told Malena.

Simone's curiosity was understandably piqued, and any thoughts she might have had about scolding me for being almost an hour late for our meeting evaporated. I told her about Margaret's birthday party, the recordings my father had made in my old bedroom, the Mephisto Waltzes, Schubert, Liszt. I showed her the reviews in *Gramophone* and MusicWeb, but not the Usenet or Yahoo! pages, because I didn't want her to know about Anthony's part in this. I didn't see how it would benefit anyone.

"It says here she was forced to retire for a while due to illness."

Simone was reading an interview with Vincent that I hadn't noticed; it followed the review on MusicWeb, and was titled: "Out of the Silence."

In the interview, among other things, Vincent went on to explain that this forced retirement had been due to "serious digestive problems" for which doctors, despite exhaustive tests, had been unable to find any explanation.

"I think her health problems have always been somewhat psychosomatic," I said.

I was startled by how callous my remark sounded, and I could see that Simone was, too. At the same time, it raised a question about how little I knew about my parents' lives during those years when Margaret was at home recording one master-work after another, and it reminded me how seldom we were in touch.

"'We thought Margaret would never play again to her own satisfaction,'" I read myself now from the interview with my father, "'for she has always been her own harshest critic. Her illness was a terrible ordeal, made worse by the fact that her doctors were left scratching their heads. I started the recordings here in the living room as a way of passing the time. Not for any other motive. And so that she could listen to herself play-ing. I thought that might do her some good. But she never did, because she had no need. Every note was etched on her memory and no recording could compete with that . . . Naturally, she was forced to stop sometimes, although she would often play through the pain. I could hear her groans when I played the recordings back. That was heartrending, of course . . .'"

Simone and I were huddled together over the desk reading the interview on the screen.

"He's eloquent," Simone said.

"Yes, he always had that," I said, and then added, to my own surprise: "The shrink I was seeing asked if Margaret might have some form of autism or Asperger's . . ."

"Does she?"

"I had never thought about it . . . He also suggested I take some tests myself . . ."

She smiled.

"What's funny?"

"He's probably never met an Icelandic Englishman before."

It was good to be able to laugh.

"Am I that bad?"

"Yes, of course you are."

Before she left I told her I had bought five copies of all of Margaret's CDs.

"As gifts," I explained.

"Good for you."

"Perhaps I haven't been such a good son to them."

have put off recalling certain events that might clarify my relationship with Simone. Not that I am trying to avoid it— not intentionally, at any rate. I started reflecting on those incidents again as part of my attempt to understand some of the things Malena said during those final months, because I still seem to be uncovering clues which, for whatever reason, I couldn't grasp at the time.

Malena and I had known each other for maybe a month when Simone first cropped up in conversation. I don't remember what the subject was, and it doesn't matter. I might have been discussing my research, or perhaps we were reminiscing about the evening we met at the Delacorte Theater. What I do remember is that we were sitting out on my balcony watching night descend over the city, the birds disappearing among the leaves on the trees in the back garden, heads under their wings. We had finished eating, and were sitting over our wineglasses; she was leaning back in her chair, her feet on my lap. A half-moon was visible between the towers of the Eldorado on Central Park West, and we made a quick bet on which direction it was moving: she said south, I said north.

We watched it silently drift behind a cloud as I stroked the soles of her feet. It was then that she said, out of the blue:

"She's in love with you."

"Pardon?"

"Simone. You know she's in love with you."

"Nonsense," I said.

She smiled.

"You mean you don't know?"

"There's never been anything between us," I said.

"You have to be kind to her," she said.

Fortunately, the moon brought the conversation to an end as it emerged from behind the cloud, now touching the southern tower.

"You see," she said. "You lost."

I was careful to mention Simone as little as possible after that, and Malena saw no reason to bring up her theory again. I'm sure I realized there was some truth in what she said, but I decided not to think about it. They got along well on the few occasions they met, and Malena was friendly and considerate toward her, for example, at hospital get-togethers where she would make sure Simone sat at our table, and always managed to get her to laugh or talk about her interests.

After our trip to Iceland, she brought up Simone's name more frequently. She did it cleverly so the context always seemed natural and I never suspected anything. Only later—when Malena was dead—did it suddenly all become clear.

Still, it would be wrong of me to use Malena's words as an excuse, even if they were a desperate attempt on her part to prevent me from being alone after she was gone. She was looking ahead, although she probably knew there was little chance that Simone and I would get together, even with her blessing.

We were staying in Liège. It was about six weeks since Malena had died. I should never have gone on that trip, but somehow I had convinced myself it would do me good. On the way to JFK, I almost asked the taxi driver to turn around, but I pulled myself together, and again when I lost my nerve at the security gate. I had suddenly remembered the day I accompanied Malena to the airport and watched her walk through that very gate, waiting for her to look back over her shoulder. I was able to get a grip on myself as I felt my legs go weak, but I forgot to take my laptop out of my briefcase and left my cell phone in my pocket, for which I received an earful from the security staff.

That was on Monday evening. Simone had flown out ahead of me because she wanted to spend the weekend with her family, and was already at the hotel when I arrived. There was a message from her waiting for me at reception and I called her after taking a shower and hanging my clothes in the closet. She had just gotten back after going out for a restorative run. The plan was to meet Moreau and his colleagues the following day, so Simone said we should take a tour of the city, that it was time we got to know it better. I had hardly slept on the plane and was tired, but I went along with the idea since I had nothing else to do and I didn't like being alone.

We visited a few museums, but mostly strolled through the streets and parks, down by the river Meuse, which we crossed and recrossed, finally sitting outside a café in Place du Marché where we had a drink. The weather was fine, though perhaps too cold to sit outside, but we did anyway and our drinks warmed us. We chatted about nothing in particular, and it felt good to be there with her, and I soon ordered another drink.

When we got up to leave it was time for dinner, so we went to a small restaurant which Simone found on her phone, and were given a table by the window. It was getting dark outside and the waiter lit a candle. We ordered a starter and a main course and a bottle of red wine which the waiter recommended. I felt better and tried to make fun of myself, probably somewhat bitterly, as Simone leapt to my defense, though that hadn't been my intention. She said she was worried about me, and I insisted she needn't be, though possibly my words lacked conviction. I told her there was nothing I disliked more than being pitied, at which she replied that I couldn't control other people's feelings, or words to that effect. I sensed what she was getting at and took her hands in mine for a few moments. She smiled, and we finished our meal and walked back to the hotel through the still night. It was chilly, and when I saw her hunch her shoulders to ward off the cold I put my arm around her. She is a beautiful woman, smart, warm, and caring. When we reached the hotel we went straight up to her room.

We undressed each other, and I kissed her lips, her neck, her breasts as we stood in the middle of the floor; she put her arms around me and whispered words in my ear which excited me, but which I have difficulty imagining her uttering when I think about them now. We dragged each other onto the bed and she lay on her back with me on top, and we both knew what was coming when I failed. It happened without warning, as though all at once I was being shaken from a deep sleep. I crumpled and she understood instantly what was going on. I sat on the edge of the bed and buried my face in my hands.

"Forgive me," I whispered.

She said nothing but lay motionless. After a while, I picked my clothes up off the floor and got dressed. I turned around in the doorway and tried to think of something to say but couldn't and closed the door silently behind me.

I remember finding the lights out in the corridor painfully bright.

S imone discovered shadows on the images. I wasn't all that surprised; she has a sharper eye than most and is prepared to spend hours poring over the computer, contemplating every square millimeter until she discovers the minutest discrepancy. On this occasion, of course, there was her added desire to take Anthony and me to task, although I don't want to make too much of that.

She approached me discreetly with her findings and spared me any criticism or unnecessary commentary.

"Perhaps it's worth taking a closer look" was all she said.

The shadows, which could be a sign of trauma in the thalamus and the neocortex, were visible only from one of many angles in a handful of images. I couldn't find them myself, despite her precise instructions, and had to ask her to show them to me. I summoned Anthony so he could go over the images with us; he instantly became defensive and even brought up Simone's episode with the speech therapist, but dropped it when he saw that she was right. However, he couldn't resist pointing out that since it was impossible to draw any conclusions about these shadows we should stick to our guns and attempt to communicate with the patient as planned. The technicians had already started hooking up the software to the MRI scanner and had convinced Anthony that the program they had been troubleshooting over the past few weeks would be ready in a day or two. He said they were still refining it but the modifications looked promising: the images appeared on the screen faster and were much clearer than before. This was good news and I suggested we use the time to make sure the shadows Simone had found were harmless. I assumed they were, I said, but we had to make sure. Neither was pleased: Anthony thought I was paying too much heed to Simone, and Simone thought my claims were rash, but I was thinking about the tremor in her eyelid and the music that had changed the look on her face, illuminating her from inside.

"And then we have to find another name for her," I said. "I don't think Adela suits her. And we can't call her 'patient two hundred and twelve.' That's just awful."

I spoke fast and was more excitable than usual, and they both looked at me rather strangely. That didn't bother me, and I attempted to cheer them up by making a joke. It failed but I found it amusing. As I left the lab I told them I had absolute confidence that they would reach a consensus.

Perhaps it was the weather that had this effect on me, the sunshine when I woke up that morning, now flooding the lawn surrounding the hospital and the fields down by the sea. I walked over to the window and flung it open and my thoughts were as bright as the day.

I seized the opportunity to think about Malena. It's rare for me to be able to do so without sadness, but now I let the memories emerge as I stood by the window gazing at the village of Cold Harbor in the distance.

With hindsight, I must have suspected something wasn't right when she called to say she was taking the train up to Connecticut to see me. Of course I was busy, barely able to answer the phone and make a mental note of what time her train arrived, and yet I still don't understand how I could have been so unprepared for the news.

She had stayed on longer than planned in Buenos Aires. When she took off, I checked her flight on the computer, saw when she landed, and called her. She didn't pick up, but shortly afterward I received a text message from her saying she had arrived at her mother's house.

I talked to her only twice while she was in rehabilitation. Both were brief conversations, the first because she was sitting down to a meal with her family, and the second because she was on her way to yoga. She spoke rapidly both times and said she missed me, but I should have sensed she wanted to get off the phone. On the other hand, she sent me regular text messages, which were brief and frankly rather forgettable. When she had been away for about a month, I sent her a text telling her I wanted to visit her, that I had found a cheap flight leaving Thursday evening and returning late Sunday, we could spend the weekend together. But she responded coolly, saying she had promised to accompany her mother out of town that weekend to visit her relatives and didn't want to break her word. I suggested I come the following weekend, and then she said she was thinking of moving up her departure and would probably be back in New York no later than Sunday. Naturally, I welcomed the news and was surprised when she changed her plans. Her mother had taken ill, she told me, and she didn't want to leave her until she got better.

Of course I could sense that something wasn't quite right. But I blamed the injuries, told myself it was only natural she felt a little depressed and disoriented, that it was actually surprising how well she was holding up. Not only had she been forced to pull out of two dance performances, but on top of that she was unable to fulfill her teaching obligations. She was used to dancing alongside her students and had more than once talked about how she couldn't stand at a distance and explain what she meant: she had to show them.

Yes, it must be the injuries, I told myself, and then it was only natural that her family in Buenos Aires would want her to stay on so that they could spend time with her when she wasn't in physical therapy or practicing yoga. I had to be patient to make sure I avoided pressuring her in any way.

Occasionally I would ask myself how well I really knew her, but then I had only to imagine her in my arms, her eyes, her mouth, and I felt better.

I was shocked when she called me on Wednesday morning to tell me she was back in New York. It was nearly eleven and I was on my way to a departmental meeting.

"Are you at the airport?" I asked.

"No, I'm at home."

"When did you arrive?"

She paused.

"This morning."

"Why didn't you let me know?"

"I didn't want to bother you. You'd have had to get up at five to come and fetch me."

"So what?"

"It was really unnecessary."

I could hear from her voice that my questions were futile.

"How are you?"

"Fine. I'm fine."

"And the rehab?"

"It went well."

"You should have let me know. I have a meeting. But I could take the train home when I'm done."

"No," she said, "don't do that. I need to go to school. I'll be there all day. I'm so behind with everything."

"But you feel all right?"

"Yes, I feel good."

"I can't wait to see you this evening."

"Me, too."

"I'll buy some groceries."

"Okay."

"We can cook dinner together."

I was longing to see her, to hold her in my arms, and it came through in my voice. I stopped talking and for a moment we listened to the silence through the telephone, and then she said, so softly I almost couldn't hear:

"I love you."

She hung up before I had a chance to respond in kind. But I held the phone to my ear, as if the echo of her words might vanish if I put it back in my pocket.

We cooked dinner and ate outside on the balcony. It was as if she had never been away.

That was on Wednesday. On Thursday evening she went to a dance performance in the East Village and slept at her apartment because the show ended late. I thought nothing of it, and we said good night over the phone before going to sleep.

It was Friday when she called me at the hospital to tell me she was taking the four o'clock train to see me. I remember standing at the window, looking down toward the sea, and deciding there and then to reserve a table with the pharmacist's daughter, who had just opened a restaurant after a long stay abroad.

S imone and I have never spoken about that evening in Liège. The next morning, we met in the lobby and walked to the hospital together. Having decided to leave early, she was wheeling a small suitcase behind her and was going straight to the airport after the meeting. It was chilly outside but not raining and patches of blue sky showed through the clouds. I had slept very little and she looked tired, too; neither of us said much. When we were halfway there, I managed to repeat a stuttering apology, at a red light. She looked away and I had the sense to say nothing more.

I have sometimes wondered whether, given the situation, it wouldn't have been more honest of me to continue. Obviously, I am not trying to disguise the fact that this would undoubtedly have had other, possibly more complicated consequences, but at least I wouldn't have humiliated her.

I was delighted when shortly afterward she started seeing a fellow who worked for a pharmaceutical company. He was a few years her junior and seemed pleasant enough. I told her so, perhaps a little too insistently given that I scarcely knew him. In any event, he was polite and his handshake inspired trust. Sadly, the relationship didn't last long. Anthony maintained she had driven him away, but he knew nothing about it, of course.

I think we've both managed to forget that evening or at least come to terms with it in a way that doesn't affect our relationship. And yet when I look at her sometimes, I can't help remembering. It's always painful, and I feel terribly guilty.

Anthony and Simone knocked at my door late in the day to give me a report on their joint assessment of our patient. They stood side by side, and it seemed there had been some major reconciliation between them. Anthony praised Simone for having noticed the much-discussed shadows, and Simone in turn said that a detailed study had shown that Anthony was right: the shadows themselves couldn't account for the woman's present state. They must be the result of an old injury or a viral infection, not even a serious one.

I nodded as they spoke, occasionally posing a question to show my interest, although nothing they said surprised me. I looked alternately at one, then the other, and when Simone sat gently on the edge of my desk and brushed the hair from her cheek, I suddenly started thinking about that evening in Liège. I could see her standing naked with her arms around me and whispering the words I won't forget. Those memories had usually depressed me or made me ashamed, but this time they had no effect. I managed to concentrate on what she and Anthony had to say, and was quick to respond once they finished their report.

I felt good in those days, brimming with optimism. I would get up early and arrive at the hospital before my colleagues, eager to get to work. In fact, there was a reason for that, which I kept secret. I don't know why, as there was no need for me to feel guilty about visiting our patient, either in the morning or in the evening when the others had gone home. And yet I decided not to mention it to Simone or Anthony, much less to Hofsinger. The busy ward nurses paid little attention to me, and besides, they were used to doctors coming and going as we pleased.

I spoke to our patient, told her where she was, described her surroundings. I talked about our research and tried to reassure her as best I could. Sometimes I would tell her what the weather was like, especially when it was nice. The stereo was still in place, and I would play my mother's recording of Schubert, as well as a CD of popular Mexican songs which I had bought.

I felt sure her expression changed whenever I came close. Sometimes when I took her hand I could feel it grow warm, and then I also thought I noticed that inner light which occasionally lit her face. I saw it, too, the first time I put on the Mexican CD. It was late in the day, I was the only one left in our group, having seen Anthony and Simone walk out to the parking lot, first her, then him half an hour later.

I sat with her for longer than I had intended that evening, and when I finally realized the time, I had missed the last train home. I made up a bed in my office, fetched a sheet and blanket from the linen cupboard, but it took me a while to fall asleep. I had a restless night, and when I awoke just before three, I was convinced someone was calling me. Still in that state of confused semi-sleep, I was sure it was Malena's voice, only it was coming from Mrs. Bentsen's room. My conviction remained as I rose to my feet, even though it was as unlikely that I would be able to hear someone all the way from the west wing as it was that it should be Malena calling me.

Gradually, my head cleared, but instead of lying down again, I got dressed. All was quiet and my footsteps resounded through the corridor, despite my attempts to make as little noise as possible. I could still hear the faint echo of Malena's voice, and I had an unpleasant feeling of disorientation, as so often happens when one wakes from a strange dream.

The lights were switched off in her room. The buttons and

monitors on the machines glowed, and outside the streetlamps next to the steps in the parking lot gave off a faint light. The ventilator hummed. I assumed she was asleep and sat in a chair near the window rather than beside the bed.

I felt better in there with her than on the sofa in my office. The chair was low and comfortable, and when I leaned back and stretched out my legs, my eyelids started to grow heavy. I listened to the soft, rhythmical pulse of the ventilator, and before I knew it, I could hear the sea.

I met Malena at the Cold Harbor station. She was late, but the weather was warm and, even though it was almost six o'clock, still good to be outside. Some of the trees had started to change color, but otherwise there was no real sign of fall. I stood in the sun while I waited, glancing every now and then down the tracks where they bend next to the old timber yards, but mostly I turned my face toward the sun and enjoyed feeling the warmth on my cheeks.

We spoke about the weather on our way down to the village, and she told me she had seen a woman on the train who reminded her of Madame Roullard.

"It was absolutely extraordinary," she said.

"Was she French?"

She told me she didn't know.

"Perhaps she was a poet," I said.

She smiled.

We held hands. It was good to feel her hand in mine, and yet every so often her fingers seemed to twitch. The first time I felt it, I glanced at her instinctively, but she didn't respond so I said nothing and started thinking about something else. There are two ways from the train station to the village of Cold Harbor: one close to the old country road, not much used but paved; the other, to the north, a trodden dirt track dating back to when cattle roamed freely. I described both, and she said she wanted to go along the track even if it took longer. I wasn't surprised, as I had told her it was prettier and quieter; that you could see the ocean in the distance and on the way there was a pond with marshes next to it full of birdlife.

The breeze down by the sea had an autumn feel. We lingered on the beach and I taught her how to skim stones. She was clever at finding the right ones, but gave up after two failed attempts. We met no one apart from an elderly man walking his dog; we said hello and he said hello back, and Malena bent down and patted the dog.

We didn't talk much on the way, and yet far from being ominous our silence enabled me to concentrate on her hand in mine, until I let go of it and put my arm around her. Then she slipped her arm around my waist and we continued walking toward the village as the rays of the afternoon sun were rippled by the waves, and I told myself how happy I was to have her back. A few days earlier, it had for a moment entered my head that she might be settling back in her home country.

I started telling her about the village where time seems to have stood still. We were outside the old café next to the pharmacy, and I remember two children, siblings I supposed, biking past us down the street. I said that apparently the street hadn't changed since the fifties, I pointed to the "H" that had been missing from the sign above the door to the pharmacy since I first came there, and showed her the Old Spice poster in the window, and the pharmacist's recommendation hanging on the door: *Live a healthy life, avoid medication.*

Then I pointed to the restaurant across the street and was about to tell her about the pharmacist's daughter when suddenly she took hold of my arm, not in an anxious way and yet I instantly stopped talking and looked at her. And then she said the words which have echoed in my head ever since:

"Magnus, I'm not well."

Maybe it was her choice of words that confused me for a second, or her expression, which showed concern for me, not for her.

She repeated the same words and added: "But there's no need for you to worry."

"What's the matter?" I managed to say at last.

"I don't want to talk about it."

Silence.

"Not right now. But I had to tell you. I've been meaning to for a while."

I stood motionless, my heart pounding as my whole body drained of strength.

"Right now I just want you to show me the village, for us to have a meal and drink a little red wine before we take the train home. That's all I want. There's no need for you to worry."

I longed to tell her that she couldn't leave it like that, she couldn't shatter everything with one sentence and expect us to behave as if nothing had happened. But my tongue was stuck, and then the children came biking back up the street, smiling at us, and she waved to them before we crossed the street.

We sat by the window in the restaurant. It was seven o'clock. The waiter filled our glasses with water and handed us the menus. It was still light outside. Malena started to talk about the dance performance they were preparing to stage later that month, but I couldn't concentrate, and her words went through one ear and out the other. I was thinking about the evening in Florence when she tripped, the walk up Snæfellsjökull, the accident on Flatey. I had been blind.

I said that to her.

"How could I have been so blind?" I said.

She had been describing the dance performance as if she could see it before her, and I had interrupted her. She fell silent. The waiter came over and recommended the monkfish served on a bed of fresh vegetables. We ordered.

The shadows were getting longer on the street. We looked out at the dusk, and she reached for my fingers across the table.

"I don't want to become your patient," she said. "I don't want that."

We ate. I tried to listen to what she was saying about the performance, about her sister in Buenos Aires and her mother who danced tango on Tuesday evenings at a senior citizens' club. I managed to say something every now and then to make it seem that I was interested, and I could see her relax. In the meantime, my brain was dredging up one situation after another, putting together words and events, surmising, concluding.

"Blind," I said to myself again, "totally blind."

She hardly ate anything, pushing the food around on her plate. She asked the waiter whether the soup contained cream and to make sure her fish wasn't salted. She had never worried about such things before.

I said nothing until the waiter brought us blueberries for dessert. It was getting a little chilly and he closed the window.

"Why did you come up here to tell me this?"

She hesitated, then seemed to decide that my question didn't violate her order not to speak about her illness.

"That way we can leave this conversation here. Take the train and leave it behind."

I could see she was getting tired, and refrained from asking more questions. The journey and her announcement had taken their toll on her, although she did her best not to let it show. The spoon trembled slightly in her hand and when she put it down her fingers continued shaking. She brushed a lock of hair away from her face and tucked it behind her ear. She tried to smile.

The waiter called a cab for us. On the way to the station we held hands in silence and looked out into the darkness. Behind us the moon shone on the bay.

We were standing on the platform waiting for the train when I said: "Salt and dairy products are harmless. But it might be good for you to eat foods which are high in carbohydrates and calories."

I tried to sound encouraging, as if to say that we were going to fight this together. But I was already fearing the worst, and my words sounded hollow.

She looked away, and I took her in my arms and held her tight as if I were preventing her from being taken away.

"It's going to be all right," I said. "It's going to be all right."

Soon afterward the train arrived and we sat, exposed, under the harsh lights of the half-empty car.

The CDs arrived in two batches; first the Mephisto Waltzes in a padded envelope, and two days later the Liszt and Schubert in a small box. Five copies of each. Both packages contained a flyer briefly describing Margaret's career, with selected quotes from reviews of her performances, and an invitation to customers to place orders for seven more CDs, which would be released in the following weeks. Those who purchased all seven CDs would receive a twenty-five percent discount and a signed photograph of Margaret.

It was only when I took the CDs out of the box that I realized three of them had been damaged in the post. The cases were cracked and the CDs themselves were scratched, two of them so badly they were unplayable. I've become quite good at shrugging off problems and frustrations, so it was strange that I should take this accident so much to heart.

I examined the packaging and concluded that it was too flimsy. The box contained no padding so the CDs were exposed, rattling around inside. What a cruel fate, I thought, if this shoddy packaging became a subject for discussion, possibly even bringing the whole enterprise into disrepute. It often took no more than that, I told myself, for all those online tributes to turn against one. Lofty reflections on the beauty of music would give way to complaints about amateurism. And then there'd be the devil to pay.

I thought I owed it to Vincent to let him know. I was due to attend a departmental meeting in ten minutes and called him at once.

He picked up after a few rings.

"Magnus! Are you in New York?"

"No, I'm at the hospital."

"In Connecticut?"

"Yes."

As always, he told Margaret that it was me who was calling.

"It's Magnus Colin!" I heard him shout. "He's at the hospital in Connecticut."

I didn't hear what she replied, but he raised his voice and repeated the announcement, or part of it, anyway: "Magnus, Magnus Colin!"

"We have a visitor," he told me then. "You met him at Margaret's party. Hans Kleuber. He's helping us out. We're terribly busy, Magnus. I hope you've been following events."

I told him I had.

"Beyond our wildest dreams," he said. "And now we're getting ready to release another seven CDs. Seven, Magnus."

I told him I'd read about it.

"Where?"

I mentioned the flyers.

"Did you order some CDs from us?"

"Yes," I said. "Five of each."

There was silence at the other end of the phone.

"Wait a moment," he said. "I have to tell this to Margaret."

Rather than calling out, he set down the receiver. I could hear his footsteps as he walked away and shortly afterward the muffled sound of his voice. I assumed they were in the living room.

I looked at the clock. The meeting was about to begin. I was getting anxious when finally he came back.

"Five, you said?"

"Yes," I said.

"Five!" he cried out. "Five of each!"

I had to go straight to the point.

"Actually, that's why I'm calling," I said. "About the shipments. Three of the CDs were damaged."

"You want them replaced? No problem."

"That's not the point," I said. "The packaging was poor. I think it could be a problem."

"We've had no complaints," he said.

"Two of the CDs were so badly scratched they are unplayable."

He asked about the packaging. I gave him a detailed description of both the box and the envelope, telling him that the former contained no padding and the CDs weren't properly protected.

"The son has taken over the company. His father ran it better. I did business with him for years. Then he passed away and Jimmy took over. He has some kind of business diploma but is incapable of thinking big. I've told him so."

"I would look into it if I were you," I said, trying to wrap up the conversation.

"But you got the flyer?"

"Yes."

"So you know there's a twenty-five percent discount if you order the luxury edition."

"The luxury edition?"

"The next lot of CDs are coming out in a special luxury edition."

I told him I had noticed the special discount.

"Rachmaninoff, Scarlatti, Mendelssohn, Chopin, Mussorgsky,

Saint-Saëns, Schumann. And I can tell you one thing, Magnus. Margaret is fabulous. She's going to take the music world by storm."

I was now late for the meeting.

"Say hello from me," I said.

"Don't you want to speak to her?"

"I'll call back later. People are waiting for me."

"Of course."

Silence.

"Well, I'll call again soon."

"I'll tell her," he said. "Good-bye."

I sat still listening to the silence after he had hung up. It should have come as no surprise to me that I felt as if somehow I had wronged them. It has always been like that.

The software had teething problems, but at last the programmers told us it was ready. They still had to add a few finishing touches, they said, but insisted that wouldn't be an issue. Simone remained skeptical from experience and grilled them about it, while Anthony and I started preparing for the tests. Fortunately, she concluded that although we might encounter a few momentary glitches, there was nothing to worry about. Having already decided to go ahead regardless, I was relieved not to have to override her.

I felt impatient, but tried not to let it show. When we had run the tests on the two patients from Boston, I had limited energy and interest, to the point where I had to force myself to go to the hospital in the mornings and would leave work early, sometimes taking the four o'clock train. But now I couldn't wait to get started and had been carefully preparing my conversation with the patient, typing the questions on my computer and instantly translating them into Spanish since we expected that English might not be her first language. Better safe than sorry, I told myself, and began practicing my pronunciation—alone at first and then with Maria, the Mexican nurse who had helped me before. I was upbeat when talking to Simone and Anthony and praised the programmers for their excellent work.

I sat with her for a while the evening before the tests began. Simone and Anthony had gone home as we had an early start the next day. I explained to her what was going to happen, what the tests entailed, and told her not to worry but to try her best to concentrate, although I knew that wouldn't be easy. Possibly I was more formal than usual, and so I felt the need to take her hand.

I stroked it gently. It reminded me of Malena's hands, long and slender. I held it longer than I intended and when I left it was already dark.

I slept little and by seven o'clock I was already at the hospital. Simone and Anthony arrived shortly afterward, and the programmers and technicians showed up around eight. We were all enthusiastic but anxious at the same time, and when the nurses finally wheeled in the patient, a silence descended upon the group. Then Anthony cleared his throat and we all settled resolutely to work.

As usual, it took a while to get the patient into the MRI scanner. The opening is small and the tube from the ventilator has to be properly accommodated to avoid any mishaps. In the end everything went well, and when I took my place by the microphone with the questionnaire I had printed out the day before, I felt nothing would stand in our way. I watched Simone and Anthony sitting side by side in front of the computer screen, comparing notes, the technicians and programmers to my right, the nurses on the other side of the window next to the MRI scanner.

The software lived up to expectations. Simone and Anthony said it was better than they had hoped, and at first they almost forgot themselves as they tried out all the new features. The images appeared on the screen with lightning speed and were sharper than before. In addition, we could examine every pixel from numerous different angles. The programmers wanted to surprise us and had kept quiet about all the changes they had made; that's the way they like to work, and we were used to it by now.

I started by addressing her in Spanish. It dawned on me when I saw the look on Simone's face that I hadn't openly discussed this with my colleagues, although of course they should have realized that was the most sensible approach. She probably found it strange to hear me speaking that language, but soon got used to it and concentrated on the screen.

First I asked our patient to imagine she was playing tennis, and when that didn't work, I suggested she imagine she was walking through her house from room to room.

"Desde la cocina al dormitorio," I said. *"Desde el dormitorio a la sala de estar . . ."*

I didn't despair, despite her failure to respond. I could see the screen in front of Simone and Anthony; they were looking inside her brain from multiple perspectives but seemed unable to detect any change to the blood flow. My voice was calm as I read slowly from the sheet of paper, not even thinking about repeating my words in English. It wasn't Simone who pointed this out, but one of the technicians, who nudged me and said: "Maybe she doesn't understand."

I was becoming uneasy. The two programmers moved their fingers swiftly over the keyboards when they thought Simone and Anthony weren't quick enough, but without result. Simone looked at me questioningly, a gloomy expression on her face. But I insisted we continue, and made a few more failed attempts before I eventually gave up and suggested we take a break.

The nursing staff took the patient out of the scanner and into the next room so that we could talk freely among ourselves. We were disappointed, and Anthony went so far as to declare that there was "nothing doing." I disagreed, saying we all knew what a Herculean task it was for patients to follow these instructions; she had barely been in the machine an hour, and we shouldn't lose heart. He relented, but I could see the hopelessness on their faces.

"Let's get some fresh air," I said. "We'll meet back here in half an hour."

They didn't stir, but I took the elevator upstairs and sat in my office. I opened the file from the hospital in New Mexico and took out the sheet of lined yellow paper upon which the young doctor had jotted down his thoughts about the patient. It had been a while since I had read them, but now I was looking to them for encouragement and hope.

"'I first noticed her blinking yesterday afternoon while I was examining her,'" I read. "'It didn't last long, and soon afterward she fell asleep. Yesterday evening, one of the nurses noticed her blink and move her eyes. I myself saw her right eye move this morning . . .'"

I had forgotten that he hadn't been the only one to see her eyes move, and this renewed my optimism. Perhaps I was beginning to have doubts. Not just about myself but about the young doctor as well. At any rate, it was strange that I should feel so relieved when I read about the nurse.

I photocopied the page before returning downstairs. My colleagues hadn't left the room, and Simone informed me that while I was away they had checked that the machines weren't to blame; one of the nurses had lain inside the MRI scanner and her responses to the questions had shown up clearly on the screen.

I made them gather around before we brought the patient back in, and read aloud to them from the sheet of paper. It was as if I were giving them a pep talk and justifying myself at the same time. That's what it felt like anyway, especially when I looked at Simone.

I tried to come across more authoritatively this time, giving clear instructions and asking my colleagues pointed questions. I could see they noticed. Perhaps now they would understand that achieving results was no less their responsibility than mine—although that hadn't been my intention.

We set to work and saw signs of change with the first question. Small yet unmistakable. I repeated the instruction: imagine you are playing tennis. We waited with bated breath, but it was only after four attempts that the motor cortex lit up on the screen. A murmur went through the group, Simone leapt up, Anthony tapped away furiously on the keyboard, bringing up one angle after another, and it was the programmers' turn to look at me as if I had taken them completely by surprise.

Normally, I would have asked her the same question again, but at that moment I wasn't concerned about statistics, knowing that we might lose contact with her at any moment. I wanted to discover as quickly as possible whether we could also see responses in the parahippocampal gyrus, and I asked her to imagine she was in her house walking from room to room.

After several failed attempts, I decided to call it a day. My colleagues weren't ready but I explained to them that the patient would be exhausted by now, and took the opportunity to discuss next steps.

I confess that I enjoyed listening to myself speak. My voice exuded self-assurance. I hadn't felt that confident for a long time.

"We'll resume tomorrow morning," I said. "You've all been splendid. Thank you."

Later that day I told Hofsinger about the results and sent a brief e-mail to Osborne and Moreau. I erred on the side of caution in my conversation with Hofsinger, and perhaps even more so in my e-mails to the other two. Hofsinger tried to interrogate, but I was discreetly evasive. In my e-mails I said it was touch and go; I would keep them updated over the next few days. They wished us well.

I looked in on her twice that day, but it was only when things had calmed down and most people had gone home that I went in and sat down beside her.

It was dark now, and the silence had deepened. In the distance I could hear a train.

I didn't turn on the light, but took her hand instead and sat like that until the nurse came to get her ready for the night.

"She did well," said the nurse, addressing the patient as much as me.

"Yes," I said. "Really well."

"Do you want me to turn on the music for the night?"

I thought about it for a moment and then nodded.

The nurse switched on the CD player and I waited for the first notes before bidding them good night and closing the door behind me. It was only when I went to my office to fetch my jacket and briefcase that I realized I was still humming the opening bars of the Mephisto Waltzes.

One evening, when I came home from the hospital, Madame Roullard was sitting at the kitchen table reading to Malena in French. She broke off for a moment when I walked in and greeted them, then carried on unperturbed. It was clear she didn't appreciate my presence and had decided to ignore me. Although I couldn't understand a word of what she read, I found her tone depressing.

I took a long shower, and when I emerged they were still sitting at the kitchen table. Madame Roullard had stopped reading, but they saw no reason not to continue speaking in French. That was the Monday after Malena took the train up to see me and we walked down to the village. The weekend had been difficult. She had avoided me, for the most part, claiming she had to attend to her pupils, who were rehearsing for an important performance. I knew better than to challenge her. She had slept at her apartment. I had been unable to sleep more than an hour or two at a time.

Instead, I had spent day and night analyzing and diagnosing her condition, reviewing all the signs and symptoms that I had missed, berating myself for having been blind for so long. By early Saturday I had confirmed my initial suspicion that she was suffering from MND, a disease in which the nerve cells controlling the muscles deteriorate and die. It probably shouldn't have taken me that long, but I was desperately hoping for another explanation.

I glanced at her questioningly when Madame Roullard couldn't see. We had agreed to spend the evening together, and hopefully the night as well, and yet here was our neighbor comfortably installed and seemingly in no hurry to leave.

Instead of getting up, Malena told me that Monsieur Chaumont was away on a trip and that she had invited Madame to dine with us.

In honor of our guest, I ordered in from a local bistro. The moment we sat down, I realized with a start that I had forgotten all about Malena's new diet, but there was nothing I could do about it now. She acted as if nothing was wrong, but ate only the rice and vegetables that accompanied the meat. It occurred to me that she might have told Madame Roullard about her illness, but when I saw her cut up the meat on her plate to make it look as if she were eating it, I realized that wasn't the case.

We didn't say much, but Madame found a reason to complain about the food: the chefs at that restaurant were Mexican not French, she said, and then talked about how much she missed Paris.

I offered to clean up after dinner, and they sat down in the living room. I was getting antsy but controlled myself. I could hear the distant sound of Madame once more declaiming poetry. Her voice was nasal and she drawled excessively.

Finally, she took her leave. Malena showed her to the door, and when she came back, our eyes met as we stood facing each other for a moment. She let me embrace her, and yet I felt we were far apart. We sat down. I could see she was dreading our conversation, but I couldn't stop myself.

"We have to talk," I said.

She was silent.

"Who is your doctor? What exactly has he told you?"

She didn't reply straightaway, but stood up and walked toward the balcony doors. It was wet outside, and when she opened them we could hear the rain on the trees in the backyard.

"I don't want to talk about it," she said.

"Malena . . ." I started to say, but she interrupted me.

"There are many unhappy people in the world," she said. "Madame Roullard is unhappy. Her life is difficult. I'm not unhappy."

I wasn't sure how to respond to this.

"What medication has he prescribed?"

"I will become unhappy if I think about my illness. That's why I don't think about it. And you shouldn't, either."

"You can't expect me to sit here and do nothing," I said. "I'm a doctor . . ."

"But I'm not your patient."

She didn't need to raise her voice for me to know that she wouldn't be persuaded. I threw up my hands in despair, and was about to ask her whether she thought it was fair to put me in this position, when I stopped myself. Instead, I said:

"What do you want me to do?"

"Love me," she said, simply, and I instantly regretted my behavior.

I took her in my arms and made sure she didn't see my face until I had collected myself.

I held her until she fell asleep. It kept on raining, and soon the reassuring murmur made it seem as if nothing was wrong.

I think that in most respects I succeeded in behaving as she wanted the next few weeks. Occasionally I could focus on the moment and ignore those fears that gripped me day and night, especially when we weren't together. I had consulted specialists at the hospital and collected whatever information I could about her horrible disease. I went as far as to contact a doctor in Germany who had recently published a noteworthy article in the *New England Journal of Medicine* and had a long conversation with him on the phone.

But no matter how thoroughly I looked into it, or whom I consulted, the conclusion was always the same.

I tried not to look at her as a doctor, but of course I failed. I kept a journal, noting down every change I saw in her. At first I hid it in the bookshelves in the living room, but then I started to worry that she might come across it, so I took it with me to the hospital and kept it there.

She deteriorated, no more quickly or slowly than I had expected, but steadily. The disease affected the limbs, but not the muscles in the neck and mouth, so she never had difficulty talking and swallowing. She became prone to dropping things, and her legs gave way more often than before. Some days were worse than others, and then she would stay away from me.

At times I would forget myself and say something she didn't like. It didn't take much. She would bridle if I so much as hinted that she wasn't well. But most of the time I was careful and managed to concentrate on enjoying my time with her.

One day when I got home from the hospital she was waiting for me in the living room. I hadn't expected her and was surprised. She wore a skirt, had her hair in a chignon, and was wearing the necklace I had given her for Christmas. She was so beautiful that I was speechless.

"Is something wrong?" she asked.

It was difficult to imagine that she wasn't perfectly fine. Her smile lit up the living room, radiating a carefree joie de vivre. When she walked over to me, her steps were so light she seemed to glide across the floor.

"Is something wrong?"

No, nothing was wrong. At that moment nothing stood in the way of our happiness, and the shadows encircling us were so far away it seemed they would never return.

She said she wanted to take me out to dinner. She had a mischievous look in her eye, and when I asked where, she said that I would soon find out. I changed my clothes, put on a clean shirt and a light sweater, and splashed some aftershave on my face. We drove in a cab through the dusk. She asked me to block my ears when she gave the driver our destination.

I didn't realize where we were heading until we turned down a side street near Juilliard and stopped at the little restaurant with the red awning. It dawned on me that we hadn't been back there since our first date. She smiled at me and I smiled back, and said:

"Just imagine, it was only eighteen months ago."

That was all I said, but instantly the smiles vanished from our lips, and I reflected about how dull my life had been before I met her, and how I feared it would become like that once more, and perhaps she was thinking along those lines, too. Then we pulled ourselves together, she first, and I gave a bigger smile than before, opened the door, and said: *"Après toi."*

As we sat down, the waiter brought the menus and filled our glasses with water.

"That's the same waiter," she whispered playfully when he had left.

"Are you sure?"

"Yes, don't you remember?"

"No," I said. "I only had eyes for you."

She smiled.

"Should I order fish and see whether he brings me chicken instead?"

I had forgotten the mix-up, and her assumption that her accent was to blame. We laughed a lot that evening, she made fun of herself, and equally of me, and when she ordered steak au poivre it didn't occur to me to ask whether she had changed her diet again. It felt as if nothing were wrong, as if we had nothing to hide, and the only time her hand faltered and she dropped her fork on the floor, we didn't let it spoil things, but instead admired the speed with which the waiter picked it up and brought her another.

At home we made love, and through the window the moon rose above the towers by Central Park. I fell into a deep sleep and dreamt about the glacier and our trip to Flatey. But in it everything was upside down. She never tripped, and the sun shone on the glacier, and the bay was like glass. We moved into a house by the shore and watched the boats come into land. When she ran down to the harbor to meet the boat, I woke up.

She was gone. It was eight o'clock. She had left a little note on my bedside table which said: *You've no idea how much I love you.*

I never saw her again.

While I was expecting the seven CDs to get a positive reception, I had too much on my plate to give it much thought. I played Schubert and Liszt regularly for our patient and had spoken briefly to Anthony about the seven discs' imminent release, perhaps showing slight nervousness. He told me he was eagerly awaiting them and assured me this was going to be a big event. I confess I had grown used to him talking to me as if I were somehow involved, and while I had no objection to that, I was careful not to let him think I knew more than I did. I was a little surprised, therefore, when this time he didn't ask questions, but I was too busy to wonder why.

I soon had the answer when he knocked on my door one day and showed me with a triumphant smile the seven CDs he had just received in the mail. At the same time, he plucked out of an envelope a photograph of my mother which, as promised, had been included in the special offer. I gave a start when I noticed that it was dedicated to Anthony in person, thanking him for his contribution to the discussions on the music forum.

"Your father got in touch with me out of the blue," he said, when he saw my reaction. "I was surprised. He sent e-mails to a few of the others on the forum as well, three that I know of. He was terribly friendly. We received the CDs four days before everyone else."

Although I understood perfectly that it was equally clever of my father to cultivate a rapport with online music enthusiasts as well as with traditional music journalists, I somehow didn't like the fact that Anthony was one of them. To be honest, I am not sure whether it was jealousy or whether I thought I saw trouble ahead. In any event, I didn't let it show and simply nodded as I took the CDs, giving them a fleeting glance before handing them back. I ignored the photograph.

"I'll start listening to them tonight," he said. "Can hardly wait. This one first," he added, holding up the Rachmaninoff for me to see. "But I doubt I'll be able to stop there. I may end up listening to all of them before going to bed."

That evening my thoughts were with our patient and the tests we had planned for the following day. I was determined not to go online and browse the forum where Anthony and his friends held court. I came close to turning on the computer once or twice, but resisted the temptation and went to bed at a reasonable hour. At about three in the morning I was awakened by a siren's wail outside and couldn't get back to sleep. I got out of bed and before I knew it I was online.

It looked as if Anthony was still up. His most recent post was from a few minutes earlier—an emotive description of Margaret's interpretation of Scarlatti's sonatas. He had been busy that evening, commenting on her Rachmaninoff and Mussorgsky, and had gotten into a minor argument with someone calling himself "pianoguru" who had dared to question whether Margaret was as versatile as everyone suggested. Those who had enjoyed the CDs in advance competed to give their opinions, and although my intention had been to take a quick peek at the computer, I didn't switch it off until I had read everything they had written. Their enthusiasm was genuine, their analyses interesting, their descriptions oftentimes quite imaginative. In addition, the forum members seemed privy to a lot of information that could only have come from Vincent.

"It is extremely interesting and explains a lot that she should have played the Rachmaninoff on the same piano he himself used during his concert tour of Great Britain . . ." "In her youth, she studied under Moiseiwitsch . . ." "I understand that she focuses on one composer at a time, playing nothing else for weeks or even months on end. For example, she practiced Scarlatti for five months straight before starting the recordings . . ."

Instead of going back to sleep, I sat in front of the screen waiting for each fresh post. Anthony had called it a day, but the others carried on, assumedly living in places where it wasn't the middle of the night. Although some of them were quite pompous, it was clear from their discussions that most of the members were deeply knowledgeable and passionate about classical music.

It was nearly five o'clock when I forced myself to go back to bed. It was still dark and after I had lain awake for a while thinking about what I had read, it started to rain. I got up, opened the window, and listened to the rain on the trees as I had when Malena was there. I always found it slightly amusing the way she became so excited whenever it rained at night; she would leap out of bed the moment she heard the first drops fall, open the window, and listen to the soothing murmur as if it held the key to a secret. She tried to teach me to listen to its rhythms, its nuances, and sometimes I pretended to know what she was talking about. But mostly I just smiled and ran my fingers through her hair as she lay with her head on my chest.

Perhaps I was asleep when the telephone rang; I am not sure. It's in the living room and has such a soft ring that I don't always hear it straightaway. A call in the middle of the night never bodes well, and my heart skipped a beat when I finally realized it was ringing and leapt out of bed. But there was nothing to fear—Vincent had simply gotten the time difference muddled up, as he was inclined to do.

"Is it really only five in the morning?"

"Yes," I said.

"Did I wake you?"

"It doesn't matter."

"Wait, are you sure it's five and not . . ."

"Yes, but don't worry about it."

I hadn't recognized the caller ID number on the screen and I soon found out why.

"I've got a cell phone. I'm calling from London. Philip and I are standing in the heart of the city, in Oxford Circus. In the sunshine, I might add."

I guessed he meant Philip Ellis, his business partner whom I had met at Margaret's birthday party. But I didn't ask.

"You aren't at the hospital yet, are you?"

"No, you called my home phone."

"Did I? I still haven't gotten used to this thing. It has a memory. My assistant put all the numbers from my address book into it. Do you have one like this?"

I said I didn't know which phone he had, but mine was two years old.

"This is an Apple phone," he said. "It's white and has lots of little pictures on the screen. Apparently you can take photos with it and go online. I tried playing music on it, but it has a tinny sound."

I said I didn't have such a fine cell phone and asked what he meant by assistant.

"I had to hire an assistant. We're up to our eyes, Magnus. I don't think you realize what's been going on."

I told him I was paying attention.

"The day after tomorrow, we're releasing seven new CDs. Scarlatti, Mendelssohn . . ."

"I know."

"We've sent them to a few influential people and the response has been tremendous."

I refrained from saying that I knew that, too.

"If you haven't already ordered them, I'll send you copies."

I told him I had already ordered the CDs.

"Good. The reason I'm calling . . ."

I waited. He was surrounded by noisy traffic but his voice boomed the way it always did when he was excited, and I was sure the passersby could hear every word he said.

"The reason is because the BBC wants to do a program about Margaret. Philip and I have just come from there. Have you been to their headquarters?"

The question was absurd, as he must have known I had never had any reason to visit the BBC headquarters. He didn't wait for a reply but carried on.

"Very impressive. And there's nothing they won't do for us."

It was still dark outside but the rain had stopped. I opened the balcony doors and felt the cool morning air.

"They want to talk to you. That's why I'm calling. I told them you probably hadn't much to contribute, that music wasn't really your thing, but they still think you'd be an interesting addition. When are you next coming over?"

"To England?"

"Yes."

I told him I was in the middle of a research project.

"That's what I thought. In that case, they might want to interview you at the hospital."

"What?" I said.

"Yes, there at the hospital, in Connecticut."

"When?"

"Wouldn't it be best for them to arrange it with you directly? I'll give them your numbers."

"Are you sure this is really necessary?" I asked.

"Philip is calling me," he said, ignoring my question. "He's just managed to get us a table at this café, it's very crowded so I'd better hurry. I'll send your love to your mother. Good-bye."

I said good-bye but kept my ear to the receiver. For a few seconds, I could hear the noise of the traffic, and Vincent muttering to himself as he pressed the wrong button on his phone: "How on earth do I turn this thing off?"

The research progressed slowly. Initially, the patient replied only to questions that tested her motor cortex, and yet her responses were quicker than before and her resilience increased from day to day. This made us hopeful, although we didn't really understand why she seemed unable to activate the parahippocampal gyrus. Simone and Anthony sat for hours on end in front of the computer analyzing the scanned images but found no explanations, and the theories Hofsinger and I offered proved tenuous. I spoke to both Osborne and Moreau, neither of whom could think of anything.

Apart from that, it was interesting how well Simone and Anthony were suddenly getting along. They cited each other when they had a chance, made sure they regularly compared notes, and backed each other up when I allowed myself to ask them challenging questions. I found it amusing, and when Simone and I were alone I told her how glad I was that she had finally discovered Anthony's qualities. She didn't appreciate my humor.

I felt buoyant during that time, convinced it wouldn't be long before our patient started to exercise her parahippocampal gyrus. To a certain extent, it was interesting that she should find it so difficult, and I would sometimes talk to her about that in the evenings as I sat with her listening to music on the CD player, or to the audiobook of *One Hundred Years of Solitude* in Spanish, which I had bought at my local bookstore. The owner had ordered it for me, and when I went to pick it up, he had asked me why I hadn't bought the digital version instead, as there were fourteen CDs altogether. He fetched the box and we both held it and remarked on how heavy it was. When he commented that I was obviously becoming fluent in the language, I played it down without divulging the reason for my purchase.

I would sometimes sit with her until close to midnight. I had never read Márquez's novel, and although I couldn't understand all of it, I somehow managed to follow the thread, and even found myself becoming absorbed at times. I assumed she was listening attentively to the saga of the Buendía family, and I found it difficult sometimes to turn the CD player off and leave her there in silence. I imagined that if she could talk she would have tried to persuade me to let it play a bit longer. *Just for fifteen minutes . . . or ten. Please . . .*

Anthony was starting to put together a complex theory when at last she responded to our calls. That was two weeks after we started the tests, on a calm, clear Thursday morning. Over the past few days, I had reworded my questions with the help of the dictionary, and although this didn't seem to change anything, it made the exercise less tedious for us.

"Imagine you are at the Buendía's house in Macondo. The sun is shining and you are following Ursula from room to room . . ."

I repeated these instructions a few times in both English and Spanish, occasionally adding some fresh detail in an attempt to catch her attention (descriptions of the room, the sound of the river, the light coming in through the window). At first she didn't respond, so after a while I made my usual suggestion that we take a break, turning to Simone and Anthony who were discussing a movie one of them, I don't remember who, had seen the night before. I happened to know it: an old French film about a man who fell in love with his neighbor, but did nothing because she was married and he was friends with the husband, a famous painter in a wheelchair. His love was reciprocated, and once they permitted themselves to hold hands on the stairs, but that was all. I remembered that the house where they lived was in an old square with a café, a bakery, and a Saturday market. On the other hand, I didn't remember the ending, and was about to ask when one of the programmers started gesticulating.

He was shifting in his seat, whispering furiously as if by raising his voice he might cause an upset. We hurried over to the screen and saw the parahippocampal gyrus light up, not once but several times with uniform breaks in between.

It felt as if a dam had burst, or as Anthony said half in jest, as if the patient had suddenly decided to do as I asked. I smiled with the others as no one took his comment seriously. And yet I remembered his words when an hour later I suggested we strike while the iron was hot and see whether she might be able to answer a few simple questions with a yes or a no. I explained to her that if her answer was yes, she should imagine herself playing tennis, and if it was no, that she was walking from room to room.

"Is that clear?" I asked, and received no reply.

I reworded the question, but it was no use.

"Imagine you are playing tennis," I persisted, trying to confirm whether we had lost contact with her. "Imagine you are walking from one room to another . . ."

"She's tired," said Simone. "We should call it a day."

I waited until everyone except Simone and Anthony had left before saying that I disagreed.

At first she misunderstood.

"You mean you wanted to carry on?" she said.

"No, but I don't think it was tiredness that stopped her."

"What, then?" asked Anthony.

"Possibly she isn't ready to answer our questions," I said.

The next day there was no response from her at all, either in the motor complex or in the parahippocampal gyrus. Simone and Anthony were concerned, and at one point I heard Simone say to herself: "Maybe we've lost her." I didn't reply, because I was convinced that our patient's silence showed that she had more control over her thoughts than we had assumed.

I said as much to her that evening when I sat with her after putting Liszt on the CD player. I added that I didn't doubt she had good reasons for her decision, while at the same time making every effort to persuade her. However, I was careful not to put pressure on her, and made fun of my limited Spanish, adding that it was better to try and fail than never to try at all.

I continued talking to her like that for I don't know how long before I realized Simone was standing in the doorway. I had my back to her, and probably wouldn't have noticed she was there had she not had to suppress a cough.

I was annoyed that she had walked in on us, but tried not to show it, and nodded as if to say she was welcome to listen in, although of course she knew that I didn't mean it.

"I didn't want to disturb you," she said when we were out in the corridor. "The nurse told me she thought you were in with her."

"You weren't disturbing anything," I said, waiting for her to tell me what she wanted. I assumed it must be urgent.

But it wasn't. She simply wanted to let me know that she and Anthony had gone over the day's images and found nothing new.

So you were just snooping, I wanted to say, but didn't.

The producer from the BBC called me when I was on my way to the subway. I had just stopped off at the diner on Columbus and Seventy-Fourth, and was holding a paper cup in one hand and a bagel in the other, enjoying my walk to Central Park West, where the morning sun shone on the trees in leaf. My phone was in my backpack, and I managed to spill some of my coffee as I twisted around to get it, so I was a little surly when I finally answered. I could see that the call was from England—Vincent's new cell phone, I guessed, as I hadn't memorized the number.

It was a woman who spoke very quickly. Could I come and do an interview next week?

"Where? In London?"

"No, preferably in Allington. At your childhood home."

"No, I can't."

"We'll pay for your trip."

"I can't."

"How about the week after?"

"No, I'm very busy."

"I see. Your father warned us about this."

"About what?"

"That you wouldn't want to come."

I had moved away from the center of the sidewalk and set my half-empty coffee cup on a low stone wall. My calm was shattered; all at once I found myself making excuses to a complete stranger.

"This is a bad time for me. I'm in the middle of a research project . . ."

"We're keen for you to take part. This program is a big thing for your mother."

She made no effort whatsoever to appear polite as she tried to persuade me. After much insisting, she finally suggested the interview take place in New York; at the earliest possible opportunity, she added, and said she would e-mail me. She spoke as if she were doing me a special favor.

It wasn't until I got off the train in Connecticut and walked to the hospital that I was finally rid of her voice echoing in my head. By then the sun was shining on the fields and on the sea in the distance, and the birds flew merrily above my head.

The day before had been difficult. The patient hadn't responded at all, and we had given up after less than two hours. Simone and Anthony had looked to me for an answer, as if I knew something they didn't, and I replied more sharply than I had intended. And so I was a bit startled when I turned into the corridor and saw Anthony hovering outside my office, clearly waiting for me. Before I had a chance to say good morning, he handed me a copy of the *New York Times*—the Arts and Leisure section, to be precise—and said: "Have you seen this?"

I took the paper from him, and he followed me into my office, studying me as I took off my backpack and contemplated the front page: a big photograph of Margaret sitting by the grand piano in the living room in Allington, and Vincent next to her, leaning against the instrument. Margaret was looking down at the keyboard, one hand in midair, while Vincent stared straight into the camera, cupping his cheek. The title was spread across the page: "Out of the Silence Comes Music," and below the caption: "Margaret C. Bergs Breaks the Sound Barrier in Her Seventies."

I read the first few sentences, but Anthony couldn't contain himself.

"A terrific article," he said, "and then a review of all her new CDs on page four. It couldn't be better."

He waited eagerly while I turned to page four, where the article from the front page continued next to the review, then quietly cleared his throat.

"I'm quoted," he said. "Here," pointing to an extract taken from the forum.

I handed the newspaper back to him and said the article seemed very complimentary, and that I must read it when I had a moment.

"Some of us fans have been hoping for a possible performance," he said then. "I mentioned the idea to your father in an e-mail. He told me the big concert halls are trying to book her, but that she doesn't think she will be up to it. For health reasons," he added.

I told him that didn't surprise me.

"You realize the pressure is only going to increase," he said. "After this article, other papers will follow suit."

"And now the BBC wants to make a program about her," I said.

Anthony didn't seem surprised, and I assumed Vincent must already have told him about it. I was going to ask, but decided not to.

When I took a quiet look at my computer in the afternoon, the article was being discussed on all the piano music forums. It had also made the news in England, and someone said they knew for a fact that the *Times* and the *Telegraph* were preparing to write about her. I thought I could detect from the wording that this information came from my father, who was clearly in contact with more people than just Anthony. I wondered whether he might have gone so far as to take part in the forum discussions himself (under an assumed name, of course), but decided that was unlikely, as he had no need. At the same time, I wondered whether I was being unfair by suspecting him of such a thing, but then I remembered my conversation with the BBC producer and any remorse I might have felt vanished.

Malena didn't answer her cell phone and the school could only tell me that she was away for a while. I got in touch with two of her friends who couldn't help me, and I saw no point in trying others. My conversations with them were awkward, because they clearly found it strange that I should be asking them about her, and they were guarded. Or so it seemed to me, and I imagined they must think I had done something wrong and that she was avoiding me. I wasn't close to either of them.

I went to her apartment, where the super said he hadn't seen her for a few days. Since I didn't have a key, I asked if he would let me in. He didn't know me, but when I explained the situation to him, showed him my driver's license and my hospital ID card, he complied with my request. I followed him into the bedroom and the living room, but opened the bathroom door on my own, and turned on the light.

"Nobody here," he said, indicating the visit was over.

However, he indulged me when I asked him to wait a moment while I opened the wardrobe and the chest of drawers, not least because I had the presence of mind to slip a ten-dollar bill out of my wallet. I tried to conceal the fact that I hardly knew the apartment, although I am not sure I succeeded. I seldom had reasons to be there.

I didn't see any suitcases and I noticed that some of her clothes were missing, too. But by then the super had started to grow uneasy. I paused in the doorway and cast a longer glance than I had intended around the apartment, before he seized the knob and closed the door.

During the next few days I discovered how little I really knew about the woman who meant everything to me. I guessed she must have returned to her family in Buenos Aires, and yet I had no address or telephone number for her mother or her sister. Nor did I know her mother's first name, although I remembered her sister was called Camila, and tried to find her online. I gave up after a few failed attempts for I was shooting in the dark; her sister was married and had likely taken her husband's name.

I unburdened myself to Simone, who had already realized something was wrong. Obviously I was incapable of doing any work, and decided to remain holed up in my office on the pretext of doing some reading. Anthony and my other colleagues didn't suspect anything was wrong, but Simone immediately saw through it. She went out of her way to help me, sat with me in my office trawling her laptop for addresses and telephone numbers, picking my brain as if we were engaged in actual research, astonished at how little I knew.

"What's the neighborhood called where she grew up?"

"I don't know."

"Palermo . . . Flores . . . Agronomía?"

"I don't know."

"How about the clinic she went to after the accident in Iceland?"

"I don't know."

"Where did she study before she came here?"

"I don't know."

She spared me any overt criticism, but I could see she was confused by my ignorance. And I found I couldn't explain it to her. I couldn't bring myself to tell her we had scarcely spoken about the past or our families, that I had purposefully avoided it and that possibly she had done the same, presumably out of concern for me. I had seen her mother once when they were talking on Skype. I was coming home from the hospital and accidentally stepped into the picture, at which Malena said:

"This is Magnus. Magnus, say hi to Mom."

I said hello and she waved to me. I waved back and then got out of the way.

When we reached an impasse, Simone suggested we go to Juilliard and try to convince them to help us. Of course I had already called them, but the woman who answered the telephone said she wasn't allowed to give me any personal details.

"We'll go there together," said Simone, "and lay our cards on the table. They have to make an exception. I can confirm that you're telling the truth, and anyway, it's probably better for a woman to be present."

I thanked her, and the next day we set off for the office at the school, arriving just after it opened. The woman at reception remembered me and repeated what she had said on the telephone, somewhat grumpily this time. But then Simone stepped in and the woman's tone gradually softened until at last she asked us to wait while she went to speak to her superior.

We sat down and Simone took my hand, pressing it gently before letting go. She doubtless meant to reassure me, and yet something about her touch reminded me of Malena, and it was all I could do not to break down. I stood up and walked over to the window, where fortunately I managed to take hold of myself.

Soon afterward, the woman came back and said that her boss was going to speak to the head of the dance department,

who was expected to return from a trip later that day. She spoke
as if she had done us a huge favor, but I felt no better. Without
being pushy, Simone asked when we might hope to hear from
them. The woman said she couldn't promise anything, possibly
the next day.

It had been over a week since Malena disappeared—nine
days, to be exact, if I count the day I woke up alone in my
bed. I was carrying the note she had left on my bedside table
in my wallet, and I had fingered it so many times since that
it was beginning to look worn. Now I wanted to take it out
again to show Simone, as if I had to prove something to her.
But I thought better of it, and as we walked down the street, I
managed to hide my feelings, and even gave a faint smile when
Simone joked about how officious they had been at Juilliard.

When we hadn't heard anything by late afternoon, I called
the office and was told the head of the department wasn't due
back until the following day. His flight was delayed. Moreover,
he had said in an e-mail that he would have to consult the
school's lawyer first. The woman was less supercilious than the
first time we spoke, and made it clear she was doing her best. I
was careful to thank her for all her help and told her that they
could call me on my cell phone day or night.

"Might she not simply have felt like a change of scenery?"
she said then, her voice changing as if we were old acquain-
tances. "Artists can be so unpredictable."

I didn't sleep much that night, but couldn't get out of bed
in the morning. I was staring at the crack in the ceiling—the
narrow crack which stretched all the way from the window
to the wardrobe, wondering if it had grown longer and wider
since I had last contemplated it—when my cell phone rang. I
gave a start and seized the phone from the bedside table. For a
split second, I thought it was the woman at the office, before
realizing that of course she wouldn't be calling me so early. Nor

did I recognize the number on the screen, much less the voice when I answered.

I think I had always suspected the worst. From the very moment I woke up and read the note she had left on my bedside table, I had feared I would never see her again.

The voice faltered.

"I . . . Is that Magnus Colin Conyngham?" she asked, struggling to pronounce my name.

"Yes."

"My name is Camila. I'm Malena Romero's sister."

She fell silent, and I had the feeling she was waiting for me to say something. I didn't reply immediately, and then she added, so softly I could barely hear:

"She's dead. Can we meet?"

Monsieur Chaumont waylaid me. I suspect he had been waiting for me to leave for the hospital. He was standing outside our building with his dog on its leash. The moment I appeared he gave a start, and the dog scurried behind him as if I were a major threat. I said good morning to him, and was about to carry on toward the station when he stopped me.

"You signed it," he said.

I knew he was referring to the rental agreement and was therefore a little surprised not to detect any hint of resentment or censure in his voice.

"Yes," I said.

"I had decided to sign it, too. Even if there is much in it that I dislike."

I nodded and looked down the street. He went on talking.

"I have lived here for twenty-three years. A friend told me about the flat when I first moved to the city. That was before I met Estelle. I had just graduated from college and planned to write a novel and teach on the side. A great novel capturing the spirit of the times, the kind young men dream about writing . . ."

I nodded.

"And then I met her. She moved in with me. Temporarily, until we found a bigger apartment. That was eighteen years ago."

I remarked that this was a good neighborhood, or words to that effect.

"Now she wants to move."

"Indeed," I said.

"Yes," he said, and then appeared to pause before adding: "Because of Malena."

He avoided my gaze, stooping to adjust—or rather, to fumble with—the dog's collar. I waited.

"She misses her," he went on at last, "and doesn't understand what happened."

"She died," I heard myself say. "That's what happened."

He seemed taken aback, and I hoped he would bid me farewell and hurry inside, but instead he held forth.

"I'm sorry," he said, almost babbling. "It's unpleasant to have to bring this up, terribly unpleasant. But I'm at my wits' end. Twenty-three years . . . I don't want to move. She says she can feel her presence, hear her voice, her footsteps, in the middle of the night, sometimes. Was it an accident?"

I don't remember what I replied. Perhaps I simply said goodbye and hurried away.

I suppose I was expecting to feel sad and miserable after the conversation. Which might explain why I was so astonished at my reaction. I am not easily riled, but now suddenly I felt at odds with everything and everyone.

I even became irritated by a man in the subway, simply because he held me up for a few moments at the turnstile while he fumbled with his MetroCard, although fortunately I had the sense to hold my tongue. I found the train too cold, and the woman who sat next to me fidgeted too much, but again I said nothing. Even so, I suspect she sensed my annoyance, as she quickly moved.

My anger still hadn't subsided by the time I got off the train, but I was able to analyze the cause of it as I made my way to the hospital. Clearly it had been provoked by Monsieur Chaumont's insensitivity and self-pity, but I couldn't help wondering whether there wasn't a deeper reason.

The shrink I went to see was expansive on the subject of grief; he spoke of denial, depression, anger, and other emotions which I have forgotten. He listed them on a piece of paper in the order in which they were supposed to appear as he sat facing me in his easy chair while I gazed out the window at the violinists in the music school on the other side of the alley. He used an ink pen, and his handwriting was neat, and I threw the piece of paper away when I got home. I could no longer recall where on the list anger was, although I was sure he had placed it high up and warned me it might flare up at any moment. I tried to remember whether he had said anything about how it might manifest itself or whom I would direct it at, but my memory was hazy. On the other hand, I clearly remembered him hinting that before I attained acceptance, as he called it, I must expect to see Malena in a different light than before. Different meaning worse, although he was careful not to spell it out.

Perhaps that was the last straw. That, and the Asperger's quiz. In any event, I saw no reason to continue my sessions with him.

Fortunately, I had no time for further reflections about the shrink or my anger, because when I got to the hospital, I was told Anthony and Simone had both been asking for me. The patient had been taken down to the MRI scanner, and the secretary who intercepted me told me they were waiting for me there. She also handed me a message she had taken, from a man who had called the switchboard moments before I arrived.

"A doctor from New Mexico," she said. "This is his cell phone. He's up early."

I opened the notes that had come with our patient to verify that this was indeed the young doctor who had been in charge of her there. It was, and I decided to call him before going down, even though I knew Simone and Anthony would be getting impatient.

He answered after the first ring and asked me to wait a moment while he found somewhere quiet as he was on duty.

"How is it going?" he then asked, straight out.

I explained in brief, and was more forthcoming than I am accustomed to, telling him among other things that my colleagues thought it was irresponsible of me to imagine she was capable of communicating. But perhaps they were right. At least that's what the latest results would suggest.

"She is conscious," he said the moment I stopped talking.

There was no trace of arrogance in his voice but plenty of conviction. He was young.

"Do you speak to her in Spanish as I suggested in my report?"

I told him we did, both Spanish and English, but said I didn't recall having seen any reference to language.

"I made a few notes on some sheets of paper which I put in with the report. I did it in a hurry; things were frantic here at the time."

I had the report in front of me and told him I saw no such instruction.

"Two sheets of lined, yellow paper."

"One sheet."

I described it to him.

"Damn it, the other one must have gotten lost on the way. But it's not so important."

"You're sure about her?" I said, because I needed some encouragement.

"She is conscious," he repeated as bluntly as before. "But she needs coaxing. She's on her guard. Didn't you see that in my notes?"

"No," I said.

"Well, I had the distinct impression that she responded differently when it was just the two of us. The moment she heard other voices she seemed to go back into her shell. It was only at the very beginning, when she was coming to, that one of the nurses saw her move her eyes. But after that, nothing."

My heart leapt.

"Are you sure?" I asked, unable to conceal my excitement.

"Yes, and it's understandable, all things considered."

"Do you mean the accident? How it happened?"

"Yes, she was probably mixed up in some drug deal. Wittingly or unwittingly. That's what the police seem to think, at any rate. There's a lot of trafficking around here."

"Do you think she's an immigrant?"

"Yes, I've always assumed she's an illegal. But I could be wrong."

I thanked him for the information.

"I should have called before. I've often thought about her. But you know how it is . . ."

We said good-bye. When I looked up, I saw that Anthony had just come through the door.

"We're waiting," he said, his impatience palpable.

S he went on as before. I gradually stepped back and let Simone and Anthony take the reins. Simone was better at Spanish, so she spoke to the patient while Anthony focused on the computers along with the technicians. I watched from the sidelines, increasingly convinced that the young doctor was right.

She kept them working, responding just enough that they wouldn't give up. She seemed to have no difficulty now imagining herself walking from room to room, although she tended to respond faster to instructions that tested her motor complex. Simone and Anthony talked about a definite improvement, comparing notes during breaks, their faces at once serious and confident.

They felt they were getting even closer to her when they managed to get her to respond alternately in the motor complex and the parahippocampal gyrus, pointing out that until then, she had only seemed able to concentrate on one area at a time. I had slipped out for a moment when this happened, but Anthony tracked me down and asked me to come immediately. It was good to see him so excited, and I hurried with him to the elevator.

Simone was standing next to the microphone.

"Imagine you are playing tennis . . . Good. Now imagine you are walking from one room to another . . . Excellent . . . Imagine once more that you are playing tennis . . ."

Anthony stared trancelike at the screen as the corresponding areas lit up, but Simone was careful not to change her tone until she announced that they were done for the time being, at which she praised the patient for her performance.

"You did very well. We'll carry on tomorrow."

They were in good spirits when we sat down in my office to go over the day's results. Simone said that I had been right, whereas she and Anthony had started having doubts, that the patient showed every sign of coming around and now we could start trying to talk to her.

I nodded, but perhaps with less conviction than she was expecting.

"You don't think she's capable of that?"

"Yes," I said. "She should be."

They left and I sat at my computer with the dictionary and started collecting my thoughts. I tried to find the appropriate words, place them in context, avoiding false friends and blatant mistakes. Normally, I would have consulted Nurse Maria, but I couldn't do that now. By the time I had finished, it was nearly eight o'clock.

I assumed that one of the nurses had put Schubert on the CD player for her. After closing the door behind me I stood for a moment, listening to the music and watching her as she lay on the bed, the overhead light shining on her face. It was bright, so I switched it off and put on the bedside lamp instead before turning down the music.

I was sure she recognized my footsteps, but I introduced myself anyway as I sat down next to her, taking the sheet of paper out of my pocket. I wasn't in any hurry, and so I read over what I had written, realizing I knew it by heart. Even so, I waited awhile longer, perhaps because I was nervous. That surprised me after all my preparations, but at last I cleared my throat and began to read.

I felt as if I were listening to someone else. My voice sounded different, stiff and hesitant. I tried to change my tone but couldn't. I thought of stopping, but of course it was too late for that.

I thanked her for having followed our instructions and told her I had always known she could.

"Not only are you able to imagine yourself playing tennis or walking between rooms," I said, "but it's also clear to me that you decide at will whether to do as we ask or not."

I told her that of course I didn't know the reason for this, but that I assumed she was being cautious, possibly even that she was afraid. I assured her she needn't be. That she was safe here with us. Once again, I told her who Simone and Anthony were, explained her situation, described her room, the MRI scanner in the basement, our research. I had done so before, but I felt I needed to repeat it for her so she could understand the context.

The following morning, she would be asked to reply to a series of questions with a "yes" or a "no." I explained the procedure once again and told her she wouldn't find it too much of a strain. I had intended this to be a pep talk, and yet my tone sounded more authoritative than encouraging. I realized that and cleared my throat, repeated my words, trying this time to come across as warm and caring, but the damage had been done.

I had intended to stay with her for a while longer but couldn't wait to get away. I tried not to let it show, turning the music up before I said good night and taking her hand in mine.

Out in the corridor, I could feel the anger I had been trying to suppress the past few days flare up again. I snatched my backpack off the desk chair and raged against Monsieur Chaumont in my head all the way to the Cold Harbor train station.

The producer sent me recordings of the interviews with Margaret and Vincent. They were short clips, unedited fragments, and with them came a message with her request that I should come to Allington. I had delayed arranging an interview in New York, ignoring her e-mails and calls. The e-mails were short, obviously written in a hurry, probably from her cell phone, as they contained no capital letters, and included numerous typos and almost no punctuation. And yet her message was clear enough: they wanted to broadcast the program as soon as possible, as this was in Margaret's best interests—as well as those of the BBC, she said candidly. The coverage of my mother would only increase, and I must understand that they didn't want others to get there before them.

Her arguments had no effect on me, for I didn't understand what they thought they would get from talking to me. I couldn't shed any light on my mother's musical talent, her service to the muse, or anything else they might possibly be interested in. And I had certainly no interest in talking about my family life or my upbringing.

Eventually, I inserted the disc into the computer. The first images were of the outside of the house, then of Margaret sitting at the piano. She played an extract from Rachmaninoff's second sonata, the work she had performed for us at her birthday party. Her gestures were the same, her movements and facial expressions identical to the ones I remembered, both in the slow passages when she closed her eyes and let her head tilt backward and in the faster, more frantic ones when she pounced on the keyboard, like a bird of prey on its quarry. The extracts weren't long, and when she stopped, she sat motionless, gazing toward the chair where Vincent always sat when he listened to her play. He wasn't in the picture, but I was certain she was looking at him, I could tell from her expression, which bore a trace of unease. *Did I do all right?* her eyes seemed to ask. *Was that good enough?*

She isn't used to the clamor of a television crew, I told myself, and yet somehow I felt uneasy.

However, in the snippets of interview that followed, she was much more like her official self. That distant look, those rambling, almost evasive replies. The questions centered on her childhood and her earliest encounters with music, the influence of her parents and teachers, creativity's demands.

"I don't remember a time when I didn't play. I can't picture myself without a piano . . ." "It would be like trying to imagine myself without a head . . ." "My mother used to say that she never felt me kick when she was carrying me, only my fingers practicing my scales . . ." "My parents loved music, and art . . ." "Our home was perfect . . ." "In my memory it is always filled with sunlight . . ."

Her creative needs? "Music is my oxygen . . ."

That was her way: you couldn't pin her down. Her words like smoke rising into the air, drifting for a moment before disappearing. As if they were never there.

She was asked about other pianists.

"My dear, I stopped listening to other pianists a long time

ago. It only confuses things. It's difficult enough listening to the music in my own head."

Vincent was true to himself when the interviewer asked him about the music world. Margaret had always remained aloof from it, he claimed, avoiding rivalries and cliques; she had dedicated herself to her art, to her vocation; she had always considered that the innate beauty of art, which she longed to bring to her listeners, was tainted by those who used it to further their careers.

When asked about Alfred Brendel or Maurizio Pollini, those pianists who were receiving the most accolades when Margaret should rightfully have been at the top of her game, Vincent's tone changed. At least, I had never heard him express himself so candidly, save at the kitchen table in Allington.

"Alfred Brendel? Talented, yes. Undeniably, in his limited way. But it's no coincidence that he never plays Chopin. And I think he's quite right. For Chopin, you have to dig deep . . . And Pollini? An amazing technician. Perhaps the best. He plays every note with clinical precision . . . It's like watching the most skilled surgeon at work: you know he will save the patient's life, but without discovering much about the soul . . ."

I realized what had happened; Vincent had got carried away, spurred on by the director's obvious delight at his antics. I watched him on the edge of his seat, saw the glint in his eyes, his hands waving about. He certainly didn't dislike being the focus of attention.

I was about to press the stop button, when I heard the interviewer mention another name.

Vladimir Ashkenazy?

I instinctively leaned closer to the screen. Vincent hesitated for a moment, stroking his cheek and knitting his brow as if he were trying to find a polite answer to a difficult question.

"I can't say I was surprised when he took up conducting full-time," he said at last. "Let's hope he finds himself there."

I couldn't watch anymore and turned it off.

I sat still, wondering how I could make the producer understand once and for all that I didn't want anything to do with this project. Hopefully, once my father had calmed down, he would ask her and the director not to use that clip they had sent me, but it was by no means certain. He was jubilant, deserved his spotlight after decades in the darkness, in silence and obscurity. There was nothing I could say that wouldn't spoil the image of my parents that was being presented.

Just as I had resolved to remain at the computer and let the producer know about my decision, Anthony knocked on the door. He and Simone had been preparing the next stage of our research, and I assumed he wanted to run something by me. After my performance the evening before, I was worried I might have made such a mess of things that we would be forced to take a break, which is why that morning I had suggested we rest the patient for two days and use the opportunity to go over the data we had already collected. Fortunately, I was able to cite the good results our colleagues in Cambridge had obtained using the same approach, but even so, I thought Simone gave me a funny look.

"Given yesterday's positive results, shouldn't we see whether she's up to it first?" she said. "Isn't she expecting us to carry on today?"

"No," I said. "I already told her we're taking a break."

"When?"

"Last night," I said, and looked away so she wouldn't be able to tell I was lying.

Although she clearly objected to my initiative, she held her tongue.

As it turned out, I could see instantly that Anthony hadn't come to talk about the patient. He was hesitant, almost shy. Still, he began by telling me that they had been going over the data and that everything was in order.

"Good," I said.

"Maybe it wasn't a bad idea to take a break," he said.

I nodded and waited.

"I got an e-mail the other day from the BBC," he said, "from the people you told me about. Because of the program," he added when I didn't reply immediately.

"I see."

"They want to interview me. About your mother. They want to talk about how we discovered her on our forum."

We. There was nothing hesitant about the way he said that, pushing himself and his fellow members forward, beating his chest.

"Naturally, I'm honored," he added. "Only they want me to go to Manhattan to do the filming."

"When do they want you?" I asked.

"As soon as possible," he said. "I was thinking I could do that in the morning, since we're giving her a rest. I'll almost certainly be back in the afternoon."

For some reason, I put off sending that e-mail to the producer after Anthony had left. Instead, I reached for the DVD she had sent me and inserted it once more into the computer.

Although Camila looked nothing like her sister—she was short and rather plump—I recognized her the moment I saw her.

We had arranged to meet at a small café on Perry Street near where Malena had lived. I came early to find that she had already arrived and was sitting by the window. The place was almost empty, and she looked up when I opened the door. I walked straight over to her and we shook hands before I sat down. I was glad she didn't go as far as to embrace me.

Language was an obstacle and yet we managed to make ourselves understood for the most part, either in English or Spanish. She had arrived a few days earlier, and although I didn't say anything, I was surprised that she had only gotten in touch that morning. She was staying in Malena's old apartment, and told me that she had been busy going through her sister's stuff. I told her there were some of her things at my place, some clothes and a few knickknacks, and I asked her if she wanted to look through them. I was relieved when she shook her head.

Perhaps I had been expecting to see something of Malena in her, a sparkle in her eye, or a nuance in her voice, a familiar

gesture, like the way she tucked her hair behind her ears. But
I didn't; try as I might I couldn't find any similarities between
them. She was extremely organized, had made a list of all the
things she wanted to discuss with me, and, like an efficient
bureaucrat, she got straight down to business. She handed me
Malena's rental agreement and asked whether I could take a look
at it; of course she wanted to terminate it—did that happen
automatically when a tenant passed away?

Possibly she finally realized how uneasy I was feeling when
instead of looking at the document, I put it aside. She leaned
back in her chair and contemplated me, silently reaching for
her coffee cup. Her gaze made me feel uncomfortable, and I
looked outside. If I craned my neck slightly to one side, I could
see the building where Malena had lived, the white curtains in
her living room, the tree on the sidewalk reaching up to the
window.

"She didn't tell me she was leaving," I heard myself say. "She
simply disappeared."

I looked at her. She didn't reply immediately; instead, she,
too, looked out the window.

"She always did what she wanted," she said at last. "She hated
good-byes. Whenever she came to Buenos Aires I never knew
how long she would stay. She was the life and soul of the party
and then suddenly she was gone."

It was strange how good it felt to hear her talk about her
sister. And at last I discovered a family likeness; their hands
were identical, although Camila's were smaller. I wanted to seize
them and tell her so, but I restrained myself. I was surprised at
my sudden need for physical contact.

"Our father was very unhappy when she decided to go
to New York to study dance," she said. "He forbade her, but
of course she didn't listen. She just left. With nothing. Mom
scraped enough money together for her fare, but said nothing

to my father about it. He was furious with her. Malena was the apple of my father's eye."

She said these last words without a trace of envy in her voice.

I think she realized how much I enjoyed hearing her talk about her sister. I guessed it brought her some consolation, too, because her face seemed to relax, and every now and then a smile would play on her lips. I was all the more taken aback when she suddenly fell silent and, straightening up and leaning forward, motioned with her eyes toward the rental agreement on the table between us.

"I really need to get this sorted out as soon as possible," she said.

I gave a start and picked up the document. Possibly because I was hoping she would go on talking if I complied with her request, I forced myself to read, although I had difficulty concentrating.

The agreement was similar to the one I had signed recently, five sheets of paper written in small type.

She studied my face as I read, sitting forward in her chair, as if she might glean from my expression what was written there. I found it disconcerting, and kept losing my place as I remembered what Malena had told me about her the few times her name had come up. They spoke regularly on Skype, and I had always assumed they were close, although Malena had never said that. But now I wondered whether perhaps I hadn't been mistaken, whether she simply tolerated her sister out of a sense of duty. All of a sudden, that seemed most likely. All of a sudden, I was convinced that Malena couldn't possibly have had anything in common with this woman who stared at me while I was reading, as if she didn't trust me, and had only gotten in touch with me because she had no other choice.

Finally, I skimmed through the contract, lingering over a few of the clauses before handing it back to her.

"Just tell the owner she has passed away," I said. "The contract will automatically be terminated."

"Does it say that?"

"Not explicitly," I said, "but the owner and Malena are the only parties to the contract, so it is clearly invalid."

"But it doesn't say that?"

I saw no reason to reply to what seemed to me a rhetorical question.

"I know someone who had to go on paying rent for his mother after she died," she added.

"Where was that?"

"In Buenos Aires."

She seemed to have a strange obsession with bureaucracy, and my reply was perhaps a little more brusque than I had intended.

"This isn't Buenos Aires."

She looked a little flustered. She picked up the contract, opened it, then immediately folded it again and pushed it toward me.

"In that case, couldn't you talk to him?"

I didn't answer her, and we sat in silence for a while. The contract lay on the table between us, but closer to me. I contemplated it, then raised my eyes and looked straight at her.

"How did she die?"

If my question shocked her she managed to hide it.

"She fell asleep."

"What?"

"She passed away in her sleep."

Her answers were so clear and direct, it felt as if she had rehearsed them.

"Was it during the night?"

"Yes."

"Where?"

"At my house."

"Was she in the habit of staying with you?"

"No, she usually stayed at our mother's, but that night she was with me."

"Why?"

She shrugged.

"She occasionally stayed with me."

I should have known I wouldn't get any more out of her, but something about her behavior clouded my judgment.

"Did she leave anything behind?"

"Like what?"

"A letter."

"No, why would she have done that?"

"And she said nothing before she died? Not a word?"

She looked at me without replying.

"Did they do an autopsy?"

"No, she was cremated."

"What?"

"She was cremated. The funeral has already taken place."

I had managed to hold myself together up until then, but now I could feel the strength drain from my body. I had a lump in my throat and my mouth was suddenly dry. I looked down and was surprised to see that my right leg was trembling under the table; I tried to hold it still but it kept moving up and down faster and faster until it hit the table. Coffee sloshed over the sides of her cup, and I took the opportunity to get to my feet to fetch some paper napkins. My head was swimming and for a moment I thought I might fall over, but then it passed.

"It got on the rental agreement," she said when I came back.

First I dried the table, then a tiny wet patch on the document. Naturally the coffee stain wouldn't come off, and that seemed to upset her. She picked up the agreement and ran her fingers over the stain as if to make sure I had done it as well as I could, then pushed it back over to me.

"She was very ill," I said.

"Ill? She'd been through this countless times. She was always spraining this and twisting that. When you're a dancer that's what happens."

As she sat opposite me, hands clasped, I had no way of telling from her face whether she herself believed a word of what she was saying. I looked at her as if somehow I thought I might influence her, but then picked up the contract.

She sat motionless when I had said good-bye, and I could feel her eyes on me as I stepped through the door. I walked slowly down the street, pausing for a moment in front of the house where Malena had lived, and gazed up at the window.

As I had anticipated, the owner raised no objections when I discussed the matter with him, and I told the sister this when I called her. My report was brief but when I was about to hang up, she stopped me. I expected her to ask some clarifying questions about the lease, unnecessary no doubt, but her voice was different. It was as if she had planned to tell me this when we met but had not been able to for some reason.

"You know she loved you very much," she said. "More than I think you can imagine."

W here exactly have you been?"

Simone had closed the door behind her and was standing in the center of my office. After a two-day break, they had resumed the tests early that morning, as she and Anthony were eager to get started. I had decided to stay away, and had spent the morning with Hofsinger and some of the hospital administrators discussing plans and budgets. I realized now that this had probably been unwise.

I had popped in to see our patient the evening before, put on the Mexican CD for her, and said a few words about the rain pounding on the windows. But I made no mention of the impending tests, and avoided falling into the same trap of lecturing her as I had the other evening. When I left, I was convinced she must have recovered from my sermon, but decided on my way to the train station that I would play it safe and let Simone and Anthony take the next step.

"Didn't Anthony tell you I was busy with Hofsinger?"

Simone looked at me as if she thought I was hiding something, then heaved a sigh.

"She isn't answering any of the questions."

"What?"

"We're getting no response from her whatsoever."

Out of a sense of duty, I questioned her a little about the tests. Her answers were brief, unsurprisingly, as there wasn't much to report. Her gaze made me uneasy.

"What exactly did you say to her?" she then asked.

"I beg your pardon?"

"On Monday evening."

"I said we were going to take a break. Didn't I already tell you that?"

"You were in there an awful long time."

I didn't like her tone, still less that she had been asking the nursing staff about my movements. However, I knew I was on thin ice and tried to act accordingly.

"I had an unexpected call," I said.

She frowned, making it clear she wasn't about to let me wriggle out of this one. But I kept my calm and asked her to sit down.

I told her about my conversation with the young doctor from New Mexico without, I believe, holding anything back. Although, admittedly, I decided not to mention his theory about the patient behaving differently when the two of them were alone. But I told her he was convinced she was on her guard, explained why that might be happening, and allowed myself to imagine the sort of life she had led, although there was little evidence to back it up. I became sidetracked for a moment in these reflections, before collecting myself and reiterating that the young doctor had no doubt that she was fully conscious.

She listened in silence and didn't respond immediately when I had finished talking. She was looking straight at me, and for some reason I found myself remembering the words she had whispered to me in the hotel room in Liège. It felt uncomfortable, and I did my best to thrust the thought aside, but there was something in her manner I found troubling. I feared she might be able to read my thoughts, so I stood up and opened the window.

"When did this conversation take place?"

Of course I couldn't help noticing the tone of cross-examination in her choice of words. I told her the truth.

"And you held off telling me this?"

I admitted it had been a mistake. I told her I realized that now.

I had the feeling she was about to get up and walk out, but she didn't.

"Might you have said something to her which would explain why it went so badly this morning?" she said at last.

"It's possible," I said. "I might have gone too far."

She asked me to explain.

"I hinted that we suspected she might be holding back. I wanted to know how she would react."

"And now we know."

"It would seem so," I said, and thought that I had shown enough remorse: "Now we know she understands everything we say."

"Or less than we thought," she said.

After I had left her in the hotel room in Liège, I paused before reaching the elevator. There was no one around but me, and the lights were blinding. All was quiet except for the occasional swish of the elevator going by. I stood still for a while, looking alternately toward the elevator and down the corridor to her room, still aware of her scent and her words echoing in my head. I wanted to get away, but finally I pulled myself together and turned around. I have no idea what I intended to say to her; I don't remember having given it a thought. Even so, I turned around and walked slowly back to her room, hesitating once on the way but forcing myself not to flee.

I waited by the door and took a deep breath. Then I steeled myself and was about to knock on the door when I heard weeping.

A soft, steady sound, so mournful it stopped me in my tracks. And yet it contained no trace of self-pity or blame, no bitterness. It seemed that it would never end.

I paused for a moment, then hurried away. I still haven't forgiven myself for leaving her alone a second time.

I remembered her weeping as I watched her talk about the research. I became lost in thought for a moment, and when at last I emerged from my reverie, I was concerned once more that somehow she could read my mind. But there was no evidence of it on her face, or in her voice when she tried to catch my attention.

"Magnus, Magnus . . . Are you listening?"

I nodded. Yes, I was listening. Perhaps she was right. Perhaps the patient wasn't in as good shape as I had hoped.

My words startled her, and possibly my impassive tone as well. She chose not to reply, stood up, and opened the door.

"We'll carry on tomorrow morning," she said.

"Yes, we will."

She paused as if she felt the conversation wasn't quite finished, then closed the door, though I hadn't asked her to.

By eight o'clock we were in the basement. Two of the night nurses, a man and a woman, helped me bring her down, and neither questioned me when I told them I needed to run a quick test. The male nurse was asking the woman's advice about a new patient on the ward with whom he had had difficulties the night before. She was smart and perceptive, and together they concluded how best to attend to the man's needs. After we had placed her in the MRI scanner, they asked me whether I needed them for anything else, and left when I told them I didn't.

"Just let us know when you're done."

I had walked down to the sea before I started, but hadn't gone as far as the village. There was no one on the beach, and I sat on a rock and looked at the light out in the bay while scribbling a few sentences in Spanish on a piece of paper. They were simple and to the point, and showed I was new to the language, but after what had happened the other evening, I thought it best not to pretend.

"We're alone," I said, without any need to take the sheet of paper from my pocket. "It's evening. I'm going to ask you a few questions. Any answers you might give me will remain between the two of us. I promise."

That was all. I paused for a moment, then went into the room next door, turned on the microphone and adjusted the screen so I could see it better. I had a clear view of the MRI scanner through the interconnecting window, and of her feet beneath the white sheet. I noticed it had slipped off her left foot, and I went to cover it before continuing. The room was cool, as usual.

I started slowly, asking her first to imagine she was playing tennis. I was assuming I would succeed in making contact with her, but I was prepared to have to work for it, especially after the trouble she had given Simone and Anthony that morning. I was therefore taken aback when the screen lit up the moment I spoke. I remained calm, pausing before I asked her to imagine she was in Ursula and José Arcadio Buendía's house in Macondo, walking from room to room.

She didn't wait for me to finish the question: I was still talking when I noticed the screen change.

"Good," I said, careful not to conceal my excitement. "Very good."

Although I knew it was unnecessary, I described the next steps in detail: I would ask her a series of questions to which she could answer "yes" by imagining she was playing tennis and "no" by picturing herself walking from one room to another. She needn't hurry, we had plenty of time, all evening and all night, and she mustn't get upset if she had difficulty focusing her thoughts in the right direction, or worry if she became confused and answered yes when she meant no; I would repeat the questions as many times as necessary.

I paused, cleared my throat, looking first at the screen and then at her feet beneath the sheet sticking out of the machine.

"Do you understand what I'm saying?"

She didn't reply immediately. A minute passed, possibly longer, and it was then that I realized how nervous I was. I had managed to hide it both from her and from myself, but now I was becoming impatient, and just as I was about to repeat myself, the screen lit up.

Yes.

I took a deep breath and repeated the question. This time she replied instantly.

Yes.

"Are you American?" I asked next.

No.

"Are you from Mexico?"

No.

"South America?"

Yes.

I didn't wish to waste precious time trying to ascertain her precise country of origin, as I knew she would tire sooner or later. And so instead I asked her whether she spoke English. She said no at first, then yes.

"Do you mean you don't speak English very well?"

Yes.

I marveled at her sharpness and was on the verge of saying so, but stopped myself.

"Married?"

No.

"Children?"

So far her answers had appeared relatively quickly on the screen, but now there was no response. I waited for a moment then decided to word the question differently.

"Do you have any children?"

When she didn't reply I added: "One or more?"

I stared at the screen in the hope I wasn't missing anything, but there wasn't a single flicker, no trace of an answer or any

sign of hesitation or uncertainty. My technical skills aren't up
to much—I can't switch angles, zoom in and out of the brain
the way Simone and Anthony do with ease, and for a moment I
feared my lack of knowledge might prove a hindrance. But then
of course it became clear I hadn't missed anything, because she
replied to my next question immediately:

"Can you hear me?"

Yes.

"Good," I said, "good. I was beginning to think I might have
missed something. I'm not so good with the computers."

I picked up a bottle of water, opened it, and took a drink.

"All right," I said, "shall we carry on?"

That wasn't meant to be a question, and so I was surprised
when I saw her reply on the screen.

No.

I became flustered.

"You don't want to carry on?"

No.

I didn't know what to say, and was about to try to get her
to explain her change of heart so that I could persuade her, but
thought better of it.

"You've done very well," I said.

I called up to the ward and soon afterward the two night
nurses came down to help me take her out of the scanner. We
wheeled her silently into the elevator and from there into the
room. The nurses were checking the monitors and adjusting
the bed when I left.

I changed my mind after Anthony went to be interviewed by the BBC. It took longer than he had expected; even so, he came to the hospital afterward and knocked on my door. He was excited and gave me a detailed account of the interview—questions and answers. They seemed very professional, he said, and he complimented the director.

"A nice guy, and very knowledgeable about music," he said. "And then he mentioned you."

"I beg your pardon?"

"Yes, during a break. I told him we were colleagues. He couldn't believe it, what a small world, he said."

I might have known Anthony wouldn't keep quiet, but I still didn't like them talking about me.

"What else did he say?" I asked, and instantly regretted it.

"He told me the producer in London had tried to persuade you to be interviewed at your childhood home, but that you couldn't leave your work. I told him I wasn't surprised, as you were extremely busy."

It was obvious he thought he had done me a favor, but I tried to make little of it.

"In any case, he is thrilled that you've agreed to do an interview in New York. They do a very good job," he said again, as if he could tell I was of two minds.

I still hadn't gotten around to telling the producer I didn't want to take part in the project. I had been on the verge of sending her an e-mail twice, but both times I had been interrupted or found reasons to delay. Now, all of a sudden, I felt duty bound, or at least that's what I told myself while I was listening to Anthony's account, although I was probably motivated by envy rather than duty. Even his gait irritated me as I watched him leave my office.

The producer wasn't as pleased to hear from me as I had expected when I called her.

"All right," she said, seemingly in a hurry. "We have a slot at nine on Wednesday morning at the studio. Can you make it then?"

I was about to put on a tie but changed my mind. I was wearing a light blue jacket and the blue shirt I had bought in Florence with Malena. I couldn't help wondering whether she would have approved of the combination. She found my way of dressing unimaginative and teased me when I tried to be adventurous.

I was trying to hail a cab on Columbus Avenue when my cell phone rang. It was half past eight; many people were on their way to work and every cab was taken. I was starting to worry that I might be late.

I glanced at the number before answering. The producer, I supposed, wanting to make sure I hadn't changed my mind.

"Colin Conyngham?" a woman's voice said.

"Yes."

"This is Mr. Conyngham's office calling, please hold."

Before I had a chance to hang up, my father came on the line.

"Magnus?"

"Yes."

"Are you on your way?"

"I beg your pardon?"

"To the interview."

"I'm trying to get a cab . . . Who was that who called?"

"My assistant," he said, as if nothing could be more obvious, as if I ought to know that he couldn't possibly have bothered to dial my number himself.

"This isn't a good time. I'm out in the street . . ."

"She worked for Lloyd Gimstead," he said proudly. "You remember him, don't you?"

I glimpsed a free cab turning the corner.

"Wait," I said, half running toward the car so as not to lose it, shooting across the street at a red light, past a man who had appeared from nowhere, apparently with the same intention as I, waving my arms furiously at the driver before leaping in the moment he slowed to a halt.

I don't know whether Vincent had heard me, because he was in the middle of listing Lloyd Gimstead's achievements when I placed the phone to my ear again.

". . . and then of course he had a chain of hotels, and a car dealership . . ."

I interrupted his monologue and asked how he knew I was on my way to the BBC recording studio.

"Oh, it was Kathryn who told me. I think they'd given up on you so of course she's delighted that you changed your mind."

I was going to correct him, to point out that I had never refused to be interviewed, however inconvenient it was for me, seeing as I was rather busy, but I let it go.

"Of course they want to describe our family life," he said. "Apparently talking about art isn't enough, people's private lives have to come into it, too, whether they like it or not. As you can imagine, we both talked about how proud we are of you, how you were always so good at school, how well you've done in your career, and about your research, although naturally we are mere laymen and only understand a fraction of what you do. But the brain is a maze, made up of so many parts, so much that is mysterious, Magnus, my boy—you of all people should know that—so much we don't understand, even about the actions of those closest to us. Margaret has a natural gift, which should now be clear to everyone, but she isn't perfect, no more than anyone else, no more than you or I . . ."

We were stuck in traffic at Columbus Circle; it was ten minutes to nine. I was getting anxious, although less so than might be expected. I was half thinking that I wouldn't mind if the traffic came to a standstill, because that way I would have a perfect excuse for missing the interview. I became lost in thought for a while, before the car eased forward again and I gave a start.

"Let sleeping dogs lie," I heard Vincent say. "Obviously, they realize how unfairly Margaret has been treated all these years, but they don't see the effect it had on her. Indeed, they are astonished by her lack of bitterness, how understanding she is, and the fact is she hasn't said a bad word about anyone in the interviews. Of course we know life wasn't always a bed of roses, Magnus, my boy, but it's not easy always being one station away. For anyone, no matter what their aspirations in life. But now she's there. Now she's finally made it . . . As I say: let sleeping dogs lie. I trust you'll agree that your memories of Allington are mostly happy. I hope so anyway. Both Margaret and I talk about how much we miss you. In the program, you see. About how far away you are. And about grandchildren—how we hope we won't have to wait too long. Although of course we don't mention that you still haven't introduced us to your sweetheart, and why would we . . ."

"Here?" the cabdriver asked, pulling up outside a tall building. "Yes."

"What?" Vincent said.

"I was talking to the cabdriver," I said. "We're stuck in traffic. I'll talk to you later."

I hung up, paid, and got out.

When I saw a food truck on the sidewalk across the street from the studio, I realized how hungry I was. I looked at my phone—it was already nine o'clock. But then I turned it off, got on line, and ordered a bagel with eggs and bacon and a cup of coffee. I found a bench to sit on and tried to forget the producer who was waiting for me.

When I finally got up, I saw a motorcycle go by out of the corner of my eye. It wouldn't be worth mentioning, if I hadn't jumped at the sight of it and hurried down the street. It was black, and the young female passenger had her arms clasped around the driver whom I all of a sudden believed was none other than Thomas Stainier, the genius who decided to disappear. When they came to a halt at a red light, I saw of course that this wasn't him. I turned around, perplexed that I had thought of him after all these years.

I took the subway two blocks away to 125th Street, then caught the train up to the hospital. The weather was brighter to the north of the city, and when we reached Connecticut the houses beside the tracks were bathed in sunlight and then the fields as the buildings vanished.

I walked briskly from the station and was still thinking about how tasty my breakfast had been when I pushed open the doors to the hospital.

Saint-Saëns, Mendelssohn, and Chopin; Rachmaninoff, Scarlatti, Mussorgsky, and Schumann. Seven CDs in a luxury edition just as Vincent had said: gold lettering on a blue background, a portrait of Margaret, seemingly recent. The packaging seemed unchanged, despite my comments. At first glance the discs seemed to have escaped undamaged in the post, and on closer inspection it was possible they had stuffed the boxes with more paper to protect them. Vincent had included a little card with the delivery. On it was printed: "With best wishes," and his signature underneath. I noticed his handwriting was shaky.

I was about to insert the Mussorgsky into the computer when the department secretary tapped on the door to tell me Simone and Anthony were waiting for me.

"I tried calling you," she said, "but you didn't pick up."

My cell phone was still off after my trip to the BBC studio, and I had no intention of turning it back on.

"They're in the basement," she added. "I don't think it's going too well."

I had no choice but to follow her, although I dreaded meeting my colleagues.

Simone was standing next to the microphone when I got downstairs. She switched it off the moment she saw me.

"She doesn't reply to anything," she said.

I walked over to the screen, as if hoping to find some answer there, and the technician pulled up an abstract of the morning's progress, tapping rather heavily on the keys, it seemed to me. Simone hadn't been exaggerating; the patient had shown no response at all.

Of course, I wished I could have told them about what had happened the evening before, talked about the patient's responses, compared notes, and discussed her progress and the next steps. But I had given her my promise—an unqualified promise, which had been the reason why she trusted me—and I couldn't betray her. Besides, I was convinced that I had no choice if we wanted results; she had proven that beyond any doubt by her silence that morning.

"Maybe you'll have more luck," Simone said, stepping away from the microphone, needlessly as there was plenty of room next to her.

She stood back against the wall, and for some reason my thoughts returned to that evening in Liège. Perhaps it was her gestures, or her expression that betrayed disappointment and despair. I paused for a moment, gazing through the window at the MRI scanner and the patient's feet beneath the white sheet, unable to look Simone in the eye.

I was relieved when our patient didn't reply. I repeated the instructions twice before switching off the microphone and saying in an impassive voice to Simone and Anthony that we should meet in my office when they had a moment.

They followed me, but instead of sitting down, Simone stood by the door, arms folded. I avoided her gaze. Anthony wasn't accustomed to having to do most of the talking when the three of us were together, but he didn't seem to notice that anything was wrong. On the contrary, he seemed to enjoy the attention, and took the opportunity to go over the research in detail, drawing conclusions and speculating with an equanimity that surprised me.

Finally, we agreed that we should take a break and meet again in the morning. Simone took her leave at the first opportunity, but Anthony glimpsed the Mussorgsky CD on his way out and paused.

"Have you listened to it?" he asked.

"No, not yet."

"A magnificent recording. Mussorgsky has never been performed so well."

I didn't say so, but I was grateful to him. It was as if his comment somehow compensated for my backsliding that morning.

Like the day before, I waited until they had gone home before setting to work. The same two nurses, the man and the woman, helped me to take the patient down to the basement. They didn't question these comings and goings, and I indicated that we had been having problems with some of the equipment recently, and were behind schedule.

She instantly showed responses both in the motor cortex and the parahippocampal gyrus, and so I began my questions without any preamble. I was careful to avoid asking her again about her family situation. I could wait till later to try to get her to confirm the assumptions I had already made.

I started off slowly. She confirmed that she could hear me, recognized my voice, and knew where she was. Did she enjoy listening to the music I had played for her? Yes, especially the Schubert. What about the Mexican CD? She didn't think much of it. What about *One Hundred Years of Solitude*? Yes, it was fine.

She was quick to answer, quicker than the night before. I had brought along the CD player and the discs with me, and I played the beginning of each work to find out how she felt about them. I was astonished at how swiftly she responded, within fifteen or twenty seconds, and how strong her opinions were. It immediately occurred to me that she wanted to get these questions out of the way and move on to something that mattered to her. Even so, I decided to take things slowly, because I didn't want to risk her withdrawing the way she had the evening before. I broached various trivial subjects, but sensed only her increasing impatience.

Gradually, I made the questions more personal. I discovered she was from Venezuela, that she had just turned twenty-eight, and had arrived in the country shortly before the accident.

"Legally?" I ventured to ask.

I got no response and decided to repeat the question. She refused to answer.

"This isn't a police interrogation," I told her. "Anything you say remains between us. I gave you my word and I won't let you down."

Silence. I cleared my throat.

"Should we talk about your reasons for being in the States?"

No.

"About the accident?"

No.

"They left you for dead. Your companion on the motorcycle didn't lift a finger to help you. He probably disappeared with the driver of the car. Is there any point in me asking you what happened?"

No.

"That doesn't surprise me," I said, unable to hide my disappointment. I was expecting her to place more trust in me than this.

I stood staring at the microphone for a while before resuming in the same vein.

"We must try to find out something about your circumstances. We need to contact your family."

She replied instantaneously.

No.

"Do you have a family?"

Yes.

"They have no idea what's become of you. We have to let them know."

No.

"Do you have parents who are living?"

Silence.

"Children?"

Silence.

"All right," I said, and tried a different tack. "I don't even know your name. The doctor in New Mexico called you Adela, arbitrarily, of course. Let's start with the alphabet. Does your name begin with A, B, C, D, E, F, G, or H?"

Silence.

I repeated the question and received no reply.

"Should I take this to mean that you don't wish to tell me your name?"

Yes.

"Not even your first name?"

No.

I was beginning to see where things were heading, and I missed not having Simone there with me. Would she carry on or end the conversation, I wondered, take a break until the next day, say good night, reflect on what course to take?

I glanced around, at the chairs where my colleagues should have been sitting, at the machines they should have been operating. Through the window I could see the MRI scanner, her feet beneath the sheet, the dark opening.

I couldn't stop now.

"Is something on your mind?"

The screen lit up, not once but again and again. I saw her

before me, hitting tennis balls with all her might, endless tennis balls, as if her life depended on it. It was strange how clear her image was in my head: she was dressed in white, moving swiftly around the court in bright sunshine, with a concentrated expression, determined not to miss a single stroke. Her features were so sharply defined that I was tempted to take her out of the scanner to make sure it was she and not someone else who had appeared in my thoughts.

I resisted. The sunshine disappeared, and darkness took over. Darkness that enveloped her and would never disappear. And the question she wanted to hear but I could never ask echoed in my head, disappearing only when I instinctively clapped my hands to my ears.

How futile. How meaningless. We had constructed a perfect machine for the sole purpose of enabling her to tell us that she wanted to die.

I held her hand until the nurses came down. It was cold and clammy, and I made sure I stroked it gently.

On my way to the train station, I realized I had never asked her if she could hear the sea when the windows in her room were open.

think I saw Monsieur Chaumont before my cell phone rang. I'm not sure, though. I remember that he glanced over his shoulder when the dog stopped next to a tree on the sidewalk and spotted me as I was closing the front door. I also remember thinking that he looked almost shamefaced, but not whether I answered the phone as I was leaving or after I had set off in the direction of Central Park West. I had been planning to walk the other way, because I felt like coffee and a bagel with cream cheese, and had been looking forward to sitting for a while at a table in the little café on Columbus Avenue. But then I would have been forced to walk past the Frenchman and his dog, which stood trembling next to the tree as though nervous about lifting its leg against the trunk.

For sure, I was still thinking about Monsieur Chaumont after I had turned my back to him. I hadn't forgotten our last conversation, and now he had deprived me of my breakfast, which I was in need of after a difficult night. I had arrived home from the hospital shortly after midnight, confused, sat up in my living room mulling over the conversation I had just had with the patient who wouldn't tell me her name. When finally I fell asleep, my anxiety spilled over into my dreams, as my heart raced and I became drenched in sweat. I had reached a dead end, both awake and asleep.

This time it was Vincent himself who called, not his assistant, on his cell phone, and he got straight to the point. I could tell from his voice that he was distraught.

"Are you at the hospital?"

"No, I'm walking to the subway."

"Magnus, we need to talk . . ."

His voice was shaking. I slowed my pace.

". . . when you have time."

The program about Margaret. I was sure that was the reason for his call, and decided to speak first.

"I didn't make it," I said. "The traffic was terrible and I was much too late. I don't think they should be expecting me."

"What?" he said, before the penny dropped. "I'm not calling about the BBC."

I waited.

"Some people can be so horribly nasty, Magnus. They'll stop at nothing. And yet you don't know what their game is. Everything is going smoothly, for once things are going smoothly, and then the next day you wake up and you're under attack. Because this is nothing short of an attack. Not on me, I don't matter, but on Margaret. After everything she has been through, all the struggles, the disappointments, the injustices, it seems some people can't tolerate the fact that she has finally been vindicated; they can't leave her alone. They pounce on her, an ambush of course, tearing her apart with shameless lies and slander."

I had halted on the sidewalk and was pressing the phone to my ear in order to hear him properly. Despite being distraught, he didn't raise his voice; it was as if he hadn't the strength. I had only heard him sound so desperate once before. That was when he came to fetch me from his brother- and sister-in-law's house in Ásvallagata.

"He calls himself 'pianoguru.' He had already posted a few disparaging comments, but nothing like this. In fact, I was so astonished when Kleuber called me to tell me about this abomination that I literally couldn't move, Magnus. I stood in the middle of the kitchen floor as though paralyzed. Thankfully, Margaret didn't see me. By the time she got up I had collected myself. She knows nothing about this, and she must never know. It would finish her. It doesn't bear thinking about."

I had let him talk without interrupting, but now he had slowed down and I seized the opportunity.

"What happened?"

I heard him sigh into the phone ("It's so unfair, Magnus, so unfair . . ."), and then he forced himself to explain all the facts.

At around midnight the night before, this so-called pianoguru had given an account on one of the forums of what he referred to as a "strange experience." The post was brief but toxic, according to Vincent. In it, pianoguru described how when he had inserted Mussorgsky into his computer he had received a message from the iTunes database informing him that he already had this CD, performed by none other than Vladimir Ashkenazy. Pianoguru insisted that he tried several times to "correct" his computer, but without success, and in the end he had had no choice but to investigate the matter. He had played the two recordings simultaneously, and as far as he could tell they were identical. "Perhaps there was some mix-up at the company that stamps the CDs," he had said, but there was no mistaking his malicious tone.

"We must nip this in the bud," Vincent said. "These sorts of aspersions can spread like wildfire on the Internet. How could he do this to her? What's wrong with the fellow?"

I believed I knew my father inside out. Every nuance in his

voice was familiar to me, and always revealed to me what he was thinking, especially when he was trying to hide something. This time I had no doubt that he was telling the truth; the distress in his voice was genuine, the fear and disappointment palpable.

"What should I do?"

I was still in the street, having moved away from Central Park West when an ambulance sped noisily by. On the sidewalk opposite, Monsieur Chaumont was still walking his dog, fortunately heading the other way.

"Vincent, I have to ask you if there's any truth in these accusations. Even the merest shred."

"Magnus, my boy, I know why you're asking. I fully realize. But this is a lie from beginning to end."

"Not an oversight anywhere?"

"No."

"Nothing in the manufacturing process that might account for it?"

"No, nothing. Out of the question."

He was pathetically cowed.

"So what's the explanation?"

"I don't know. I'm bewildered."

"How could the computer give him that information?" I said to myself as much as to him.

"I haven't a clue. I know nothing about all this technology. It confuses people. Unless he's doing this for his own amusement. He's had a grudge against Margaret from the beginning. Read some of his posts and you'll see. Who listens to music on a computer, anyway? No true music lover, I can assure you. The sound is artificial, utterly lifeless . . ."

I was about to tell him I had noticed pianoguru before, when he continued:

"Kleuber thinks I should get legal advice."

I didn't know what to say, and for a while I simply listened to the noise of his breathing. For the first time he struck me as old.

"I need you, Magnus. Could you see your way to helping me?"

It was clear from his words that he wasn't counting on my assistance and his voice revealed the same uncertainty; he sounded meek, almost apologetic. As if he were telling me that he knew he didn't deserve my help, that I owed him and Margaret nothing.

"I'll go online," I said, "and see what I can make of it."

"When you get to the hospital?"

"No, at home. I'm heading back there now. I'll call you later."

"Thank you, Magnus, my boy. With all my heart."

I felt as if I were standing in the hallway at the house on Ásvallagata. His voice was trembling as it had then, just before he broke down. I had to prevent that from happening.

"We'll get to the bottom of this," I said as I hurried up the steps to the front door.

I was surprised at how reassuring I sounded.

The post was just as he had described it, brief but nasty. I had been half expecting to discover that Vincent had been exaggerating, not necessarily on purpose, but if anything it was the opposite; for example, he hadn't mentioned pianoguru's insinuation about Margaret's interpretation of Chopin's Fantasy in F Minor, op. 49: "Am I alone in having the impression that I'm listening to Dinu Lipatti?"

So far there were only a few responses to the post. Fritzb23 had said his was big news if true, jonjon had agreed, and 3cords had used the opportunity to criticize Apple for its faulty search engines, its monopoly of the music market, and its lamentable offering of classical music. "Yes, capitalist pigs," added khammond, and there the thread ended.

I saw no need to remain at home on the computer, so I caught the train up to the hospital as planned. Before I left, I called Vincent; we only spoke briefly, but I think I managed to calm him down. I had never spoken with him about Anthony, but I guessed he knew we were colleagues. It turned out he did, and naturally Vincent sang his praises as I had expected.

"I'll have a word with him," I said.

"I'm very grateful to you, Magnus. I don't know what I'd do without you."

There was a definite if faint glimmer of hope in his voice, and I was relieved.

I had just gotten off the train and started the last leg of my journey up to the hospital when my cell phone rang. I was expecting it to be Vincent, unable to contain himself, but it wasn't him but Simone, who said, without preamble:

"Where are you? I've been trying to get hold of you."

"I'm almost there."

"It's nearly eleven."

I told her I was aware of the time.

"I need to speak to you."

I was in a hurry to speak to Anthony, so I suggested we meet around noon.

"In over an hour?"

I didn't reply, and I doubt she was expecting me to. She hung up, and I paused for a moment to send a text message to Anthony asking him to meet me in my office in five minutes.

He was there when I arrived. I closed the door and told him unequivocally about pianoguru and his antics as I took off my jacket and put my backpack down. He told me he had seen the post before he left home, but hadn't really paid much attention.

"Have you spoken to Simone?" he asked, and his expression seemed to suggest that they had already had a conversation. However, I decided not to ask him anything about that, and told him I was expecting her shortly.

I sat down at my computer, opened the forum where pianoguru had been making his claims, and beckoned Anthony over. He drew up a chair, leaned forward, and started reading.

If his mind had been on the research and whatever it was Simone wanted to discuss with me, that changed the instant he looked at the screen.

"He's always ranting about something," he said when he saw pianoguru's name. "Fritzb23, jonjon, 3cords . . ." he murmured as he scrolled down the page, ". . . no heavyweights, that's for sure. 3cords is an idiot, jonjon and Fritzb23 are both nobodies. Pianoguru can be unpredictable and pompous, but he clearly listens to music and knows something about it. However, he has all sorts of misconceptions and isn't particularly musical. I've had to straighten him out more than once," he added.

I told him that Vincent was very worried.

"I can understand why," he said. "This is annoying. But he needn't worry. No one listens to pianoguru. You can see from the responses. Only three posts. And from people who don't matter."

"Do you think he's making it up?"

Anthony said he didn't think so.

"He isn't that devious," he said. "I reckon it's his software. He was bragging in one of his posts about having merged iTunes with his own database. I'll see if I can find it . . ."

Anthony ran his slender fingers deftly over the keyboard, and in no time had pulled up all of pianoguru's posts on the screen. He scrolled through them and quickly found the one he was looking for.

"Here," he said. "In fact, there are several, because he starts off boasting about having merged the databases, and then goes on to say he has managed to fix all the resulting glitches."

He shook his head at such stupidity.

"There are so many idiots on the Internet," he said. "We do our best to keep them in check, but that's easier said than done. It takes work. They need to be dealt with the moment they start making trouble."

I read pianoguru's posts. Anthony's description was spot-on: first he announced that with the help of "computer science students here at the school" he had succeeded in merging the two databases, and in his subsequent posts he went on to list the ensuing technical difficulties and their solutions in mind-numbing detail. Finally he said he was able to proclaim victory; that was two months ago.

"As you can see, the explanation is obvious," said Anthony, when I finally tore myself away from the screen. "His database is a complete mess."

I had never suspected that Anthony's arrogance might warm my heart this way. I resisted the temptation to embrace him. Even so, I think he could sense my gratitude as we sat next to each other, leaning back in our chairs and staring silently at the screen. He was trustworthy. Steady as a rock.

"Have you heard that recording by Ashkenazy?" I ventured to ask.

He didn't hesitate.

"Yes, a long time ago. He doesn't manage to convey the longing or sorrow of the piece. Margaret does that brilliantly. He isn't a very sensitive pianist."

I breathed more easily.

"I'm wondering whether I ought to challenge him," he said then, "but I doubt there's much to be gained from that. I think I'll just say something about the CD instead."

He looked at the clock on the computer.

"I could do it now. What time is Simone coming?"

"In ten minutes."

"She isn't happy," he said. "Just so that you know."

"Why is that?"

"I don't know. She didn't want to talk about it. But we didn't do anything this morning."

"What?"

"She said there was no point in taking the patient down be-fore she had had a talk with you."

He spoke as if he and I were on the same side, standing together. I might have objected to that in the past, but right now I felt comforted.

"Thank you," I said.

He nodded and left.

I sat in front of the computer, browsing pianoguru's posts, which now appeared in a fresh light. They no longer filled me with dread, and I wondered whether it had taken Anthony to make me overcome my misgivings. I couldn't help but admit that it had, and I felt ashamed.

Simone didn't show. While I waited for her, I called Vincent and relayed to him my conversation with Anthony. I explained exactly what he had said about the databases, and couldn't resist quoting his opinion of Ashkenazy.

"You can't imagine how relieved I am," he said, but his voice remained frail.

I had expected him to perk up at the news, return to his jubilant state even, but pianoguru's attack seemed to have taken a bigger toll on him than I had imagined. Perhaps he realized this, or at least he seemed to echo my thoughts, when he said in a low voice:

"I thought we had reached dry land at last. After all we've been through, I really thought we had."

Strange as it may seem, I missed his swagger, his habitual garrulousness, his tendency to ignore what he doesn't wish to hear, to stick to his guns no matter what. I felt sorry for him; it was an uncomfortable sensation.

We said good-bye, and I opened the door and scanned the corridor for Simone. There was no sign of her, so I took the elevator up to the third floor and knocked on her door before opening it. She wasn't there, and the lights were off.

As I closed the door behind me, a nurse stepped out of the elevator carrying a blue folder. I recognized it immediately as belonging to Simone.

"She's not in her office," I said to save her the trouble.

"Really? She left her folder in the basement this morning."

"I beg your pardon?"

"This morning. After the tests. She must have put it down while we were taking the patient out of the scanner."

I nodded as though her words hadn't surprised me.

"Well, I'll just leave it on her desk, then."

I took the stairs, pausing next to the window and looking out at the traffic on the main road and the red-painted supermarket depot with its delivery trucks bearing images of canned food. In the distance I could see the train moving off toward the city.

I don't know how long I stood there. My thoughts were racing, and I found it difficult to shake off the ghosts that were suddenly assailing me. The morning had been productive, and I shouldn't forget that. I had finally been of some use to my parents, I had responded in their hour of need, taken control instead of fleeing the way I often did, shown them kindness. Perhaps not love, but kindness.

Of course I had known from the beginning that our patients would probably have doubts about the point of staying alive in their condition, but yesterday I had let my concerns get the better of me. I had put words in our patient's mouth and been reckless in my interpretation of her responses.

It was only back in my office that I started to wonder what might have transpired between her and Simone. I fumbled in my pocket for my cell phone and was about to call Simone's number, but hesitated. I decided not to send the text message I started typing, either, as I wasn't sure what to say. Instead, I resolved to look in on our patient and play the Schubert CD for her, which I should have done already, given the trouble she had taken to tell me that she actually liked it.

I gave a start when I opened the door and saw Simone sitting beside the bed, her coat on her knees. And yet I closed the door behind me, reached for a chair, and sat down opposite her.

"Buenas tardes," I said in a low voice.

Simone looked at me while I contemplated the patient, lying like an effigy between us, her head filled with memories, fears, and desires. I wished I could clasp her hand and say something encouraging, if only about the birds I had seen as I gazed out the window. But I said nothing and kept my hands to myself.

In the end I couldn't avoid catching Simone's eye. Her expression was inscrutable, but she had this going-away look that made me uneasy. It was as if she were just passing through and had popped in to say hello to a relative before continuing on her way. She sat with her hands in her lap, occasionally running the fingers of her left hand over her coat, folded and placed on her knees.

When I got back from Liège, Simone said she wanted to speak to me in private. I received her text message just fifteen minutes after I landed, which made me think she must have tracked my flight on her computer. She herself had flown back the day before, hurried home as fast as she could.

We met the following morning. She told me she was going to quit, that we couldn't carry on working together. She spoke as if she were giving me the objective results of exhaustive research.

It wasn't easy talking her around, but I succeeded in the end. I seem to recall that she gave in only when I myself had written a letter of resignation and was poised to deliver it to Hofsinger. We were standing in her office at the time, and I couldn't help embracing her, although that probably wasn't wise given the situation. And yet she smiled and said "okay," and I convinced myself we had turned a corner.

I don't know how long we had been sitting opposite each

other in Mrs. Bentsen's room when it occurred to me that the patient probably found our silence strange. I was about to say something but wasn't sure what, and so I rose and put on the Schubert CD. The volume was low so I turned it up a fraction, and instead of sitting down again I stopped by the window and looked out. It was starting to rain.

I jumped when I heard her push the chair away from the bed. Possibly she had been waiting for me to turn my back, because out of the corner of my eye I thought I saw her let go of the patient's hand and straighten up before she left.

I went after her. She stopped in the corridor and I waited for her to say something to show how upset she was with me. But she didn't speak, her face impassive. Finally I blurted out:

"I thought I could get closer to her if I was on my own."

"And you succeeded, didn't you?"

"It's no excuse, but . . ."

"I succeeded as well."

I had already considered carefully how I would go about justifying myself: bringing up my conversation with the doctor in New Mexico, reminding her that together we hadn't made progress for days.

"I couldn't let her down as well," I heard myself saying.

She looked at me. "As well?"

"I refused to recognize my mother's talent. I turned a blind eye to Malena's illness. And to you . . ."

"Don't worry about me."

"I . . ."

"Don't."

I was about to tell her that I had felt vindicated every time my mother got a bad review or encountered failure of some sort. That Malena's illness had been staring me in the face for months. That what I had done in Liège was unforgivable. But I had the sense to keep quiet.

"How did you find out?" I asked instead.

"The night duty reports, Magnus. How on earth did you think you could get away with it?"

Her voice betrayed no accusation, only surprise and disappointment. But I had no time to reply because she quickly said: "Perhaps it's just as well. Now we know where we stand."

The nurse I had bumped into outside Simone's office half an hour earlier came down the corridor with a medical student she was showing around; they paused, and she fetched a wheelchair and a walker in a small alcove off the corridor, then opened the linen cupboard and placed a towel and sheet on the wheelchair. I gave a start, as if they had caught us doing something wrong. The nurse gestured to us and said: "You found her, then." I tried to smile as she added: "Simone, I put your folder on your desk. You left it in the basement this morning."

I followed Simone to the elevator. She was holding her coat as if she were unsure what to do with it.

"Where are you going?" I asked.

"I don't know."

"We mustn't give up, just because our patient seems to be having doubts," I said.

"Did she seem in any doubt to you?" she asked. "She didn't to me."

"You didn't ask her directly, did you?"

She didn't reply.

"What were we expecting, Magnus? What exactly were we expecting?"

The elevator doors opened. She stepped inside and pressed the button. I stood watching her until she disappeared, only collecting myself when she had probably reached the ground floor and was perhaps already on her way out of the building.

I still wonder whether I should have read something in her eyes the moment before the doors closed.

S imone didn't come to work for the rest of the week—she called in sick and didn't answer calls or e-mails. Anthony ran the tests while I took a back seat. Unsurprisingly, he got limited results from our patient—but enough for him to keep trying. She was admirably resourceful.

His post about Margaret's performance of Mussorgsky's work was both erudite and forceful. Naturally, he acted as if pianoguru didn't exist, and instead of responding to his innuendos offered what I considered a detailed and insightful comparison of Margaret's and Ashkenazy's playing. I said this to him and he appreciated the compliment, adding that he hoped this would be the end of the affair. And as far as I could see he was right, because the tone of the debate instantly became more objective and restrained. Fritzb23 and jonjon behaved as if they had never even read pianoguru's posts, much less contemplated his accusations, fervently agreeing with Anthony's analysis of the zeitgeist in late-nineteenth-century Russia, as well as his reflections on the inner life of the composer, in particular when he was writing *Pictures at an Exhibition,* which Anthony described as a "masterpiece and a challenge for the pianist, at once mournful and uplifting." 3cords kept a low profile, but more surprising, there wasn't a peep from pianoguru himself.

I spoke with Vincent every day, and gradually he seemed to cheer up a little. His voice sounded stronger, and when he called the following weekend I couldn't help smiling. I was sitting in the café on Columbus with tea and a bagel, watching the traffic and the soft sunshine on the naked branches of the trees along the sidewalk, pleasantly light-headed after my lap around Central Park.

"Magnus, is that you?"

"Yes," I said, "were you calling someone else?"

"No, your voice sounded different, but now I can hear that it's you. Are you at the hospital?"

"No, it's Saturday."

"But you work on Saturdays."

"Not always."

"It's been four days," he said. "I'm counting. Kleuber says that if this kind of thing doesn't get traction within two or three days, it's over."

"I think we've seen the end of it," I said.

"You do? You really think it's over?"

"Yes, I'm sure of it," I replied, surprised at how categorical I was.

He reminded me of a patient whose test results come back negative, but who has trouble believing it and keeps questioning the doctor just to be doubly sure.

"You can't imagine how relieved I am, Magnus, my boy. Isn't it astonishing how little it takes to cast a shadow over all that is good in life?"

He didn't wait for a reply, but cleared his throat forcefully before informing me that *Gramophone* had nominated three of Margaret's CDs for their annual music prize: Liszt, Schubert, and Mussorgsky. This was big news, as it was the first time the magazine had ever given an English musician more than one nomination. He also told me in confidence that after the weekend, the *Guardian* would be publishing a retrospective of Margaret's career, in which the paper's lead music critic had gone so far as to describe her as one of the most important pianists in the history of the United Kingdom, and without a doubt the most versatile.

"I haven't even told Margaret about it. In case anything should change . . . Least said soonest mended."

Before we broke off the conversation, he told me he had gotten rid of his new cell phone.

"That iPhone," he said. "I can't bring myself to use it again."

I said he needn't give up his phone just because pianoguru had indirectly implicated iTunes; the Californian technology company wasn't to blame.

"To my mind they're one and the same," he said. "There's even a picture of this iTunes on the phone. I find it most uncomfortable."

I finished my breakfast after we said good-bye. They had forecast fine weather, and I couldn't decide whether to go to Chelsea to see a gallery opening I had been invited to—stroll around the neighborhood, possibly along the High Line that had recently been transformed into an elevated park, or down to the Hudson where I could sit on a bench and read a book, something I had been too restless to do for a long time. I ordered another cup of tea, as I wasn't in a hurry and enjoyed watching the Saturday strollers on the sidewalk, lovers brushing noses, people window-shopping, a young couple pushing a baby carriage up the street.

When I awoke that morning, I noticed to my surprise that I was able to stave off the anxiety that had been plaguing me recently. I even fell asleep again, or dozed off at least, the way I often did on weekends when Malena was alive. My dreams were strange, as they usually are between sleeping and waking, and

I kept thinking Malena was lying beside me. I even gave a start when I thought I had brushed against her and felt her lingering touch on my arm.

I was brimming with newfound optimism when I got up, opened the balcony doors, and heard the birds in the back garden. It was then that my thoughts returned to our patient, and I told myself that both Simone and I had failed in our duty, given in to despair, and behaved badly toward our colleagues—I more than she. Of course it was only to be expected that our patient would have doubts about staying alive; anything else would have been unnatural. For all we knew, our colleagues in Liège and Cambridge had experienced similar situations, only they had wisely decided to keep those incidents to themselves.

That's what I told myself as I pulled on my exercise clothes and jogged in Central Park. I also concluded that it was fortunate that Anthony had taken over from us, because he would never fall into the trap we had, much less give up. He would never grow weary of repeating the same questions over and over, perhaps with an occasional variation, believing he would finally wear the patient down. Only the day before, he had come to announce triumphantly that he had discovered she was from Peru. I congratulated him, even though I knew she was only toying with him.

After the weekend, Simone and I would join the others again and carry on the research as if nothing had happened. We needed to regain the patient's trust and that would take some time. Surely in the end she would want to meet her loved ones, let them know she was still alive, receive the warmth which her friends and family would undoubtedly give her.

I went to the show in Chelsea. The artist was from Argentina, an acquaintance of Malena's. It was the first time I had seen him or her other friends since she died. I had replied to those who had e-mailed me, but otherwise avoided them.

The exhibition was a smorgasbord. In one corner, a toaster

dangled over a bathtub brimming with bright blue water, the power cord attached to the ceiling. The work was called *Beware— Sunset.* In the room, there were several other household appliances displayed in an unusual context. The artist glimpsed me as I walked in and came over to embrace me. I met more of Malena's friends and did my best to speak to them in Spanish. I was amazed to discover that I had missed them, and promised we would meet soon. We exchanged telephone numbers, and I even accepted an invitation to a birthday party the following weekend.

Only as I was about to leave did the artist take my arm and lead me to a sculpture by the main entrance. It was a leg in a tango shoe which I had paid little attention to when I walked in. I had assumed it was made of glass, but now he told me it was ice and would melt in two days. Beneath it was a large tray; I saw the drops of water already falling into it.

"In memory of Malena," he said. "I hope it doesn't offend you."

"It doesn't offend me at all," I told him, and we embraced once more before I left.

The afternoon sun shone on the cobblestone streets as I set off for the High Line, and bathed the brick houses in crimson. I felt at peace and was looking forward to a relaxing evening. I thought I might buy some groceries and cook a meal for myself, listen to music, then watch a movie on television.

I sat down on a bench on the High Line, fished my cell phone out of my pocket, and called Simone. She didn't pick up, but I left a long and rather upbeat message, telling her where I was calling from and asking her to try me back at her leisure.

Sunday couldn't have had a better start. I didn't sleep in as late as I had the morning before, but my feeling of calm and well-being was so overwhelming that I had to lie still for a moment to make sure I wasn't imagining it. I made coffee, put Margaret on the CD player (Chopin's Études), then opened the balcony doors and felt the cool air drift in from outside. Above the houses on the other side of the backyard, the sky was so blue and translucent that it seemed very far away and somehow unconnected to the light flooding the kitchen and living room.

I hadn't been sitting for long at the kitchen table when scenes from my childhood slowly began to resurface. I was surprised because I couldn't recall having thought about them for years or possibly decades, and therefore had to fumble around in my memory for them. At first the images were hazy then gradually brought into focus by the soft, mournful melody. It was his Étude no. 3, op. 10, which the composer considered the most beautiful music he had ever written.

We had just moved to Allington, and I was coming home after football. The rain had turned the pitch into mud, which didn't stop us, but attempting a sliding tackle I had managed to twist my ankle. It hurt a great deal, but I put on a brave face to my friends as I hobbled off home, only bursting into tears as I approached the front door.

Margaret was home alone. She heard me come in and appeared in the hallway where I was sitting at the bottom of the stairs. I wouldn't say she became flustered, but she looked as if she didn't know how to respond. Finally, she sat down beside me and stroked my cheek hesitantly. I was so unused to this behavior that out of sheer astonishment I instantly stopped sniveling. She slowly drew her hand away and we sat side by side in silence until she rose, beckoning me into the kitchen, where she poured me a glass of milk. Then I followed her into the living room where she gestured for me to sit in Vincent's chair, before installing herself on the piano stool.

She played that same Chopin Étude for me, which was presently echoing through my apartment: no. 3, op. 10. Although I had no ear for music, I understood that she was trying to comfort me—with the notes that expressed her thoughts when she couldn't find the words. A half-smile played on her lips, and her expression was tender and healing.

I don't remember whether Vincent came home before she stood up from the piano, but I don't think so. She slipped out of the living room, went upstairs, and I sat motionless, clutching my glass of milk, as I tried to hold on to the music echoing in my head, proving what I had always hoped was true but had never known for sure: that in spite of everything, my mother did love me.

It had grown chilly in the apartment by the time the music finished, so I closed the balcony doors. I thought about putting on another CD but didn't. I hadn't eaten and was debating whether to make myself some scrambled eggs or go out to the café on Columbus when the telephone rang. It was in my bedroom and the ringer on so low that it was pure coincidence I heard it.

"Magnus Conyngham?"

"Speaking."

"Perhaps you won't remember me. Hans Kleuber. We met at your mother's seventieth birthday party."

I told him I did, but his call was so unexpected that he could scarcely have found my reaction welcoming. At least that's what I told myself later.

"Forgive the intrusion. I've been trying to get ahold of you all morning, but you didn't answer."

He fell silent, as though waiting for an explanation, but I said nothing.

"Could we meet?"

"Meet?"

"I'm here, in New York." And then he added: "It has to do with your parents."

I was going to ask him what this was all about, but I changed my mind; Margaret and Vincent were fond of him and I owed it to them to show him courtesy.

"Of course," I said, clearing my throat gently. "Where are you staying?"

I took the train down to Soho before noon. He was at a small hotel north of Canal Street and was waiting for me in the lobby. We greeted each other with a firm handshake, and I made an effort to compensate for my abrupt manner on the telephone. He didn't seem to hold it against me, and bowed with an almost childlike sincerity as he shook my hand, remaining like that for a moment longer than necessary before straightening up.

We sat in a small library, beyond the reception area. He told me he came to New York once a year to attend musical events; he had been to see the Philharmonic the night before and was going to the opera that evening.

"*Orpheus and Eurydice,*" he said. "I can't wait."

We sat by the window. Outside the sun was creeping down the walls of the houses opposite. I had eaten before I left home, and when the young waitress came over to ask if we wanted anything we ordered only coffee.

"I am indebted to your father," he said as the girl walked away. "He stood by me when I got divorced. And yet we barely knew each other. Your mother, too. I visited them twice in Allington, and we sat in the living room listening to music late into the evening. It helped me a great deal. He didn't have to be so kind to me."

He picked up the envelope he had placed on the table between us and opened it.

"I had a call from Ellis yesterday."

"Ellis?"

"Philip Ellis, your father's business partner."

"Yes, of course," I said.

"He looks after the money side of things. General management . . . accounting . . ."

I remembered the red gemstone on the ring finger of his right hand, the tobacco-stained beard at the corners of his mouth.

"He received an e-mail yesterday. Or rather, the company did. He called me straightaway. I was on my way to the Philharmonic, but I read it when I got back to the hotel and printed it out."

He reached his long fingers into the envelope, drew out a folded sheet of paper and handed it to me.

"It's from pianoguru. His real name is Caspar Bouwer. Dutch. He lives in Massachusetts, where he is associate professor of physics at a university just outside Boston. Single, according to Facebook. He has views on everything. Most of them unusual."

I opened the piece of paper, but flinched from reading it.

"What does he want?" I asked.

Kleuber put down his coffee cup and clasped his hands together.

"He claims he can prove that the recording of Mussorgsky is plagiarized."

I glanced at the sheet of paper.

"Is that the word he uses?"

He nodded.

"What exactly is he up to?"

"He also says he has bought your mother's Chopin Études and wonders whether she is a fan of Minoru Nojima."

"Who is that?" I asked.

"A Japanese pianist. Well-respected in professional circles, but eccentric, doesn't do many recordings, is practically a recluse."

"But he has recorded Chopin's Études?"

He nodded again.

"Have you listened to them?" I asked.

He said he had, and that he probably had this particular recording in his collection, but couldn't say for sure.

"Very different from your mother," he said. "He possesses an extraordinary technique, but has none of the lyricism that distinguishes your mother's playing."

"What is it he wants?"

Kleuber pointed to the piece of paper.

"He says that unless Margaret and the recording company come clean he will make his discovery public. He has given them until Wednesday."

"Do you think he's serious?"

Kleuber looked out the window, clasping and unclasping his fingers.

"Shouldn't we assume that he is? He is clearly not right in the head."

"What does Vincent say?"

"He knows nothing about it. Philip got in touch with me

and the two of us decided it was best not to tell him anything about it. Not for the moment."

"How did you get my number, then?"

"Philip found it for me."

I picked up my cup but the coffee had gone cold, so I left it. It was only lukewarm when the waitress brought it.

"I thought about contacting a lawyer," he said, "but that might just wind him up. Still, I think someone ought to try to talk him out of it."

"Massachusetts?" I asked.

"Waltham," he said. "Just west of Boston."

I looked at the sheet of paper. "'I wonder whether Mrs. Bergs is a fan of Minoru Nojima?'"

I picked up my cell phone and keyed in pianoguru's e-mail address (or rather that of Caspar Bouwer, associate professor of physics), introduced myself, and said I wanted to meet him. My fingers were shaking, with rage not fear.

Before pressing send, I passed the phone to Kleuber. He read the message and nodded.

"As soon as possible," I had written. "As soon as possible."

The highway follows the coastline for the first hour, before turning inland in a long, slow curve westward. There the urban sprawl gives way to a vast expanse of tree-covered hills that turn blue where they meet the horizon. The monotonous landscape is soothing and relaxes the mind, especially on a glorious autumn morning when the pale sun shines on the hills and everything seems so far away.

He had replied to my e-mail while I was on my way to the subway, having taken my leave of Hans Kleuber. His message was brief: I was welcome to pay him a visit, but he doubted it would be of much use to my parents. We arranged to meet in his office at the university; I told him I would be there at ten the following morning.

I picked up the rental car on Sunday evening and found a parking space in my street after driving around for forty minutes. I set off at six in the morning and pulled up outside the university at half past nine, after stopping twice on the way to get gas and stretch my legs. I got slightly lost after I left the highway on the outskirts of Boston, and had the sense to ask someone for directions when the ones on my cell phone were confusing.

Having parked the car, I made my way to the physics department. It was on the north side of the campus, which stood on a hill outside of town, a mix of brick and glass structures, green lawns, neat flower beds, a pond here and there. There were many students milling about, on their way to or from lectures, and I stopped at the student center to get a cup of coffee. I could see the highway in the distance, continuing westward to the city by the sea.

He can't have been much older than thirty, of medium height, with dark hair and spectacles. He was waiting for me at the main entrance, and I could tell from his expression that he had been hoping I wouldn't turn up. We said hello and he asked me to follow him up the stairs.

"I'm on the second floor," he said.

His office was small and very tidy. It contained few personal belongings apart from some CDs and a framed photograph of a woman I supposed was his girlfriend or wife. He invited me to sit down and turned on his computer.

All I had with me was the envelope Kleuber had given me. He glanced at it and said:

"I assume you have looked at the data I sent."

I told him I had an e-mail, opened the envelope, and pulled out the sheet of paper.

"What about the data?"

"What data?" I said.

He asked if he could see what I had. I passed the piece of paper to him.

"There are two attachments missing," he said. "Haven't you seen them?"

I admitted that I hadn't.

"Now I understand why you made the journey," he said, turning to the computer and suggesting I bring a chair up to the desk so that I could better see the screen.

First he opened the document in which he compared Margaret's interpretation of Mussorgsky to that of Ashkenazy.

"I can print it out if you want, but it might be easier if I just take you through it on the screen."

He seemed more at ease once he had the data in front of him and was able to focus on it: a scientist discussing the results of his research, objectively and without any sentiment.

"Let's start at the beginning," he said. "*Pictures at an Exhibition.*"

He pulled up two graphs.

"We're going to look at the waveforms side by side. The horizontal line measures time," he explained, "the vertical line amplitude. When I press the button you will see your mother's recording on the top graph and Ashkenazy's on the bottom."

He looked at me as if to make sure I was following him. I nodded.

He raised his forefinger higher than necessary and let it fall onto the keyboard. The Promenade's first notes rang out jauntily inside the office, out of tune with how I was feeling.

"I'm playing both recordings at once," he said, "although you can't tell. You see as well that there's no difference between the two graphs . . ."

"It doesn't exactly jump out at me," I said, as the wavy lines sped past.

"I'll freeze them," he said.

He enlarged the two graphs, placing one on top of the other. They were identical.

"If I enlarge them further and play the music slowly, you can see even better," he said. "The red lines are Ashkenazy, the green your mother."

He started the music again, gradually slowing it down until they were playing only one note at a time. The two wavy lines moved across the screen in perfect harmony.

"The entire work is the same. No difference between the recordings."

He showed me an example of "Gnomus" and "Il Vecchio Castello" to prove his point.

"Do you want to see more Mussorgsky?"

I had stopped following, and shook my head.

"The other document is particularly interesting, and shows a comparison between your mother's playing of Chopin's Études and that of Minoru Nojima."

I slipped off my jacket and hooked it over the back of the chair, using the opportunity to wipe the sweat from my brow. I wished I could take my leave, hurry away, and each time I looked out the window my gaze was drawn to three little chapels standing in a semicircle around a small pond. The path ran right past them, toward the student center and then up to the parking lot. I sat down again, forcing myself to listen.

He went through the same motions, pulling up two graphs, comparing them. Études 1 and 2, op. 10, looked identical on the screen, as did nos. 4 and 5. However, when it came to no. 6, the music clashed, jarring on the ear, and the two graphs revealed two different recordings. I felt a glimmer of hope, which faded as he said:

"It took me a while to find it, but I finally succeeded. Maurizio Pollini, a recording from 1990."

He pulled up the graph of Pollini's interpretation and played both recordings simultaneously. There was no difference between them.

I had a hard time sitting still, and Bouwer could tell.

"Look at this one," he said. "Number seven."

He leaned back in his chair. Chopin's music rang out once more, but suddenly started to reverberate in my head and I had difficulty distinguishing the notes.

Bouwer raised his forefinger and brought it down decisively on the keyboard.

"It happens right there. The lines diverge. For the first time. You heard the echo, didn't you?"

I nodded.

"But then they join up again," he said, pressing play once more. "For twenty-two seconds. After that they go their separate ways."

He played the Étude through to the end, without looking at me, his eyes fixed on the screen.

"So, it isn't the same recording," I said.

It was as if he had been waiting for me to make this observation.

"That's what I thought, too," he said. "Until I examined the graphs more closely. The amplitudes are identical."

He pulled up the two graphs again, superimposed them, and pressed play. The echo was clearly audible, and then he pressed a few keys on the computer until it disappeared and the two sets of lines merged.

He looked at me. His smile was that of a contented scientist who has solved a riddle, and bore no trace of malice.

"The performance has been sped up in several places, and slowed down twice. But it's the same recording. Maurizio Pollini. Whoever did this has a remarkable ear. With those few changes, the recording released in your mother's name is better, incredible yet true."

He reminded me of Anthony: earnest in his diligence and unwitting ruthlessness.

"Number three is the only one that eludes me," he said then. "I can't find it anywhere."

He clicked on Étude no. 3, op. 10, on Margaret's CD and played it on its own. We sat motionless in our seats in front of

the computer; he was slightly hunched over, I was paralyzed. I
tried to thrust my memories aside, telling myself this wasn't her
playing, but someone else, that it was simply a matter of finding
out who. And yet I couldn't convince myself; once more I was
back in the living room in Allington, once more I was that boy
holding a glass of milk listening to her comfort me.

We sat still till the end. When it was over I felt too weak to
get up straightaway. He switched off the computer.

"You're a scientist," he said ruefully, and then added: "I
googled you . . . This is self-evident. I'm sorry."

I paused on the path next to the chapels. The sun was shining on the pond and an overhanging oak tree. A few leaves clung
feebly to its branches; the slightest gust would blow them away.

When I looked over my shoulder, I saw him watching me
from his office window.

still find it difficult to comprehend what happened over the next twenty-four hours, which is in itself worrying, as it wasn't that long ago. For example, I don't recall starting the car and driving off campus, although I have a clear image of the transit officer who came over to me when I accidentally went in the wrong toll lane for the highway. I can see him shaking his head before taking the payment I passed through the window and lifting the barrier that was blocking my way. A small line had developed behind me, which I noticed only when impatient drivers leaned on their horns.

I drove for about an hour before stopping for gas. There was half a tank left, but I needed a rest, so I filled it up before leaving the car in the short-term parking lot outside the service station. It was no different from any other such constructions you find on a highway: an anonymous, one-story building with fast-food restaurants and a convenience store, restrooms by the entrance, plastic tables and chairs next to the windows overlooking the highway. There was a stench of fried food in the air and a long line for coffee.

It was only when an elderly man asked me the time that I

remembered my phone in my pocket. I had put it on silent before my meeting with Caspar Bouwer and forgotten about it. I had nine missed calls and many unread texts, but I put the phone back in my pocket without checking further. I needed peace and quiet, solitude. I had nothing to say to anybody.

It was only one o'clock and there wasn't much traffic on the highway. It would likely get heavier as I drove south. I switched on the radio, searched through the channels, but found nothing I felt like listening to.

It seemed unlikely that Kleuber was an accomplice. He was gullible but honest, and would have been taken in by my parents' charade, the attention they lavished on him, the kindness they showed him when he was having problems. I was convinced that Philip hadn't shown him the attachments when he urged him to get me involved, undoubtedly at my father's behest, who of course must have known about the whole thing.

"I've only looked at these two CDs," Bouwer had said. "What is the likelihood, do you think, that the others aren't tarred with the same brush?"

How did Vincent think he could get away with it? I asked myself as the car sped along the highway, and the answer I came up with was that he had failed to take into consideration technology: computer programs and databases with their infallible memories. That world was a closed book to him; he had always been leery of it and made an effort to stay away from it.

My phone lay on the passenger seat. It was still on silent, but I could see out of the corner of my eye whenever the screen light up. It was Kleuber, understandably impatient, but I didn't feel up to talking to him. I was thinking about my mistakes. My naïveté. Trying to fathom how I could have let Vincent fool me after everything I had been through with him. I was ashamed.

When I got down to Connecticut the traffic was at a standstill. An illuminated sign by the roadside said an accident two miles south had closed three out of the four lanes and we could expect long delays. I was sitting in a dip and could see row upon row of cars in front of me going up a tree-lined hill.

I was in no hurry, and in some respects I welcomed the delay. I had automatically slowed down the last half hour, driving in the far right lane, below the speed limit. I had felt my despair grow with every mile, and I knew that if I didn't collect myself, it would get the better of me. I tried to picture the graphs which Bouwer had shown me, but the lines would disappear somewhere in my mind and instead I found myself looking at the computer in our lab, the screen lighting up, tennis balls flying over the net in bright sunshine. When I heard her calling my name from the scanner with Malena's voice, I pulled over and stopped in the break-down lane to shake it off. I felt I was losing my mind.

My phone continued to flash on the passenger seat. The traffic barely inched forward. The sun started to fade above the hills, casting shadows on the road. It was almost four o'clock; the days were growing shorter.

By the time I approached the accident site, I had begun to marshal my thoughts. I managed, for example, to arrive at the obvious conclusion that I should avoid my parents and anything related to them. They were their own worst enemies and there was nothing I could do to change that. I had only been a child when I realized the destruction they could cause, but I had let down my guard. Why?

I had failed our patient and betrayed my colleagues. In fact, I had shamefully been on the verge of giving up in the face of what were predictable problems. I needed to see to her immediately, take charge of the research, talk openly with Simone and Anthony, and possibly even Hofsinger, too. I owed it to them to behave honorably, to get my act together. I owed it to myself.

Science had always been my escape. The place I went when I felt cornered, the sanctuary where I could find order and discipline, whatever else was going on.

A delivery truck had overturned on a bend and was lying on its side across the road. The flashing lights of police vehicles and fire trucks were visible in the distance—the ambulances were long gone. Two automobiles had veered off the road, but neither looked badly damaged. When I finally inched past the site, I instantly recognized the images of canned foods on the delivery truck.

I decided to stop at the hospital on my way back to New York. It was only a slight detour, a fifteen-minute drive from the highway at most. I wanted to organize the following day's research, speak with Anthony—and with Simone, if she was there—find out who had been trying to get a hold of me, help them with whatever they needed. I wanted to look in on the patient. Above all, look in on her and say a few words, hold her hand, try to reassure her. And remove from her room Margaret's CDs. I should never have played them for her. I should never have poisoned her mind with my parents' deceit and falsehood.

It was nearly five by the time I parked in the gravel lot behind the main building. The lights glowed in the windows; it was getting dark outside.

I planned to talk to Anthony first. I was going to warn him not to take part in any further discussions about my mother. Not to respond when pianoguru posted his accusations, to keep a low profile. I would explain later, but I was too tired now, far too tired, I planned to say when he asked me why.

I didn't get to talk to him, however, because no sooner had I stepped out of the elevator than our secretary came running over to me.

"Where have you been? We've been trying to get ahold of you all day."

She caught me off guard but didn't wait for me to reply. "She's dead."

I felt as if I was a spectator, looking at us from far away in the brightly lit corridor. She said something else, but I couldn't make it out because of the hissing noise in my head. But I do remember her lips moving and someone seizing me by the arms as my legs gave way, and then nothing more until I came to on the sofa in my office.

The waters of the Hudson are deepest where it flows past the village, wide and calm. The far bank is rocky but there is sand on this side and an old dock which appears to be used only by pleasure boats, and mostly in the summer. Today, the water at the river's edge is frozen over, although the ice doesn't look very thick to me. The forecast is for continuing frost.

I took the train up and am seated in a small diner down by the river. The journey took only about an hour, and on the whole the views were pleasant, more so the farther we advanced. This area is sparsely populated and tranquil, the houses quaint, and there are a few interesting buildings close by, such as the mills I saw from the train, and the foundry, which used to bring people up here in the old days. It's a museum now, and the workers' cottages have been renovated and are rented out to tourists during the high season.

It is eleven o'clock. We arranged to meet at twelve, but I wanted to play it safe and took an early train. I had nothing better to do. I haven't been back to the hospital since she died, which was almost six weeks ago.

When I came to on the sofa in my office, Hofsinger and

Anthony were both standing over me. Our secretary had fetched a glass of water, which she handed to me the moment she thought I was able to hold it, and I dutifully lifted it to my lips, even though I wasn't thirsty.

Both men wore expressions of concern and embarrassment. Embarrassment mostly, I expect.

It occurred to me I ought to explain my behavior to them, tell them about my journey, my overwhelming fatigue when I finally got out of the car, but I didn't have the energy.

"Are you all right?" asked Hofsinger.

I nodded.

"Where's Simone?"

"She's gone," Anthony said, and the secretary added: "She was with her this morning when she died."

I set the glass of water down.

"It's unfortunate," said Hofsinger. "Very unfortunate. We're back to square one."

They said she had probably died of a stroke, and I didn't ask any questions. They left soon afterward, Hofsinger first and the secretary last, not before fetching me a cup of coffee and a doughnut from the pantry.

I glanced around. My office looked strangely unfamiliar, the chair, the computer, the bookshelves, the papers on my desk, the sofa I was stretched out on. Our secretary had pulled the door closed when she left, but I could hear footsteps in the corridor and rumbling noises. Then everything went quiet.

I got to my feet. The CDs I had ordered were mostly still in their boxes on the desk. The Mephisto Waltzes in the padded envelope. I picked them up, one by one—Liszt, Schubert, Saint-Saëns, Schumann. Chopin and Rachmaninoff. Mussorgsky. I looked at them for a moment, wondering how I should get rid of them, before putting them down again.

I don't know what I was expecting from Mrs. Bentsen's

room, but I felt the need to go in there. I hesitated for a few minutes, then put the CDs back in the boxes and the envelope, before pushing the chair under the desk and slipping into my jacket pocket the photograph of Malena and me which I had pinned to the bookshelf above my desk.

It was as if she had never been there. The machines were gone, the bed freshly made, ready for the next occupant. A gentle breeze stirred the curtains, and the streetlamps by the path to the parking lot cast a dim light that reached over to the door where I stood, motionless, having closed it behind me.

I was surprised not to feel her presence. I walked over to the bed and sat down on it, running my hand absent-mindedly over the sheets. I tried to imagine her before me, but her face refused to appear, and after a while I stood up. The CDs I had brought for her were next to the stereo system in the corner. I gathered them up and dropped them in the trash bin on my way out.

On the table next to the door are some newspapers, which the breakfast customers appear to have read thoroughly, and tourist booklets affectionately if modestly depicting the village and its surroundings. I picked one up on my way in, along with a four-page real estate brochure, but I left the newspapers, as I haven't been following the media for the past few weeks, not since a few days after Caspar Bouwer disclosed his findings.

Kleuber continued to call me while I was at the hospital, and after the fifth or sixth time, I felt I had no choice but to pick up. I was on my way to the parking lot by then, and asked him to hold on while I searched for the key and started the engine. I automatically strapped on my seat belt, but didn't drive off or switch on the headlights. The evening had grown cold but the car soon warmed up.

He seemed flustered, and for a moment he had difficulty finding his voice. I only half listened to his apologies: he had been relentless, but hoped I would understand, given the situation, given what was at stake. Through my windshield, I had a clear view of the streetlamp that illuminated Mrs. Bentsen's room, and I noticed the bulb was flickering.

I told him about my trip and left nothing out. I was taken aback when he instantly went on the defensive, declaring that he didn't trust Caspar Bouwer—or should he say, pianoguru—who had repeatedly proven he was a two-faced egomaniac, not to put too fine a point on it. He himself had listened to Ashkenazy's recording of Mussorgsky, and although it was some time ago, he clearly remembered that his interpretation, while technically perfect, was superficial, nothing like that of Margaret.

He said he wasn't surprised Bouwer had pulled up graphs on his computer; the man had already shown his partiality for effects and trickery. If he refused to listen to reason we must seek legal advice. As soon as possible. Could we meet to discuss it tomorrow morning?

He was intense and yet he spoke clearly and with his usual conviction. He said he had delayed his return flight, that he owed it to my parents to help me "deal with the situation" and would do everything in his power to put an end to these attacks.

"I believe him," I said then.

He seemed stunned and I felt sorry for him until he spoke again.

"I am aware that you haven't always been on good terms with your parents, but I can't believe you would let that influence you."

I was exhausted and his tone irritated me. I asked him whether it didn't strike him as odd that he hadn't been sent the attachments which clearly showed the results of Caspar Bouwer's investigations, and whether he thought this omission was an accident.

"I would have been spared the trip had I seen them," I added.

"There were no attachments," he said. "Of that I am sure."

It was hot inside the car when I drove off. I said good-bye rather abruptly and rolled down the window to get some fresh air. I was half expecting him to call back, but he didn't, not until the following morning.

"I apologize for calling you at home, but your cell phone isn't ringing."

The relief in his voice was palpable, and he went on to tell me that the whole thing had just been made absolutely clear to him. "The whole thing" was how he referred to it. Naturally, after our conversation the evening before he had been concerned, but he had just gotten off the phone with both Ellis and Vincent, and he now knew exactly what had happened.

"Not ideal," he said, "but understandable, and demonstrates clearly how fond your father is of Margaret. Understandable and all too human."

I waited for him to continue, but instead he suggested I call Vincent, who was ready to tell me everything.

"I don't think that's a good idea," I told him, but he persisted.

"You must give him a chance to explain. You owe him that much."

I capitulated, but not before having breakfast followed by a shower.

"Are you at the hospital—in Connecticut?"

His voice was slightly faltering, and yet this time I didn't have the feeling he was trying to make me pity him.

"I'm at home."

"I did something stupid," he said, clearing his throat. "I alone am to blame."

He went on to give me a detailed account of how the recordings had gone in Allington. Well, on the whole, except that Margaret had been forced to take breaks.

"The pain," he said, "came on without warning."

They had resumed recording from the beginning when she

had recovered, but on a few occasions the cramps had been bearable and thankfully short-lived so she was able to play through them. It was only later, when he was preparing the recordings for release, that he noticed the groans in the background. It was more complicated than one might think to have Margaret replay the necessary fragments, but he had managed it all the same. Except in two instances: one of the études and *Pictures at an Exhibition*.

"That's when I made a mistake."

He went on to describe how out of desperation he had been tempted to erase her groans by stealing approximately sixty seconds from Vladimir Ashkenazy's recording, and forty-two from Minoru Nojima, splicing them into Margaret's performances.

"It was a mistake, Magnus, my boy. I got ahead of myself. And now your mother is paying the price."

I told him that Caspar Bouwer maintained the plagiarism was far more widespread.

"He's making it up. That man will stop at nothing. He's been through every CD and is making a mountain out of a molehill. But I confess that I laid myself open to it."

"Does Margaret know about this?"

"No, she knows nothing. And she must never find out. Never."

"Are you sure there is nothing more?"

"I'm telling you the truth. It saddens me that you don't believe me, but I do understand. Forgive me."

It's a well-designed booklet and the photographs are attractive. Most if not all are taken in summer or early fall with the trees beginning to change colors. They show the main street bustling with people dressed for the warm weather, filling the tables outside the cafés and restaurants. One photograph is of the bicycle repair shop, announcing bikes for rent at reasonable prices and a few suggested routes for enthusiasts. One alongside the river, but two or three up into the hills overlooking the village.

I must say I was pleasantly surprised that Thomas Stainier should remember me when I called. His voice had the same mischievous ring but was even more youthful than I recalled. It hadn't taken me long to find him when I sat down at my computer between Christmas and New Year's Day, as there is only one bicycle shop in the village and he seems to have stayed put there since he gave up medical research.

"Yes, by all means drop in," he said, seemingly quite happy to hear from me. "Maybe I can interest you in a bicycle."

After my conversation with Vincent, I told Kleuber I wanted no part in any action against Caspar Bouwer. I was hoping he would take my decision at face value, but of course he didn't and tried to pressure me for an explanation. Finally, I was forced to admit that I didn't trust my father, which was more difficult for me than I had imagined.

I haven't spoken to Kleuber since, and I have no idea whether he made good on his intention to hire a lawyer to try to put a stop to pianoguru. In any event it did no good, as Caspar Bouwer published his findings according to plan late Wednesday evening, following them up two days later with an even more detailed report. As was to be expected, other Internet warriors instantly picked up the story, followed by trade magazines such as *Gramophone* and *International Piano,* and then one newspaper after another. They were merciless, since after all Vincent had tricked and embarrassed them. Anthony took my advice and kept a low profile, while technicians the world over went to work examining all of Margaret's recordings. Unfortunately, their findings came as no surprise.

I stopped following the coverage, and have so far managed to avoid the media. I've kept to myself and am grateful to Hofsinger for allowing me to take unpaid leave while I try to gather my thoughts. It has been good to have some time alone, and the holiday period wasn't as difficult as I had feared. It snowed on Christmas Eve and I sat in the living room watching the balcony become white, the table and chairs, the trees in the backyard. I fetched a packet of birdseed from under the kitchen sink, scraped the snow off the table and scattered some seeds on top of it. I thought I could hear birds tweeting in my sleep that morning, and when I woke up, the seeds were gone.

On Christmas Day I took the plunge and called my parents. Vincent answered at the first ring, as if he had been waiting by the telephone.

"I've grown old," he said. "Perhaps I slipped somewhere, I don't know, it's all so confusing . . ."

"I just wanted to check in," I said, "it is Christmas after all."

"Margaret's having a rest," he said.

"Give her my regards. I won't be easily reachable for a while."

He was distracted and didn't try to prolong the conversation. I didn't ask how they planned to spend the day, and we said good-bye, incapable of wishing each other a Merry Christmas.

I didn't look at my phone again or check my e-mails, text messages, or missed calls until the day after my visit to Caspar Bouwer. In fact, I left my cell phone in my jacket pocket after I got home from the hospital that night, and the next morning the battery had run out. It was late in the day when I reluctantly charged it.

It came as no surprise who had been trying to get a hold of me: my colleagues at the hospital, Kleuber, Vincent, Anthony from his mobile. There were no interesting e-mails, and I scarcely glanced at them. The same was true of my text messages, until I came across one from Simone.

I suppose I felt relieved; in any case, I paused for a moment, stroking my thumb over her name on the screen before opening the message.

I remember her words—how can I ever forget them?—but the moments that followed are lost somewhere in my mind, and I still haven't been able to recover them. When I came to I was sitting at the kitchen table trying to delete her message, the phone shaking in my hand.

"I had to do it."

Nothing more, only that brief sentence, as simple as it was devastating.

What did she want me to do? Expose her? Applaud her? Comfort her? Run to wherever she was and fling my arms around her? What?

My hands trembled as I watched her words disappear from the screen, and for a brief moment I felt as if I had accomplished something. But of course they existed somewhere in the Cloud or inside a computer, evidence I was so eager to get rid of.

The next day when I spoke to Anthony and told him I had discussed taking a break with Hofsinger, he mentioned that he had just received the results of the autopsy.

"Suffocation, not a stroke," he said.

I managed to reply that we might have expected it.

"Yes," he said, "I guess it isn't all that surprising. But damn, I thought we were getting close."

I have had no contact with Simone. She resigned, and according to our secretary she is living in France. But not a day goes by when I don't think of her, and I will get in touch with her soon, if only to hear her voice.

On New Year's Day, I made a call to Camila, Malena's sister, in Buenos Aires. I didn't know how she would react to hearing my voice and was surprised by how pleasant, even kind, she was on the phone. She said they had been thinking of me, the family, and when I told her that I wanted to visit her sister's grave, she encouraged me to make the trip. I hadn't expected this, but she had surprised me before. "You know she loved you very much," she had said the last time we spoke. "More than I think you can imagine." It's strange that I should take such comfort in these words, which I play back every day, but maybe I needed someone to corroborate my own beliefs.

I've booked a flight at the end of January and practice my Spanish diligently. I must say that I'm making decent progress, but of course I still have a long way to go.

A red-and-white ferryboat is sailing upriver, making slow headway against the current. I fold the real estate brochure and put it in my pocket. It is full of useful information. The rents here are much lower than in the city, and there is more inventory than I had expected. For example, I saw an ad for a nice two-bedroom apartment in an old house down a small side street, charmingly renovated, judging from the photographs.

But I am getting ahead of myself. It is true that when I decided to call him, working as an assistant in his bicycle shop seemed like a convenient—if somewhat hasty—solution to my situation. But since then, I've slowly been getting my bearings, and now I'm just hoping that Thomas Stainier will be able to lend a hand. How, exactly, I'm not sure, but I've always held him in such high regard and believe that he has the ability to solve problems that others can't. His voice confirmed that when I called him, bright and cheerful, slightly naughty, as if to say: "Don't worry, I've figured it all out."

The ripples the ferryboat makes break up the thin layer of ice along the riverbank. For a moment I wonder if I've made a mistake coming up here, but then I realize I've nothing to lose. At worst, I'll learn something about fixing bicycles.

Despite everything, I had the presence of mind to ask for her ashes. Our secretary was very helpful, so the only thing I had to do was pick them up and sign the necessary papers. She made it easy for me, printing them out and putting them neatly in a folder. At first, I wasn't sure what to do with her remains, but eventually I found my way to the village the first week of January. Despite it being a cold morning, it reminded me of the day I had picked Malena up at the train station and we walked down to the sea. I stopped on the beach where I had taught her to skim stones and watched the small waves lapping at my feet, little servants offering their assistance. And that's when I opened the jar and scattered her ashes. The waves took them and gently brought them away from me until I could see them no more. I managed to say a few words, and while they are not worth repeating, they made me feel better.

I put on my coat and wrap my scarf around my neck. It is ten to twelve and I want to be punctual. As I open the door and set off up the street, I feel a refreshing wind on my back from the river.

OLAF OLAFSSON was born in Reykjavík, Iceland, in 1962. He studied physics as a Wien scholar at Brandeis University. He is the author of four previous novels, *The Journey Home, Absolution, Walking into the Night,* and *Restoration,* and a story collection, *Valentines.* He is executive vice president of Time Warner and lives in New York City with his wife and three children.